THE NAIL COLLECTOR

ARLA BAKER SERIES 4

ML ROSE

D1519534

PROLOGUE

Debbie Jones couldn't keep her eyes off her date for the evening. His dark blue eyes were fixed on her face, and she kept watching his sexy mouth move as he chewed the last morsel of food, then swallowed. A large hand reached for the glass of red wine. The lights in the restaurant were lowered, throwing soft shades of yellow, and the soft chink of cutlery sounded occasionally.

"So, where were we?" he asked. He lowered the glass from his lips, and his tongue flicked out to lick wine off his lips. Debbie swallowed, a sudden heat rushing low in her belly.

Her right hand fluttered up to touch her collarbone.

"Sorry," he smiled. "You asked me what I did before I became a lawyer."

He had a nice smile too. Full, sensual lips, white teeth. He was attentive and interested in her. When he picked her up from her apartment, he had brought a bouquet of roses. When was the last time a man had brought her flowers? She couldn't even remember.

Debbie cleared her throat. "Yes."

"Well," he said, "Just college and a law degree. Usual stuff."

*****

Dinner concluded, they strolled out into the warm night. The restaurant was on the border of Clapham Common. The red and yellow ribbon of traffic on the A3 glowed like LED lights in the distance, the sound muted by trees and grass. A velvety dark night lay like a glimmering shroud over the Common, its colours deepening from indigo to a clot of blackness that claimed the trees. The trees were still visible in the moonlight, still and hushed, as if drowsy from the day's heat. It was sticky and hot, the kind of summer night that presses against the skin and makes sweat trickle down the back of necks.

When his hand touched hers, she didn't move it away. Gently, his warm fingers enveloped hers, and she held his hand. It seemed natural on a night like this. A fat moon bounced over the trees, so low it could almost be touched. It shone like a silver plate, which served to show the scars on its face that much clearer.

"Beautiful, isn't it?" he murmured.

"Yes," Debbie said. She noticed they were headed into the dark breast of the Common, where no lights were visible.

"Where are we going?" she asked.

"Not there," he said, pulling on her hand slightly. She moved to see where his hand was pointing. A row of lights at the end of a path illuminated what seemed like a carpark.

"My car's parked there. Shall I give you a lift home?"

Debbie let out a breath of relief. Going into the dark belly of the Common with a man she had met twice was risky, even if she really liked him.

"That would be lovely, thanks."

Once the car stopped in front of her apartment, she asked the question which had been playing on her mind the whole journey.

"Will you come up for some coffee?"

"Only if it's okay with you," he said graciously.

"Of course," Debbie smiled.

They rode up in the elevator, Debbie conscious of the heat of his body. She could reach out and touch him. But she wouldn't. She didn't want to show how desperate she was. She hadn't been with a man for almost a year. She wanted those big hands on her body, her lips on that wicked mouth of his. She remembered that he had asked who she lived with. Alone, she had answered truthfully.

2

She opened the door and switched the light on. He came in behind her, fast, his body bumping into hers. She turned, surprised, but his hand came down to clamp over her mouth. He pressed her body against his, kicking the door shut with his heel.

The hand gripped her mouth like an iron vice. Debbie felt herself spin, then cried out as her back hit the wall. A blow slapped against her face, and her vision rocked as pain exploded inside her skull. She opened her mouth to scream, but his hand clamped over her mouth again, and he hit her in the stomach. The blow was like being pierced by a spear, and she fell to her knees. Her eyes were blurred, nausea rose in waves into her mouth, and she retched bile on the carpet.

He dragged her by the hair into the dark lounge as her legs kicked the floor weakly and in vain.

His knee sank on her chest, and she looked up, terrified, at the black shadow of his form looming over her like a demon risen from her darkest nightmares.

"Now it's time to make both of us famous," he whispered. A metallic glint caught her eye. A knife had appeared in his right hand like magic. She tried to scream again, but pain blossomed in her head as his fist slammed into the side of her face.

"Go on, fight," he panted. "I like a challenge."

CHAPTER 1

Detective Chief Inspector Arla Baker threw her warrant card on the table and took off her cardigan. She wiped sweat off her brow and flopped down on the office chair. It was too hot to be outside. Her eyes closed in the comforting coolness of the air conditioner. They snapped open when her door opened. The lanky, wide-shouldered form of Detective Inspector Harry Mehta leaned against the door frame.

His eyebrows raised, lips open without speaking as he stared down at her. His milky coffee-coloured cheeks were shaven so smooth that flies would slip on them. Even in this weather, he had a tie and waistcoat on. Harry was the only copper she knew who dressed like a banker.

"I knew it," he drawled slowly, staring at her. "I'm too hot to handle. Wearing you out."

Arla sighed and leaned her neck back on the chair, staring at the ceiling. She knew his banter was exaggerated, a smoke screen he hid behind. But that didn't stop him from being infuriating. She wanted to slap him across the face. In fact, slapping a different part of her body was exactly what Harry had done last night. Her cheeks coloured at the memory. She swung her legs down and massaged her forehead.

"Get me a coffee," she mumbled. Anything to get rid of the big oaf. More trouble than he was worth, sometimes.

"What's the magic word?"

"I'll give you two. Fuck off."

Harry angled his head. "Now there's two words I like to hear. I like the first one more but the second..."

She jerked her head up. "Shut your face," she hissed, frowning. Her eyes darted past him to the detectives' open plan office where desks were arranged in rows. The nearest figure was far enough to not eavesdrop on their conversation. But still. It would be the ultimate nightmare. Harry knew it too. He straightened, filling up the doorway.

"I think you need something cooler. A Frappucino maybe?"

She nodded. He turned and stalked down the office without a word. She watched his easy, loping gait, perfected by decades of growing up in south London. Appearances were deceptive though. Harry was the toughest cop she knew.

Lisa Moran appeared in Harry's place. Arla narrowed her eyes. Her Detective Sergeant had always been close to her, and she wondered if Lisa suspected. If Lisa did, she did well to keep it to herself.

"How did it go?" Lisa asked. Her chestnut locks framed her pale cheeks.

"Bloody great. All the Albanians had run off. But the warehouse was full of weapons." Arla's wing, the SCU or Serious Crime Unit, had been tracking an Albanian gang who had settled in London. Plenty of Eastern European criminals had arrived in the capital lately, trafficking everything from cocaine to women.

"SFU should have a field day," Lisa said. Specialist Firearms Unit.

"Yes, but we still need to catch Gorshkin." The leader of the Albanian Mafia was hiding in London at the moment, and it was in his honour that the weapons were being stored. The police were tipped off, which resulted in the dawn raid by SCU and SFU.

There was movement behind Lisa, and the corpulent form of Robert Pickering appeared, a sergeant in the SCU, with whom Arla had worked closely. Despite the coolness, Robert had a sheen of sweat on his brow. He breathed heavily, eyes widened a fraction more than normal.

Arla had worked with him long enough to know the signs. She half rose from her seat.

"What is it, Robert?"

Robert huffed and took a deep breath before he spoke. "There's a body, Guv. Dead woman. Out in the Common."

CHAPTER 2

Uniforms had cordoned off the section with blue and white tape. Harry parked the black BMW, tires crunching gravel. Arla felt a rush of heat, mixed with that humid, diesel smoke infused smell from the car. The sun was blinding already. A yellow haze lay over the Common, turning the normally green grass to straw coloured. Five days without rain. That was like five days without booze in London.

Arla was wearing sensible flats, and she brushed away Harry's supportive arm. He had the petulance to look aggrieved, but she ignored him, walking down briskly towards the crime scene.

She took in her surroundings as she walked. The Common had a lot of flat open land; hence, it was popular with football players and families. But it also had densely wooded sections, and this was one of them. She followed the path that led into the trees from the clearing where they had parked.

The shade provided by the trees was embracing, cooling. Green foliage kept the malevolent, winking sun at bay. Just as well, Arla thought with a grimace. It would delay the body's decomposition and allow forensics to get more clues. One of the uniformed Sergeants, Darren Maddy, looked up as she got closer.

"Morning Ma'am," he touched his hat.

Arla grinned. "Guv is fine, Darren. Ma'am makes me sound old."

Darren shrugged. He took out a clipboard with a paper stuck on it and signed them in. Scene of Crime Officers, or SOCO, hadn't arrived as yet, but they still had to put on gloves and mask, and shoe coverings. Duck boards were already laid on the ground for them to step on. Killers left valuable clues on the floor, which were lost forever if shoes trampled on them.

Arla could see the kneeling figure of the London Met pathologist, hunched over the body on one knee.

She ducked underneath the tape and went first, Harry close behind. This time, she didn't mind his proximity. She hated stepping on the duck boards. Her shoes slipped on them, and she had lost count of the time she had almost fallen off them. Dirty Harry, as he liked to call himself, had stopped her from landing on her butt more than once.

The man had some uses.

Arla stepped off the duck planks onto the tarpaulin that was spread on the ground around the body. Her insides constricted as she took in the scene.

The body was fully clothed in an above knee, strapless evening dress. The woman lay on her back, bruise marks on her face, small cuts evident on her arms and legs. She was young, in her late twenties or early thirties, Arla surmised.

But what bothered her more was the ring of stones that circled the body. At the head, the stones had been piled up into a triangle formation. Like a shrine. Flower petals lay around the body and at the base of the triangle of stones.

What the hell was this?

"Weird, I know," a voice said from below her.

Arla looked down to see the bespectacled face of Dr. Banerjee, the erstwhile pathologist, and her long-time confidante. Dr. Banerjee was in his sixties and married to his job. Detective Colombo of the South London Met, his colleagues called him. With his shuffling gait and stooped posture but sharp analytical mind, the resemblances to the TV detective were numerous.

Arla knelt down to his level.

"Morning, Doc. What do you make of it?"

Banerjee shook his head. "Sad. Young girl." His voice was muffled as he spoke through the surgical mask. He looked down at the dead woman.

Arla recalled Banerjee had two grown-up daughters. She pressed on his arm, and the older man looked at her. She could see the smile behind his mask.

"Same old, I know. Doesn't make it easier though."

"Too right," Arla said. "What have you got so far?"

Banerjee pointed a gloved finger at the ground. "Observe the surroundings before the body. What do you see?"

The brown earth had turned to shades of black around the victim. "Blood?" Arla asked.

"Yes. Seeped into the ground for a while. It's the way she died." Banerjee pointed at the wrist closest to them. "Lacerations in the radial artery, both arms." He shifted, and Arla stood, stepping away from him.

"Look at the neck. Marks in the region of the carotid artery and jugular veins."

Arla saw the long, jagged marks on either side of the neck. She shivered. This was a horrible way to die, blood slowly seeping out of the body, while the person was still alive.

"That took care of the upper body," Banerjee said in a grim tone. He pointed to dark patches that blossomed on the light coloured evening dress, at the groin. Again, on both sides.

"The femoral artery. The main conduit for the legs. If this artery is lacerated, then death occurs within hours."

Arla grimaced, glad she was standing. There was a smell closer to the ground, and it wasn't damp earth. A strange metallic smell of blood, mingled with something else. A rotting odour.

"Time of death?" she asked. Harry stood, suddenly visible. He was kneeling next to Banerjee, observing silently.

"Given that the ambient temperature is already twenty degrees, and her rectal temperature is about ten, I would say between midnight to three am. I need to get the body on the table to be more precise."

"How did she get here?" Harry said. He was stroking his cheek, staring at the body. Arla knew he was asking the question aloud, directed at no one in particular. She was wondering along the same lines. He looked up, and their eyes met. Their brains worked in synch most of the time. She had never thought it possible, but it happened. She read about it in books but couldn't imagine she would one day have a relationship like this.

Mired as they were in this ghastly scene, she felt something warm and full-bodied move inside her like a summer breeze. Gentle, comforting.

She looked away from him. This was no time for personal feelings.

Banerjee said, "I don't know. But judging by the bruise marks on her face, I would say she was knocked out cold first. Not easy to make these precise cuts when the victim is struggling."

Arla said, "So he hit her till she passed out, then made the cuts?"

"That would be my guess."

Arla thought to herself. He could've lured her in here for sex, then started his evil torture. Or did he pick her up from somewhere, knock her out, and then bring her here?

She looked at the face. Pale, almost white. Hair the same colour as the earth, stuck to it now with dried blood.

Banerjee said quietly, "I'm afraid that's not all."

Something in his voice alerted Arla. The pathologist glanced up at her and jerked his head towards the body. He shuffled over and picked up a dead, cold hand in his glove.

"Look at the little finger," he said. Arla and Harry kneeled closer.

Arla drew her breath in sharply. The nail on the little finger was missing.

"It's the same on the other hand as well as the feet. Nails in the small toes are missing."

Something sharp scratched at the back of her mind. It ripped open a gash, and suddenly a dark memory bounded out from her subconscious like an animal, its dripping fangs and hooked claws raking deep cuts in her mind.

Her mouth opened; her vision dimmed. The dappled sunlight from above dulled and faded, like she was sinking underwater, eyes still open.

"No," Arla gasped.

CHAPTER 3

Arla felt an iron grip around her arm, steadying her. "You okay, Guv?" Harry asked softly.

She blinked. Green, gold and yellow swirled like a kaleidoscope of colours. Shafts of sunlight filtered in from the canopy above, trickling into the recesses of her brain.

Recesses she'd kept buried, hidden.

Arla took a deep breath and immediately wished she hadn't. The faint waft from the body was nauseating. She shook her head like she was trying to shake off a spider on her hair.

"Yes. I'm fine." She looked up to find Harry's chestnut brown eyes hard like rocks, blazing at her. His lips were set in a tight line.

"Fine," she repeated, more for him than for herself. But she was lying. It would take a

long time for her to be fine.

Banerjee was standing as well. He looked anxious. He stripped off his gloves and came forward. "Is this upsetting you?"

Arla snorted, despite herself. "You should know better than to ask me that question, Doc."

Banerjee raised his eyebrows. "What is it then?"

Arla closed her eyes and that strange floating sensation, like she was adrift in an invisible, watery current, assailed her senses again. *Fuck this.*

She opened her eyes quickly. The two men were looking at her with blank faces. It struck Arla that these two men were the only ones she trusted. And perhaps, the only ones who cared for her.

Apart from her father, of course, whom she barely saw these days. Her relationship with him? Complex, to say the least.

She took a deep breath and came back to the present.

"There was a killer who had the same MO as this. He was nicknamed the Nail Collector by the press. He removed the nail on the little finger of each hand and the small toes."

Harry said, "I remember that. More than ten years ago, if I'm correct. Killed four young women, right?"

"Yes."

Banerjee was frowning. "Don't think I was involved in that case, was I?"

"No, you weren't."

Harry said, "But you were?"

Arla looked at him and nodded. "At that time, it was the biggest case of my life. Lots of media attention. People went crazy. Those killings happened in the summer too."

Harry narrowed his eyes. "Hang on. Are you saying the Nail Collector is back?"

"There's no chance of that," Arla said quietly. Her eyes met Harry's till he understood.

He said, "He's in prison. Or is he dead?"

"In prison, serving a life sentence."

Arla saw light dawn in both their faces.

Harry rubbed his forehead. "Shit. A copycat killer?"

"Let's not jump to conclusions," Arla said. She had recovered her composure. Those heady summer days, ten years ago, had consumed her memory. It was the case that made her a Detective Inspector, from Sergeant. From then on, she was a rising star in the London Met.

She turned to Banerjee. "Anything else?"

"There's a lot I can't tell you without a proper examination. But there are a few observations."

Banerjee moved back to the body as Arla caught movement behind Harry. Three men had arrived with suitcases and duffel bags. They were getting changed into white sterile suits at the end of the perimeter. One of them looked up and waved at her. It was Frank Parmentier, head of the south London SOCO.

Banerjee had moved to the foot of the victim. Arla followed. The pathologist donned new gloves and turned the left foot. Arla took a sharp breath inwards. She didn't need this. Not right now, while the city was experiencing a crime wave.

Harry was leaning closer. "Is that what I think it is?"

"Yes," Banerjee said. "It's a black rose. Painted over the outside ankle bone. The lateral malleolus."

Arla kneeled herself, hearing her joints creak. "This is what the Nail Collector did as well. He had a fixation on black roses. When we raided his home, there were black roses everywhere."

"That settles it," Harry said. "This has to be a copycat killer."

Arla said nothing. She asked Banerjee, "You took the rectal temperature. Any signs of sexual activity?"

"Not in the anus, no. But I've not examined elsewhere."

"Hello," a cheerful voice said behind them. It was Parmentier. "Another stiff in the morning. Just not civilized, is it?"

He caught the looks on their faces and stopped. "Sorry. Did someone die?"

"Not funny, Frank," Arla ground out. "Hurry up and do your job."

"I came here because the great DCI Baker was attending a crime scene."

"What do you want, a medal?"

Parmentier grinned. "Some DNA will do." He was in his late forties with a belly hanging over his belt and big teeth that made him look like the dog from Scooby Doo. An appearance he was now following up with his act.

"Then you'd better start looking," Arla retorted, moving away.

This was just what she needed. Heat brought all the violent criminals out. It was a well-known phenomenon. In American cities and across Europe, summer acted as a trigger for bloodthirsty freaks to act out their sick fantasies.

And this freak, Arla knew, was just getting started.

CHAPTER 4

Sunlight glinted off the windows of the council block apartments as Arla watched from the window of the black BMW. The tall buildings surrounded Clapham Police Station like a forest. Arla often wondered how many lives were packed in these giant Lego blocks of bricks and mortar. Bedsheets and clothes hung from balconies far above her head, flapping in a breeze. They looked like the pages of an open book, words stripped by the wind, meaning lost in the endless smoke and smog of this behemoth, archaic city. Lost lives, imprisoned in five hundred square feet of living space.

After five minutes, the grand parade of Victorian mansions that lined the Common came into view. Arla shook her head. London's contrast of poverty and wealth were like oil and water, mixed into the same canvas, a painting of polar opposites. Somehow, the opposites didn't crash and learnt to live side by side. No doubt helped by the high taxes the rich had to pay. It remained a strange painting, and she was one of the tiny, invisible figurines on that canvas.

She wound the window down, feeling the breeze from the Common flirt with her dark hair. The sun was stronger now; it was almost midday. She had stayed at the crime scene while the forensic photographers took photos, then sent a drone up in the air to get aerial shots. These views would be analysed with digital enhancement later at the lab.

She had stayed because a sense of unease was burrowing through her bones like an army of termites inside a log. She had put the Kevin Anderson, aka the Nail Collector, behind bars. She had been stationed in Balham then, not far from Clapham. She could still recall the dull, dead gaze that Kevin gave her across the courtroom as the sentence was read out. It filled her with cold fear. She couldn't meet his eyes for long. Kevin had told her he would come after her one day. That she would die in his hands.

And now, it was all happening again.

This body turning up on her patch couldn't be a coincidence.

But Kevin was behind bars in HMP Full Sutton, up in Yorkshire, north England. Full Sutton was one of the seven Category A prisons in the country, where the most dangerous criminals were kept. Kevin had always maintained that he was innocent. That the evidence against him was circumstantial, and he'd been mistaken for someone else. But that wasn't true. DNA from the victim's bodies had identified him. So had a long and arduous police investigation. For almost 18 months, a large team had picked up evidence painstakingly, while Kevin carried on terrorising south London.

From the street, a child pointed at Arla as the BMW sped past. She closed her eyes.

Damn. She could feel the tightness in her gut, a sense of danger moving like cool fire into her limbs.

This was more than just a case. This was a message to her.

But who? And why, after all these years?

"Take it easy," Harry said. He had an annoying habit of knowing what she was thinking or at least making a good guess. She didn't reply and ignored the warm fuzz that spread across her chest. She knew he was glancing at her as he drove, and she ignored that too.

"Don't assume this has anything to do with you, just because you caught that guy. He's behind bars anyway."

"I'm not assuming anything. Keeping an open mind." Her training meant she had to. But she couldn't silence the little voice whispering at the back of her head.

Arla walked inside the station briskly. Harry went off to see the pool mechanic for some repairs on the BMW. The rear exit parking lot was full of unmarked Met CID and some uniform squad cars. Two uniform constables were smoking outside, and they nodded at Arla as she went in. She barely acknowledged their greeting.

"Uptight bitch," one of them said under his breath.

Arla wasn't listening. She was more concerned with powering her laptop up and getting inside the Crime Files Database to access Kevin Anderson's records. She stopped to pour herself a coffee from the new coffee vendor.

The green Lino on the floor made the wide corridor look like it belonged in a hospital. The paint was peeling off the walls, stacks of notice boards had photos of missing people, and chart printouts showed the rate of crime in different boroughs of London, the worst boroughs red coded.

It was a fluid, moving thing. The one graph she was interested in was smack in the middle of the largest noticeboard - a squiggly line showing the rate of crime in different seasons. Always up in the summer.

"Guv," a voice said from behind. Arla picked up her paper coffee cup and turned. It was Warren, a curly-haired, tall, broad-chested uniformed sergeant.

"Hi Warren," Arla said, blowing into her coffee.

"I'm on desk duty, Guv, and DCS Johnson left a message for you."

Arla stiffened. Wayne Johnson had been her boss for several years, and they got on like a house on fire. Arla had work to do; she didn't feel going into a skirmish with Johnson right now.

"What does he want?"

Warren shrugged his wide shoulders. He was black, and his close-cropped hair glowed dully in the bright overhead light. "Dunno." His handsome face broke into a grin. "You know what he's like. Always huffing and puffing."

Arla grimaced and fell in step with Warren as they walked towards the offices. "Don't I know it. Did he seem in a bad mood?"

Warren raised his eyebrows, and they both laughed.

"When is he not in a bad mood, right?" Arla said.

"You read my mind Guv," Warren smirked.

"Catch you later," Arla said, as they parted ways at the bulletproof double doors that led to the main desk area.

She walked down a similar corridor, but one where the paint was fresher and the blue Lino on the floor laid new last year. This section housed the Detectives and Uniformed offices.

Noticeboards lined the walls, mug shots of wanted criminals next to a list of their crimes stared blankly at Arla as she walked briskly down the corridor.

She went through the open plan detective's office into her own at the back. She dumped her bag, then went back out. Wayne Johnson's office used to be on the ground floor, but now that he was weeks away from being Commander Johnson, his office had moved upstairs. Arla took the stairs, two at a time. By the time she got to the fourth floor, she was panting, but the burn in her thighs felt good. She hadn't been for a good run in more than a week.

She knocked on Johnson's door, and his gruff voice barked from inside.

"Come in."

Johnson was in uniform, which meant he had some media function to attend to. Probably to take credit for some case the detectives downstairs had solved or lubricate himself with some politicians. He wasn't a bad person. Like most senior police officers, he knew the value of keeping the right people happy. He valued his career more than anything else, which Arla couldn't blame him for. But it also meant he put his needs above others.

His recommendation had promoted Arla to the DCI level, and she had worked closely with him for several years. Johnson knew about Nicole, her lost sister, and everything else.

"You asked to see me, sir," Arla said, standing with her hands clasped behind her back.

"Sit down, Arla," Johnson said in his baritone voice. His silver-grey hair was cut close to the scalp, and his smooth cheeks were lit by the sunlight from the window behind him.

Arla did as she was told.

Johnson said, "What's this about the body in the park?"

Arla was astonished. She shut her open mouth quickly. In this day and age of instant media, why was she surprised?

"Let me guess," she sighed. "Twitter?"

Most reporters and journalists lived on twitter. Tweeting about everything under the sun, but especially bad news seemed to be their purpose in life. Nothing sold like bad news. Bad news over good news, every time. Twitter was the bane of a policeman's life.

"Yes. Some reporter was jogging through the park on his way to work and saw the blue tape. He took photos of the crime scene on his phone before the uniforms could stop him."

Johnson leaned over and slid his phone across to Arla. She picked up the iPhone and scrolled down the Twitter feed.

Crime scene in Clapham Park. Is that a dead body on the ground?

The photo showed the blue tape and the back of a uniformed officer but cleverly blurred the rest of the image. Only the hint of a shape lying on the ground was visible.

The image already had hundreds of shocked and crying face emoji's and had been shared fifty times. Arla passed the phone back.

"Great. All we need."

Johnson coughed into his hand. "As you know, it's only a matter of weeks before I change jobs."

Arla nodded, keeping her face impassive. She knew what was coming next. Johnson wanted this managed quickly and with the minimum of fuss. He wanted to leave the DCS job with his near-perfect record. Near perfect, thanks to Arla and the detectives sitting downstairs.

And what did she get?

It was high time to broach the topic. If Johnson was vacating his role, surely it was Arla's turn to take over as DCS? She had been a DCI for almost six years running. She felt ready for the job but was also wary. She'd be doing little police work and more managing, more schmoozing with the big bosses. She felt conflicted. It was time for her to move on. If that meant more people management than day to day police work, then so be it.

Arla asked tactfully, "Who will be replacing you, sir?" She arched her spine, sitting up straighter, holding Johnson's eyes. She saw his jaw go slack. He pressed his lips together, then let go. For some reason, it concerned Arla. Her heart knocked into gear, suddenly drumming against her ribs.

"Um, yes, about that."

Arla tried to control her breathing and failed. "About what?"

Johnson didn't reply immediately. Arla filled in for him. "Do you mean the DCS job?" She hooked an eyebrow. Her tone hardened. "The job that was promised to me?"

Johnson lifted both palms. "Now, hang on, Arla."

Arla frowned. "Hang on for what? You were backing me on this. The Secretary of State was putting in a good word for me, right?"

In Arla's last case, she had saved the Secretary of State from deep trouble, and the senior politician had made it clear he would support Arla's bid for the job. The role of DCS was a major step up. Arla would be responsible for the working of a large area of south London, with more than ten police stations. She had never seen a woman fill the role in her twenty-five years of police work. She intended to change that.

"Yes, I am supporting you, Arla, and Sir Nicholas will too, I am reliably informed."

"What's the problem then?"

Johnson shifted in his seat and blew out his cheeks. "Well, there are some external candidates."

"What do you mean, external?"

"From other parts of the country."

"Sir, I know south London like the back of my hand. I grew up here, lived here...

"Arla, this is not my choice. The Commissioner's Board has decided to open the post up to applications from elsewhere."

Arla felt her pulse surge, and heat spread across her face. Her nails dug into her palms. She grit her teeth, trying to stop the words that were rising up like a black tide inside her but felt powerless. Moisture beaded on her forehead.

"Let me guess. The Board gave you an order, and instead of standing up for me, you just gave in."

"Arla!" Johnson thundered, his voice booming like a foghorn. He stood up, and with his six feet five inches, he was an imposing presence. He planted both fists on the table and leaned over.

"I will not tolerate this talk from you."

Arla swallowed and glanced down. Her eyelids closed for an instant. Johnson was right, of course. She couldn't speak to a superior officer like that. Her jaw flexed, nostrils flared.

But damn it. I'm pissed off.

She exhaled slowly, then looked up. "I'm sorry, sir. I didn't mean that."

Johnson's tightly bunched forehead relaxed. But his eyes remained grey flints, staring down at her.

"I did put in a good word for you as it happens," Johnson said quietly. He turned his back to her and looked out the open window at the parking lot below. "You've solved big cases. Big enough to make a career. For the record, I do think you're the right person for my job. You've earned it."

Arla swallowed, fighting a myriad of emotions. Surprise, elation, and a sense of dread.

"Thank you, sir."

Johnson half turned towards her. "The problem is you ruffle too many feathers, Arla. People don't like your attitude. And when those people happen to be in high places, your reputation goes down like a lead balloon."

They want someone who kisses arse and keeps her mouth shut.

Fortunately, the words remained inside her mouth.

Johnson said, "The Americans have a phrase for this. I think it's kick ass and take names."

"If you say so."

"I do. Assistant Commissioner Deakins isn't your biggest fan, as you know. He called to inform me of the Board's decision."

Arla shook her head. She couldn't keep the bitterness out of her voice. "Remember the last case? If I had followed his suggestion, we would never have found the killer."

Johnson faced her. "I know, Arla. Everyone knows that. But there is a right and wrong way to do things. You can't stomp your feet and shout at people who are your bosses."

Arla raised her eyebrows. "Kick ass and take names?"

The hint of a smile appeared on Johnson's lips, then vanished. "That's what a drill sergeant in a Hollywood movie does. Not you." He became serious. "So, I have to go with the Board's decision. You will need to prove yourself and keep out of trouble. Got it?"

Arla flung her head back and looked up at the ceiling. She didn't care that Johnson was watching. In fact, she didn't care, period. These senior management dipshits just didn't get it. And she was tired of trying to tell them.

"Yes sir," she said in a resigned voice. "I got it."

"Good." Johnson sat down, making the leather arm chair creak as his ponderous bulk folded on it. "Now tell me about this body."

Arla told him. Johnson frowned when she finished. "Missing nail on the small digits? Didn't we have a killer with that MO?"

"Yes, we did. The Nail Collector, from ten years ago. Kevin Anderson, his name was."

A frisson of fear shuddered down Arla's spine as she remembered the time when they broke into his ghastly garage turned laboratory. Where he had tortured the women. Where Arla found the necklace made of nails, that he kept hanging on the wall like a work of art.

She recalled the dead, icy look in his eyes as she stared at him for the first time. That horrible smile that slowly spread across his face. It made her want to turn around or run or reach out with a baton and smash his face in.

"Evil man he was. But he's now up north somewhere, right? In a Cat A prison."

"High Sutton, sir, in Yorkshire."

Johnson rubbed a palm against his chin, eyebrows lowered. "This has the potential to become a shit storm."

After a pause, he continued. "If the tweets are spreading, it's only a matter of time before it becomes a headline." His eyes narrowed. "I might have to make a statement."

Arla groaned inwardly. Johnson was always dreaming of appearing before the cameras, calmly reassuring the public there was nothing to fear from a crazed killer.

"There's only been one body, sir. I think we're quite far away from you having to make a statement."

Her comment was tongue in cheek, and Johnson looked up sharply. Arla kept her face impassive.

"In which case," Johnson said, "You'd better make sure there are no other bodies, DCI Baker. Your future career depends on it."

CHAPTER 5

T he detective's office was busy when Arla came down. Harry looked up from his desk as she walked past him.

"Get Lisa and Rob," Arla called out to him. "Meeting in my room."

She had opened up her laptop when Harry entered, on his own. He shut the door and leaned against it.

She tapped on the keyboard, ignoring him. Harry said, "Johnson wants this case cracked quickly, right?"

Arla got into her email folder and scanned it. Nothing back yet from Banerjee. She knew it was early, but sometimes the old man was very quick. She picked up the remote control and flicked on the AC, but it didn't work. Harry came forward and took it from her hands. He went out and came back in a couple of minutes. The remote was working now.

"New batteries," Harry said, putting the remote back on her desk.

"Thanks," she said, meeting his eyes for the first time. He stared back, face blank. She had grown used to this game they played, keeping their personal life separate from the professional one. It wasn't easy. She was his boss, after all. Luckily, despite all his machismo and Elliot Ness clothes, Harry was actually quite a humble sort. He didn't mind hanging back, letting her take the lead.

"Don't let this get to you," Harry said gently. She was about to reply when there was a knock on the door.

Rob poked his head in. Arla waved them inside. When all three were facing her, she asked, "Do we have an ID?"

Lisa said, "She had a credit card in her pocket. We traced her name down." She consulted her files. "Debbie Jones. Lives in

Lambeth." She looked up, and Arla saw a shadow pass across her face. Rob shuffled close to her and put a hand on her back in support.

Arla felt a cold hand curl around her heart. Lisa's eyes were clouded like she was thinking to herself.

Arla stepped forward. "What is it, Lisa?"

Lisa was a stalwart of the Met Force. She had seen enough in her time not to be fazed by the most macabre of murder scenes. But she seemed to have trouble speaking.

"Debbie Jones worked here, Guv."

"What?" Arla felt a hollowness spreading inside her ribcage. She forgot to breathe.

Rob spoke up as Lisa was clearly shocked. "Jane worked on the switchboard. She was one of our telephone operators. She'd been here for almost a year this summer."

For a while, none of them spoke. Arla and Harry looked at each other. This was too much of a coincidence.

Rob continued. "She didn't have any past convictions, no PCNs, no prints on IDENT-1. She wasn't known to any of the Forces in the UK. In any case, all of this would've been checked before she got the job."

Arla hung her head for a while, trying to think. "Any jealous boyfriends or violent ex-partner?" In her heart of hearts, she knew the answer. No jealous boyfriend or ex-partner would be *this* twisted.

Rob shook his head.

"What about her family?" Harry asked.

"She used to live alone in a single bed apartment, but her mother lived close by. Her father's dead."

"Where did they live?" Arla asked, dreading the answer.

"Balham," Rob said.

Arla was perched on the edge of the table, and her hands gripped the sides, hard. Her jaw clenched tight as an icy numbness spread tentacles into the tips of her toes and fingers.

Balham Park was where Kevin Anderson had killed his victims. For more than two years, he'd terrorised that neighbourhood.

Arla clutched her forehead. She needed to get a grip. This was becoming unreal very fast. She couldn't jump to conclusions. Surely, this was the strangest of coincidences and nothing more.

Harry spoke up. "Gather the Incident Room. Put the victim's photos and details up on the board. We need to get cracking."

Arla lifted her head and glanced at Harry. He asked, "Is that okay, Guv?"

"Yes," Arla said, clearing her throat. "Get everyone in. I'm going to tell them a story."

CHAPTER 6

Jane Crouch was a sucker for dimples. They got her, every time. And this guy had them. His dark hair was swept back from his forehead, and his large, attentive blue eyes were focused on her. Like he was drinking her in with his stare. But it wasn't creepy. He gazed at her between smiling and answering her questions. Every time he did, her heart skipped a beat. Apart from his lean face, strong jawline and sensitive, full lips, he also had an athletic build, trim, wide-shouldered. Jane wondered what it would be like to hold on to those shoulders, then looked down at her food quickly to hide the heat creeping up into her face.

She was meeting him for the second time and both times, they had met during lunch. He was a lawyer, and she had checked out the office, not far from where she lived in Clapham. He was genuine. She liked the fact that he didn't mind meeting in the daytime, unlike some of her other dates. And she could tell he was interested in her. Her job as a media liaison officer in Clapham Police Station was boring, but he was keen on finding out all about it while respecting the fact she couldn't give out classified information. Which he understood, of course, being a solicitor.

"How long have you worked there?" He asked, taking a mouthful of his pasta.

"A long time," Jane laughed, "feels like it anyway." She was in her forties, and he was younger than her. She found that intriguing as well. She had never been out on a date with a younger man. Was he one of those men who liked older, single women like her? Only time would tell.

The conversation flowed easily as they finished their lunch. Neither had anything to drink as they were going back to work.

He insisted on paying the bill. Jane liked that, too. Then he looked at his watch and exclaimed.

"Gosh, I'm late."

Jane reached for her jacket. "Hope I didn't keep you too long."

"I'd stay for longer if I could," he said when she turned back around. She stopped when he saw the serious look on his face. Then he smiled slowly, and god, she loved those dimples.

This was on. It was definitely on. Jane hadn't felt like this about a man just after two dates, and her mind cautioned her, but her body and heart were saying otherwise.

"Have you got a client?" she asked, as he held open the restaurant door for her.

"No. I'm doing some building work at the house, and I have to take delivery of a chandelier."

Chandelier.

He must have money, she thought, to afford a house in Clapham. And chandelier? Jane loved chandeliers. She even went to the Victoria and Albert Museum this year to look at the Glass Exhibition.

"I'll drive you back," he said.

"No, don't be silly. I'll take the bus back."

"And then walk? No way. Either I call you an Uber or drive you back. I live near the High Street. The station's just two minutes further."

Jane hesitated. Why was he being so nice? She looked at him, his eyes frank and sincere. He seemed to read her hesitation. He put his palms up.

"I'm sorry. I didn't mean to press. Whatever you like." He grinned. "As long as we meet again, I don't mind."

Jane wrestled with her own mind. What harm can it do? It's only a lift. And maybe she'd get to see his house as well. From the outside, of course.

"Okay," she said.

His car was parked near the station. It was a Range Rover, and he held the passenger side door open for her. They drove down the High Street, and then through some side roads till they stopped in front of a semidetached house that was clearly being renovated. A white van was standing outside.

"Goodness me, they're here already," he said. He dashed out of the car and into the entrance, which was open. He came out in a few seconds, a little out of breath.

"Sorry about that. Are you okay to sit here for a minute while I show them where to put it up? Then I'll take you to the station."

Jane wrestled in her mind again. The thought of seeing a chandelier being lifted to the ceiling was so enticing. Wasn't her Facebook feed full of chandelier photos? Even her twitter feed. One day, when she had some money saved up, Jane wanted to start her own glassworks studio.

The temptation won over.

"Can I have a look at the chandelier?"

He looked surprised. "Really?"

"Yes. I, uh, I like chandeliers."

He shrugged. "Sure, come and have a look."

He walked behind her as she went up to the door. He reached from behind her and pushed the door open. Jane stepped into a dark hallway. She was suddenly blinded from the sun outside and couldn't see much apart from some dark shapes.

The door slammed shut behind her. A hand grabbed her face from behind, closing around her mouth. Before she knew what was happening, pain exploded at the back of her head as she was smashed against the wall.

She screamed, but only a croak emerged. She had slid down to the floor, and a heavy weight descended on her chest, pinning her down. The hand clamped over her face again. Eyes bulging, Jane stared as he came low over her face.

"Just relax," he whispered. "We're only getting started."

CHAPTER 7

Arla faced the room full of detectives and uniformed policemen. There was a buzz in the incident room. There had been a slew of gun and knife crimes and a couple of armed robberies, but this was the first murder of the summer.

Arla knew that word had already spread about the strange crime scene, and gossip was rife about the killer. But what made the tension palpable in the room was how close this killer had struck home - Debbie was one of them. Maybe not rank and file, but she worked on the same premises, and many had spoken to her while she worked on switchboard.

Harry stood next to the whiteboard, on which the victim's face was stuck, along with an old file photo, blown up to A4 size of Kevin Anderson.

Officers stood at the corners of the room, leaning against the fax machines or desks with phones and laptops on them. Arla stepped forward, and the buzz in the room stilled. She cleared her throat.

"As you know, the victim's name was Debbie Jones. Did anyone know her?" Her head swivelled around the audience.

"I spoke to her a few times, Guv," a uniformed inspector called Weston said. "She connected my satellite phone to the station as I was in a scene without any reception."

"Me too," another voice said. Several heads nodded in agreement.

"Good," Arla said. "So we know this is personal. Whoever killed her will pay what he or she did to her."

She took them through what had happened since the morning. She turned back towards Harry when she finished.

"Any news from Parmentier?"

Harry said, "They found shoe prints, which they ran through the database and found nothing." The shoe print database was new and surprisingly useful. Criminals didn't always think to change their footwear, it seemed. Several burglars had been caught as they wore the same shoes to different crime scenes.

"Anything else?" Arla asked.

"Not much. They have taken samples of the soil around the body and from the victim as well, obviously. Too early for results."

"Pathology?" Arla asked.

"He's working on it. Said he would be ready to give you a run down in one hour."

"Good," Arla was pleased. Banerjee had got to the body quickly. It wasn't uncommon for him to have three or four cases to deal with in the mornings. Especially in the summer.

She walked back to the board and tapped on the photo of Kevin Anderson. "Anyone remember this guy?" She knew the new guys wouldn't. Her eyes fell on Jason Beauregard, a DI who was also her adversary and was pissed off that he'd never got her job.

Jason grunted. "Isn't he the Nail Man?"

"The Nail Collector, to be precise. The victim had nails removed from the smallest digits of her limbs. She also had a black rose painted on the left ankle. She was killed by exsanguination, which means blood drained out of her body till she died."

There was a collective indrawing of breath in the room. Arla found a grim, set look on the faces as she carried on.

"This is the same MO as Kevin Anderson, aka the Nail Collector. I know because I put him behind bars. He was, and still is, a very sick individual."

James, a new detective sergeant, raised his hand. "But isn't he in jail?"

"Serving life in HMP Full Sutton. So, yes," Arla said. A murmur rose up in the room, hanging over their heads like a cloud.

Arla raised her voice. "One swallow does not make summer. As you know, we need three victims before we can declare a serial killer, but that's textbook. In reality, this is looking very disturbing."

Jason said, "You interrogated, then arrested this guy, right? And then gave evidence in court as well."

Arla gazed at Jason, who had a smirk on his face. He was clever and knew how to get under her skin.

"So?" she asked.

Jason shrugged. "Just saying. He knows who you are and where you work."

"If you have something to share Jason, now would be the time," Arla said, keeping her voice even.

Jason gave her a shit-eating grin. "I mean it's a huge coincidence, isn't it? A victim is killed in the same MO as your biggest fan. Right on your doorstep, so to speak."

Arla said, "I have many fans, Jason. You're one of them, aren't you?" There was some tittering across the room. Arla continued. "Or do you wish you had caught the Nail Collector?"

She grinned back at him, watching the smile fade from his face, replaced by a scowl. She said, "Sure you'll get your chance, Jason. One day."

Sounds of smothered laughter came from the back benches. Arla suppressed her own smile and turned back to the whiteboard.

"I pulled out his file and had a look. Kevin was abandoned at birth and grew up in foster homes. He enjoyed torturing small animals when he was a teenager. His foster mother from Balham reported that. He left that foster home when he was sixteen and worked varieties of odd jobs as chef and builder. Came back to this area in his early thirties. Over the course of two years, he killed four young women. All looked the same. Dark hair, dark eyes. All Caucasian. He got to know them as he was a good looking man. Then he brought them home and tortured them in his garage before driving to Balham Park and leaving the bodies there."

Arla tried to ignore the nightmare visions screaming across her memory like the black wings of a giant bat. She didn't succeed.

Sensing her pause, Harry picked up smoothly. "He was caught when a waitress identified him on a photo as the man who was speaking to one of the victims. His DNA matched the semen found inside the victims. Yes, he sexually assaulted them as well."

Arla nodded at Harry, grateful for his intervention. She said, "Despite the mounting evidence against him and the DNA match, Kevin maintained he was innocent. He accused us, well me, mainly, of putting semen that matched his DNA inside the victim's bodies. He was clearly psychotic with deranged belief systems."

"One of his key thoughts," Arla continued, "was that someone else killed the women. As you know, the term psychopath is obsolete now. Psychopaths have severe personality disorders or PD. The malignant narcissist PD is what Kevin had, according to his psychiatrists. He was a classic Jekyll and Mr. Hyde, charming and smooth till he suddenly flipped and became a cold-blooded killer."

There was silence for a while. Then Jason said slowly, "So, if Kevin Anderson is in jail, who is killing now, using his MO?"

CHAPTER 8

The question settled over the room, weighing over everyone's mind.

Arla said, "The odd thing about this murder was the ring of stones around it. And the triangle of stones arranged like a shrine at the head of the victim."

She swallowed. *The victim* made it sound so impersonal. It was designed to sound impersonal, so the detectives could distance themselves from the case emotionally. But now it sounded crude, even cruel. Arla might never have met Debbie Jones, but she used to work just a few metres away from where Arla was standing now. The thought was heartbreaking.

As she re-focused, a granite-hard determination took shape in her mind. She would be ruthless in finding this killer.

She addressed the crowd again. "We are still in the early stages, and let's hope this idiot doesn't strike again. But given the shrine-like setting, it's possible this is a copycat killer, who is doing this in homage to Kevin."

Internally, she shuddered at the thought.

Harry said, "And don't forget that the media is already aware, thanks to the Twitter account of some random reporter who happened to be jogging in the Common."

"Yes," Arla nodded. "Mouths shut, please. No comments to any media vulture." She pointed a finger at her colleagues. "Any word leaks out, we know it came from this room. The boss upstairs, *Commander* Johnson, has given this priority. So I need volunteers to help with my team." The mention of Commander caused a round of laughter, mainly because Johnson wasn't present in the room.

Arla ticked off on her hand. "I want a full search and forensics of Debbie's house. With a door to door within two square miles of her home, to see if anyone saw something suspicious. We need a breakdown of her daily routine - from when she woke up till she went to sleep. Ask her switchboard colleagues. Ask her mother. Ask as many people as you can to get a detailed picture. Every little thing is important. Where she picked up her morning coffee from, what newspaper she read. Get on her social media pages. I want phone logs and call sheets. We need to interview every single friend she had."

Arla paused to take a breath. She glanced towards Harry and Lisa. Harry was watching her closely, while Lisa and Rob were scribbling on a pad furiously.

Arla said, "Any volunteers to join the team?"

Two of the new detective sergeants raised their hands, as did one inspector. Warren and two of his uniformed colleagues did the same.

Harry said, "What about posters of Debbie showing her most recent photo stuck on popular routes in the Common and outside the tube stops?"

"Good idea," Arla said. "Anything else?"

Detective Constable Pamela Das, an Asian woman of slight build, opened the door of the Incident Room. "Sorry to interrupt Guv, but the deceased's mother is here, asking to see the body."

"Great," Arla said. "Did someone not tell her to visit the morgue?"

Das shrugged. "The Family Liaison team called on her this morning, but she was out. They left a message for her to call back. She just came right here."

Harry stood. "I'll go see her. Relative's room?"

"Wait," Arla said.

It was the part of her job she liked the least. There was no good way to break bad news, but there was only one way to do it. She had to be direct, repeat herself, and then explain. She hated looking into the shocked faces of relatives, watching the vacuum in their eyes spread till it enveloped their faces in a mask of rigid incomprehension. She had seen grown men collapse to the ground like their legs had been chopped off.

Arla didn't know how people coped.

Or maybe she knew exactly how. Nicole's face wavered in her eyes, adrift like an image projected into water. The ripples spread to the rusty corners of her heart, lapping against the old, hardened walls.

"You stay. I'll handle this," she said to Harry. "Send Emily over to the room," Arla instructed Das, who nodded and left.

The meeting broke up. Harry moved closer. "Go," he said, "We have plenty to get stuck on. I'll see you in fifteen, and we'll head for the morgue to see Banerjee?"

"Right," Arla said. "And we can take the mother with us if she wishes."

Arla strode out the door and walked briskly down the corridor. She saw Emily Fairbrother, the Family Liaison Officer, standing outside the relative's room. They greeted each other.

"Does she know?" Arla asked.

"Yes."

Arla tried not to show the relief on her face. Emily said, "I met her when she came down to the station. I had to tell her, Guv, hope you don't mind."

Emily was in her late twenties, chubby with ginger hair and a cluster of freckles on her nose. She looked mildly anxious, and Arla put a hand on her shoulder. "Don't be silly. You did the right thing. The worst thing to do is keep them waiting."

"Thanks, Guv."

Arla knew Emily didn't know any details about the case. She knocked on the door and went in. Mrs. Jones was sitting in one corner of the sofa, sniffing into a tissue. She looked up with red-rimmed eyes when Arla walked in. She was a small, shrivelled woman, lines etched deep on her face. Arla sat down next to her.

"I'm so sorry, Mrs. Jones. Debbie was a colleague. I can assure you we will get to the bottom of this."

Mrs. Jones pressed the tissue over her nose. "That won't bring Debbie back, will it?" Tears spilled out of her eyes. Emily knelt in front of her, rubbing her arm.

When she had settled, Arla asked, "I know this might not be a good time, but was there anything unusual about Debbie's behaviour over the last few days and weeks?"

Mrs. Jones closed her eyes and rocked. Arla gave her some time. Then the bereaved woman opened her eyes.

"Yes. She had started going out more in the evenings. She was seeing a man. I overheard her speaking to him once, arranging to meet…" her eyebrows furrowed. "Olive something, near the common."

Arla wrote the name down and circled it. "Anything else you can think of?"

"She was wearing a cream-coloured dress that night…," the older woman's head lowered, and her shoulders shook with emotion. Arla reached out and rubbed her shoulder.

"I'm so sorry."

She gestured to Emily and stood. Emily occupied the vacant spot on the sofa as Arla went out of the room.

Harry was leaning over Lisa's desk, staring at her laptop. Arla moved around Harry to see. The laptop screen was divided into four with grainy black and white images in each section. It was the CCTV footage from the cameras on the streets surrounding the Common.

"There's three of us checking the northwest side of the park," Lisa explained. "Where the body was found. If we see anything, we'll let you know."

"Good work, Lisa. Any luck with the phone?"

"SOCO are in her apartment at the moment. They haven't found a phone in there."

"He must've taken it." Arla thought to herself. "But her mother heard her speaking on the phone to him yesterday. Must've been a few hours before she saw him. From the phone number, we can get the IMEI digits, then get the call log."

"I agree," Harry said. "Even if her phone's off or destroyed, we get a signal for 5 days, so it's worth checking."

Arla consulted her notebook. "Can we search for a restaurant in Clapham where the name includes Olive?"

Rob had joined them, along with Gita, one of the new detective sergeants.

"I'll look into it," Gita said.

Arla said, "Debbie was seeing a man. Her mother seems to think so, anyway. She was going out to meet him, and on the night of the murder, they probably went to this restaurant or pub."

Harry met her eyes, and she read the excitement in them. A flame touched the insides of her gut as well.

She said, "If we can get to this Olive place and access their cameras, then we could have a visual of the potential suspect."

"If she went there," Harry corrected. "We don't know for sure. They could've gone somewhere else." He grinned. "Let's not get our hopes up too quickly."

"Always have to be the naysayer, don't you, Harry," Arla said, frowning.

"I keep this place under control. You know that, Guv," Harry said, craning his neck back and swivelling his head till the joints popped.

Arla snorted. "You do what I tell you to. Remember that. And stop making that weird sound with your neck."

Harry grinned again. "Thought you liked my weird sounds."

"Like hell I do."

The others laughed as Arla felt the warmth rising up her neck, fanning into her cheeks. She glared at Harry, which only served to make his grin wider.

Arla turned away quickly. "Get the car ready, Harry. Do something useful for once in your life."

"Is Mrs. Jones coming with us?" Harry called out.

Arla stopped. "No. Let Emily take her. I don't have much to go on right now, till I see Banerjee."

CHAPTER 9

Arla and Harry waited while a visibly shaken Mrs. Jones was taken away by Emily and another Family Liaison officer. Once she had gone, Harry stood and rang the buzzer on the double doors of the morgue. Arla shivered while she waited, standing close to Harry. The morgue was in the basement of a building in Lambeth, and she hated the place. It was so quiet, she could hear a pipe dripping behind a wall somewhere. The grey walls were drab and cold. She was glad when the click sounded, and the door swung open.

Lorna, Banerjee's Chinese assistant smiled at them. She was wearing green scrubs, and a surgical mask was lowered to her neck.

"Come in," she said. "He's with the body at the moment."

Arla and Harry put on aprons, and although they didn't need to, Arla put a pair of gloves on. There had been the odd occasion when a piece of bone or other body part was handed to her for close observation.

Banerjee was at a gurney, leaning over the body of Debbie Jones. He looked up as they approached and put down a saw. With a gloved finger, he pulled his mask down.

"Ah, here you are. Just at the right time. I'm all done."

"Anything new?" Arla asked.

"Yes and no. Vaginal fluids showed sperm and evidence of sexual intercourse. Sperm's been sent off for DNA analysis, don't expect that back before tomorrow at the earliest."

Banerjee moved to the head. "Evidence of blunt trauma to the right temple." His gloved hand turned the head away from them, and Arla saw the angry black bruise above the right ear.

"She was hit twice in the same spot. That must have rendered her unconscious, or nearly so."

He moved to the hands and lifted one up. "Some skin scrapings on the nails, which I'm betting belonged to the suspect. She fought back, but he obviously overpowered her. Evidence of nicotine stains on the nails and also on hair follicles of the scalp. She was a smoker."

"There's bruise marks in the chin and jaw as well, where she was scratched." He pointed to the neck, "More bruise marks but minimal."

"Cause of death?" Arla asked.

"What I suspected. Exsanguination. The cuts here," he pointed to the neck, then moved down the body, pointing to the wrists and then over the ankles, "Here and here, are all at major arteries. Blood would have flowed out, eventually stopping her heart and causing cardiac arrest."

There was silence for a while. Arla asked, "How were the nails removed?"

Banerjee raised a gloved finger. "Good question. There are tiny lacerations around the nail beds affected, and on the finger pulp, a blunt, shearing force. I would say he used common pliers. The type you can buy in a hardware store."

Arla grimaced.

Harry whispered, "Sick bastard."

Banerjee moved down to the left ankle, where the black rose was drawn. "I've taken skin samples to find the type of ink used already. Waiting for results to come back."

Arla asked, "Any drugs or alcohol?"

"Ethanol found in the bloodstream, over the driving limit. She was on a night out, clearly. Drugs? Don't know till toxicology comes back in three days. If we're lucky."

"Fingerprints?" Harry asked.

"The ones on her body match nothing on IDENT-1. Whoever did this is not a known convict." Banerjee glanced at Arla. "Any news from SOCO?"

"Not the whole report. They've taken samples from the earth around the body." She gestured towards the gurney. "What was the time of death?"

"Between midnight and one in the morning. Rigor Mortis was early when I saw her in the Common, only in the small muscles. So, she wasn't there for more than eight hours. Together with the tissue turgor and core temperature, that's what the computer tells me."

Arla thought aloud. "So she went to the restaurant or wherever, then met up with his guy. That wouldn't be at three in the morning as she went out around 7-8pm, according to her mother."

Arla pursed her lips. "So, when was she assaulted? Before she was cut and left to bleed, I assume?"

"Yes. The bruise marks are older, and she needed to be dazed, if not out cold, when he was making the cuts. Otherwise, she could fight back."

"Unless," Harry said, "he wasn't alone. They were a team, one holding her down, while the other did this."

"Good point," Arla said. "So, if she was assaulted first, then it must have been where no one could see them. Deep inside the Common, as it's a warm summer night? Maybe they got frisky. Or back in her apartment?"

"Uniforms said no signs of break and entry in the apartment. SOCO are taking prints now."

"She could have let him in," Arla said. She hoped they'd gone back to her apartment. It would be easier to hunt for clues in there. Parmentier was fond of saying the crime scene was like a book. One just needed to look for the right pages. Which was fine in a confined environment, but in open nature, looking for forensic clues was a nightmare. Moisture and temperature destroyed evidence.

"Thank you, Doc. As soon as the DNA results are back, will you let me know?"

"I will, and let's hope we get a match."

CHAPTER 10

Arla got out of the BMW into the blinding sunshine. It was late afternoon, and London was in the middle of a heatwave. The pavement was baking hot, and Arla felt the burn of sunlight on the nape of her neck.

Harry had parked on Balham High Street, a busy intersection. He left the blinkers on. People stopped and gaped at them. There was a pub opposite, with its doors wide open, already half full with punters swilling from long pint glasses. A betting shop lay next to it, and a row of men stood outside it, watching Arla with interest.

"This way," Harry said. He had to raise his voice above the din of traffic and bubble of voices, that constant, cacophonous cocoon that surrounded London, a subversive radio station eternally switched on.

They dodged other people and arrived at the apartment block that was above a row of shops on the high street. It didn't look great, but on a switchboard gal's salary, Debbie had done well to get her own place in Balham. Only a mile away from the maelstrom of the High Street lay rows of lovely terraced buildings that housed families and sold for million-pound price tags. Arla knew the answer to how normal people lived in south London - they rented like she did and would for most of their lives.

The two uniformed constables standing guard at the entrance nodded at them when Arla showed her warrant card.

Upstairs, SOCO had set up a white tent on the small landing, and there was barely any space for Arla to put on the shoe coverings, never mind Harry.

Inside, Parmentier was bent over the carpet in the living room. Two white-suited men were collecting samples from the window sills.

"Anything?" Arla asked, kneeling down to Parmentier's level.

"Careful," he said. A shape was drawn in white chalk on the dark carpet.

Arla said, "You didn't find a body here, did you?"

"Yeah, and we didn't tell you," Parmentier said.

Arla rolled her eyes. "Come on then, Charlie," she addressed Parmentier by his first name. "What is this?"

"Signs of a struggle. Very subtle, but it's there. My guess is he didn't have time to put down a tarp or dust sheet before this happened. The carpet fibres are all twisted, there are a few drops of blood, here and here," he pointed. Arla could barely make out the blackened blood marks against the dark carpet.

Parmentier rose, and Arla followed. An island had been created on the small hallway, and Parmentier plucked out the plastic stands embedded in the carpet.

"More blood marks," he pointed. The carpet was lighter coloured here, and Arla could see the dark marks clearly.

"In a cluster," Arla said. "Like someone stood or was held here, while they bled."

"Exactly."

She looked at the door, which was an arm's length away. "Maybe he held her in a fireman's lift while he turned the lights off and opened the door. She was passed out by then."

"Maybe," Parmentier said, "Hence the cluster in one spot." He pointed to the doorframe of the kitchen behind Arla. "Paint chipped off here. Something, or someone, banged against this." He pointed to the floor, and Arla followed the direction of his finger. Small white flakes of dry paint lay on the carpet.

"This blow was new," Parmentier said. "No one cleaned up after."

Harry had come up behind them, and he hunched down on his knees. "No blood here by the looks of it."

"No. I suspect he needed to surprise her, hence some damage had to occur. He could have cleaned up better though. I've seen more organised killers in my day."

Arla shook her head. "Thank God there ain't too many of those. Can we get a DNA match of this blood with Debbie's?"

"No problem," Parmentier said.

"Send me a full report, please. I'm heading back to the station." She turned to Harry. "Can we call Jeremy Melville, the psychologist? I want him to go through Kevin Anderson's files. I think it's time we spoke to the prison warden at Full Sutton as well."

Arla's phone buzzed. She checked the screen and froze.

"What is it?" Harry asked. He leaned over to look.

It was an image from a Twitter feed. The photo showed a white forensic tent outside the crime scene in the Common.

"Who sent you that?" Harry asked sharply.

"Johnson," Arla said. "He's keeping an eye on the media storm. Bloody hell, there's more."

She scrolled down the feed to see scores of images of the crime scene. She shook her head. There was no censoring the press these days. Instant media had worked wonders to unmask serial abusers, but they also hampered police work.

She looked up at Harry. "Who is our Media Liaison Officer?"

Harry frowned. "Jane Crouch, I think. Not sure. Shall I call her too?"

"Yes."

CHAPTER 11

HMP Full Sutton
Outside York, North England

Kevin Anderson, aka The Nail Collector, stared back at the woman sitting opposite him with a blank face. They were in an interview room, down the corridor from his cell. A glass box on the wall allowed viewers on the other side to monitor the progress of the interview and to keep watch in general. On either side of the table, within arm's reach, stood two stout guards. Both men were former military and not to be messed with. Two more guards were standing outside the door.

The woman's name was Rochelle Griffith. She was a consultant psychiatrist, specialising in severe and dangerous personality disorders. Kevin didn't care about her title but liked the fact that they thought he had a personality disorder. Kevin knew he had done bad things, but they'd happened at times when he couldn't control himself. When the need raged inside him. The need to impose control over nature. The women he had killed knew this because he had explained it to them. Once he controlled them, he also purified them by draining their blood. Then the women, his victims as they were so callously called by these people, were pure. The women he killed weren't victims. They ascended to a higher zone when he had branded them, made them rise above the slime of this filthy world. A higher place that he, Kevin Anderson, inhabited. Free from the muck and ooze of common people. He was sure many people aspired to be where he was, but only a few got there.

Did he regret the killings? Yes, a part of him did. But he only did it to make them understand. Once they were dead, they would always be a part of him. Death was not the end. Death was the beginning. Why didn't anyone get that? If anything, it was life that was fragile. Broken easily. Death was permanent, a void that stretched for eternity, like a night sky without moon or stars.

He didn't mind dying. Death would be welcome. But it would be on his terms. He couldn't explain any of this to anyone. And this Dr. Rochelle Griffiths, did she understand? She always acted like she did. But did she really?

"I spoke to the psychotherapist, Carol," Dr. Griffiths murmured. "She is pleased with your progress."

Kevin didn't speak. He continued to stare back at her.

"What do you think?" the psychiatrist asked.

"Dr. Griffiths, you've known me for a while now. You should know better than to ask me that question."

"Afraid I don't follow. And you can call me Rochelle."

"OK, Rochelle." Kevin put his elbows on the table. One of the guards moved forward a step. Kevin was aware of it, but he ignored it.

"Carol keeps asking me about my childhood. How I felt about my foster parents. How I spent my days bunking off school."

"I think those feelings are important. They make you who you are."

Kevin noticed Rochelle's vivid blue eyes. She had light brown hair, which she dyed blonde. Kevin knew to look for dark roots. But he had to admit, the doctor was easy on the eyes. If she wasn't such a hard nut, he would like to know her better.

"Does your childhood make you who you are?" he asked, gazing at her intently.

"Of course," Rochelle murmured in that soft voice of hers. Kevin found it irritating. If this room wasn't so quiet, it would be hard to hear her. He wondered if she spoke like this normally.

"It does for everyone, Kevin. Among other things, of course, like our genes and the social situation we grow up in."

"Whatever, Doc. The point is, I don't like talking about my childhood. I don't mind Carol like I don't mind you, but it gets boring. She might think we're making progress, but all I do is feel like going to sleep on that couch."

"Being relaxed is vital for psychotherapy. You are allowed to enter a dream-like state, so all your repressed memories come out."

Kevin smiled. "Do you have repressed memories, Doc?" he raised his voice. He wanted to challenge her. He always cooperated with the doctors. He knew it was a game. They thought he was like a jigsaw puzzle they would have to piece together, and then voila, one day the whole picture would emerge. Why he did the things he did. The stupid fact was, he told them, but they barely listened. Or they didn't understand.

Fine. They could continue to poke, but he would have his fun with them as well. He enjoyed the mind games. What the doctors didn't realize was that he was examining them just as they were examining him. It worked both ways.

Rochelle said, "All of us have repressed memories. Virtually every human being has thoughts they suppress. Thoughts that lead to jealousy, anger, even rage. Sometimes violence. But we are programmed to suppress those thoughts."

She tapped her forehead. "That's why humans have a large frontal lobe, compared to other animals, including primates. We control what we think, say and most importantly, do."

"I don't, Doc. I'm thinking right now, I like your red nail polish, and I just said it." He grinned when he saw the scarlet wave moving up her neck, into her cheeks. She curled her fingers, and moved her right hand from the table to her lap, away from his sight. Both the guards shifted on their feet.

Rochelle swallowed and blinked.

Kevin smiled. "Gosh, I didn't make you feel uncomfortable, did I? Just admiring your taste in nail polish, that's all."

Rochelle's lips were set in a tight line. Her eyes were a dull, glazed blue. Kevin could see that he had upset her, and he was pleased.

"Continue with the psychotherapy, Kevin. We will meet again in two days."

"Oh, I'm sure we will, Doc. Look forward to it."

CHAPTER 12

The man arrived before the woman. He always did. He took a seat at the back of the cafe, a baseball cap pulled low over his head. The cap covered his dark brown hair, and a pair of sunglasses effectively shielded his eyes. After ten minutes, the woman arrived. She wore a hat, wide-brimmed and angled to cover her face as much as possible. Her blonde hair was tied up in a bun, not visible. They never visited the same cafe twice. Developing a pattern meant people would take notice.

Without a word, the woman took a seat opposite the man. He got up and went to the bar to order two cups of coffee, then returned to the table.

She hadn't removed her hat or glasses, but he had taken the sunglasses off.

The cafe was in a side street, off the main drag of Clapham. The maze of streets was a combination of terraced houses and the occasional council apartment block. It was quieter here, and the cafe was frequented mainly by local residents.

They had the last table in the place, facing the wall. She took her sunglasses off and sipped her coffee. She contemplated him over the fumes, staring into his dark blue eyes.

"It's started."

He nodded. "Yes." He held her eyes. He knew she could see the bitter, twisted truth. But he also felt the excitement that was obvious in her eyes. The hazel irises sparkled at him.

"Did you...." she left the question unfinished.

"Yes, I did," he confirmed. His breath quickened, mirroring hers. She reached out, and they held hands over the table.

"I can't believe you went through with it."

He shrugged. His baseball cap was still on, dense hair curling around the sides, over his ears.

"It wasn't as hard as I thought it would be."

She closed her eyes. "If only we could let Kevin know."

He smiled. "Soon, the whole world will know."

She shook her head. "There's no Facebook in prison. And we both know the police will try and keep it from the media as much as they can."

"It's already on Twitter," he snorted. "If they want to keep it under wraps, they're doing a pretty poor job."

She leaned back on the seat. Her fingers toyed with a knife on the table.

He said, "We have to be very careful now. Every step we take will be monitored. You know that."

She frowned at that. "But they don't know who we are."

"No, and it will be difficult for them. But that Inspector Arla Baker is on the case. The one who put Kevin behind bars in the first place."

She took a deep breath. "I didn't know that. How did you find out?"

He merely sipped his coffee in response, but his eyes twinkled at her. Her mouth fell open.

"No, you didn't!"

He smiled. She gasped. "You stayed in the Common to watch them?"

He nodded. "Yes, I did." His face clouded over. "Seeing Inspector Baker there was a blow, actually. I know what she's like. She won't let go. She's going to take this personally."

Her jaw clenched. "Well, the bitch did lock Kevin up. How dare she!"

He said softly, "And now she'll pay. With her own sanity."

"Yes," she whispered, fervently. Her eyes took on a distant gaze as if she was daydreaming. Then they snapped back to him. "I checked the messages today. Already hundreds. From around the world. It's crazy."

"And it's going to get crazier." He leaned forward subtly. "This is why we need to keep our feet on the ground, okay? There's going to be a storm. Kevin is a big star, partly thanks to us. When this hits the main global news channels, we might become stars as well."

They gazed at each other, struck by the enormity of what they were thinking.

"But," she said, "How far are we going to take this? What if it…"

His eyes became flat, steely. "We take it as far as it's going to go. Can't you see," he gestured with his hands, becoming animated. "This now has a life of its own. It's taken wings. This thing will now fly away, and people will take notice. They'll know what a hero Kevin was."

"You think so?"

"I know so." His voice dropped. "But I need to make sure you're with me on this. No one will find us, I can guarantee. Just be careful at your workplace. Never open Facebook, Twitter or Instagram on the work laptop. Just use your phone."

"I know. And when I use my phone, make sure the GPS is turned off." She swallowed, and her voice faltered. "But we need to think of the worst case. If that Inspector Baker finds out who we are…

"She won't," he interrupted. "She won't have the means if we are careful enough." He narrowed his eyes as he stared at her. He grasped the meaning in them.

He sighed heavily and held her hands again. "I won't let anything happen to you."

She smiled, relief washing over her face like sunlight emerging from clouds. "You sure?"

He winked at her, feeling a need for her throb in his pants. "Of course, I'm sure."

56

CHAPTER 13

Since she had come back from Debbie Jones' apartment, Arla's afternoon had been swallowed up in two lengthy meetings to discuss the new five-year plan for the London Met. The Met's Assistant Commissioners were in attendance, and as one of the DCIs, Arla had to be there.

Harry met her outside the meeting room when she emerged. "Did you fall asleep?" he asked, handing her a cup of coffee.

"Thanks," she said, taking it gratefully. She peered at him over the fumes of coffee. There was a hint of stubble forming on Harry's coffee-coloured cheeks. Harry was as vain as a peacock. He wanted his cheeks smoothly shaven all the time. She tried to keep her eyes away from his lips and the jutting jawline, but he was leaning forward with a lusty look in his eyes. She stepped backwards.

"It's you who looks tired, Harry. Not me. Got a stubble forming on your cheeks."

He bent his neck and glared at her. "Get your own coffee next time."

She grinned, happy that she'd managed to rile him. She could tell from the way his lips curled upwards that he was dying to reach out and slap her on the butt. She wouldn't mind at all in fact, but not while they were at work.

They walked down the corridor, side by side. Harry said, "One piece of news. There's a shoe print outside the door of Debbie's apartment. It matches the print in the Common, next to the body."

Arla's guts tightened. "Excellent. We have a link now to prove that he was at both places."

"Although the defense would say it's only a shoe, and anyone could be wearing that shoe."

She frowned and looked up at him, only to find him grinning. She shook her head.

"Anything else?"

"Parmentier will have a report ready for early tomorrow morning."

"Any word from the psychologist?"

"Yes, he's waiting in the office. But no word from media liaison."

"Jane Crouch, right?"

"Yes."

"We need to her to track these Twitter accounts and shut them down, if possible. Where is she?"

Harry shrugged as they entered the large, open plan area of the detective's office. "They said upstairs that she didn't turn up today."

Arla sighed. "Right. Find out if someone else can do it and leave a message on her phone to call me."

Arla beckoned towards Lisa and Rob, and the four of them went into her office.

Arla opened the blinds on her window, and weak sunlight streamed in, although it was almost seven in the evening. Arla massaged the back of her neck, then rubbed her eyes.

Lisa spoke up.

"There is a restaurant called Olive Garden in the north of the Common, at the corner with Wandsworth Road," Lisa said, "But they don't have CCTV inside, which is a pain. But I got videos from the cameras outside."

"Their security cameras," Rob corrected. "We got the footage from that, and I have two sergeants going through them now. Also got hold of the street CCTVs. What time period are we searching from?"

Arla said, "Given the time of death, and the fact that she was more than likely assaulted at home *before* she was taken to the common and killed, I would say, between eight pm and midnight."

Rob smiled. "Not the worst times. Fewer people around, that's for sure. But harder to identify faces."

"I know," Arla said. "But the sooner we get an efit, the better. Then we can put the CGI image all over south London."

There was a knock on the door. "Come in," Arla said.

The long-haired face of Jeremy Melville appeared. He let himself in, then shut the door. He looked around at the four figures in the room. "Busy, are we?"

"Like you won't believe," Arla said. She shook Jeremy's offered hand. With his long locks, ripped jeans, and Doc Marten shoes, Jeremy more like an aged hippy than a psychologist. But Arla knew a sharp mind inhabited that messy cranium. Jeremy had been analysing criminals for many years, but only in the last year had he transferred to the South London Metropolitan Police Force from North London. He had been of great help in catching the killer who had almost got rid of England's Secretary of State.

It happened less than a year ago and was a case Arla wouldn't forget easily.

She put her elbows on the table and leaned forward. "So, Jeremy. You want to tell us about Kevin Anderson?"

Jeremy said, "You caught him. What did you think?"

Arla had been thinking about nothing else. "Cold and calculating. He loved himself, too." She gritted her teeth as the memories came tumbling back. "But one thing is sure. He was adamant that he was innocent. Even when he was caught red-handed."

"That could've been his deranged mind and split personality. But remember, he kept insisting he was sane. He was also judged to be sane; hence, there was no sentence of diminished responsibility."

Arla frowned. "Yes, but he did have that personality disorder stuff, right?"

"Yes. All serial killers suffer with what we call severe malignant personality disorder. It allows them to have a split personality, effectively. So, they can be loving fathers and also cold-blooded killers."

Harry said, "But he wasn't a family man, was he?"

"No," Jeremy said. "He was an orphan, abandoned at birth. No one knows who his parents are. He never got married, so no children. He worked as a builder and did odd jobs. Even worked in a primary school for a while. Can you imagine?"

"Guess they didn't have CRB checks in those days," Lisa smirked. Criminal Records Bureau.

Jeremy said, "That's the thing. Even if they did, his record would've been clean. He had no prior convictions. We will never know if he assaulted other women if they didn't come forward to report him."

After a pause, Jeremy continued. "He was in Broadmoor for a while, while he had his psychiatric evaluations. Then he was transferred to HMP Full Sutton, where he has been incarcerated for the last eight years."

"Any trouble while in prison?"

Jeremy shook his head. "Category A prisons are maximum security, as you know. Only 580 inmates live in Full Sutton. Security is so tight even a mouse can't get into the cells where people like Kevin Anderson are kept. In addition, there's a Close Supervision Cell inside most Cat A prisons, including Full Sutton. This is a prison inside a prison. Every aspect of the prisoner's life is monitored, even when they are in the toilet."

"Ew," Lisa said, scrunching up her nose.

Jeremy said, "I went through his files, then contacted the In-reach psychiatrist who visits Full Sutton. She looked after him at Broadmoor as well. Dr. Rochelle Griffiths."

"And?" Arla asked.

"He cooperates with his psyche evaluations. Full Sutton has a PIPE - Psychologically Informed Planned Environment, which means making these areas suitable for treating these people and hopefully, converting them back to normality."

Harry said, "I doubt that ever happens. By the way, is there any indication that Kevin knows about these murders?"

"Rochelle didn't mention anything. I had to tell her why I was calling, of course. After seeking prior approval and having my credentials checked by the prison Governor."

"Did you mention my name when you spoke to Rochelle?" Arla asked.

"Yes, I did. She knows you by name, of course. But have you two ever met?"

Arla shook her head. "There's never been a need to, but as this case proceeds, we might well have to meet."

CHAPTER 14

Arla could see Harry, hands folded behind his head, watching her from the bed. She had showered and just put on her clothes. She leaned towards the mirror, putting on her mascara.

"It's only 6.30," Harry grumbled sleepily. "We had another half hour, easy."

Arla wouldn't mind spending the next thirty minutes in bed with Harry. But she had work to do.

"By the time I get in, it'll be past 7," she said. "Then you need to come."

"I last came at midnight," Harry smirked. "Only once. But you came more than me, right?"

Heat fanned Arla's face, turning her cheeks crimson as she looked in the mirror. Harry had been particularly skillful with his fingers and tongue last night. They had been to the pub after work, with the team, then left together but discreetly.

"Hey," Harry said, his voice softer. "Don't let this case get to you. It's not about you, right?"

"Well, if it is a copycat killer, then I do feel I'm the best person to deal with it."

"We don't know that yet. Just take it easy."

She finished her makeup, then picked up her purse and warrant card. She went back to the bed and gave Harry a kiss.

"Get up sleepy head. Time to do some work."

"When was the last time we had a shower together? You're always leaving before me," Harry said.

"Stop whingeing," she said, going out into the hallway. Her one-bedroom apartment was on the ground floor. It was small, but big enough for her and now for both of them. Not that Harry had left his home in Mitcham. His mother and sister still lived there.

Arla came out into the inner city streets of Tooting Broadway. Caribbean mothers with slow gaits mingled with the commuter crowd rushing to catch the early tube. Afghan and Pakistani drivers leaned against the wall of a cab station, smoking and watching the river of humanity. Arla dodged them all, joining the great migration into the bowels of the tube. It was five stops to Clapham Common and then a twenty-minute brisk walk to the station. She enjoyed the walk; it helped to clear her head.

The canteen was almost empty, save for a team of uniformed officers finishing off the night shift. Arla waved at them. She got a hot muffin and coffee, then picked up the two files left in her in-tray by Lisa. She settled in her office, going through the files. One held the call record of Debbie's phone. The phone itself was still missing. Her Facebook account was also visible, and Arla checked her phone for the link.

She went through the call sheet first, circling the numbers that appeared regularly, numbering them. Debbie had called a number before she left, and the time was 19.15. She would've been at her mother's house, and this was the call that her mother had overheard.

Debbie had called the same number several times over the last eight weeks, more than once a day. Arla could only assume this was the man she met that night. Until Lisa got the voice records from the phone company, this was all she had.

She made a note of the number and sent an email to Lisa and Rob. Then she opened her laptop and logged into Facebook. Her heart twisted when she saw Debbie's happy, smiling face on the profile photo. Debbie had been a nice young woman with a long life to look forward to. Arla flicked through the photos on her account. She scrolled past the holiday and pet photos and stopped on one where Debbie was wearing a sleeveless evening dress. The photo was taken inside a restaurant in the evening; a candle lit on the table where Debbie was sitting.

It was a recent photo. Who had taken it? Arla brushed her thumb over Debbie's glowing face.

"Who are you smiling at, Debbie? Tell me his name. How did you meet him?" Arla whispered. The smiling face stared back at her, silent but expressive.

Arla closed the laptop and went outside. On the far wall of the open plan office, there was a huge map, showing London in granular detail. Her fingers hovered over the northwest corner of Clapham Common. Several large roads congregated there, and there would be a lot of CCTV images to comb through. She knew the address of the Olive Garden restaurant. There was a tray at the base of the map with marker pens and red pins. Arla picked up a pen and stuck it at the restaurant's site. She saw a problem immediately; the restaurant could only be accessed by a path through the common. No CCTV would have access there. If Debbie and her companion had exited through the common and arrived the same way, then there was little hope of finding anything on the cameras.

She stared at the map, arms folded across her chest. She was beginning to realize this wasn't any ordinary killer. He had planned this meticulously. She now had to assume he had parked inside one of the Common car parks as well, where again, no cameras existed, as they weren't used very often.

Her reverie was broken by the sound of fast-approaching steps. A uniformed sergeant almost ran into the office and pulled up short when he saw Arla.

"DCI Baker." He panted. Sweat was pouring off his face. The flushed look on his face made a cold slab of fear hit Arla's chest.

"What is it?" she asked.

"Another body, Guv. Left in the same way as the last one, in the Common."

CHAPTER 15

Arla could hear a buzz inside her head, like a nest of hornets let loose, growing louder by the second. A wave of dizziness overcame her. She took a step back, bumping into the map on the wall.

"Who reported it?" Arla asked when she finally found her voice.

"A beggar. He slept underneath the bandstand and then went hunting for tidbits in the morning. Came across the body and called 999."

Arla breathed heavily, trying to dispel the mist circling her. "And this body also has a ring of stones around it?"

The sergeant, whose name was Chris, nodded. "And looks like she bled to death as well, Guv. We took photos, and they're going through the database as we speak."

"Please inform SOCO and Duty Pathologist." She looked at her watch. "Get me a squad car to the crime scene. Where in the Common is it?"

"South side, near the church."

Arla clamped her jaws tight. The Holy Communion Church, a place she knew very well indeed.

Chris hurried off, and Arla sent texts to Harry and Lisa.

The sun was shining when she came out on the rear parking lot. The rays hit her face, a baleful, malicious presence. London seemed better shrouded in mist, rain and cold. Or was it just her state of mind, wishing darkness to envelop this city, mired as it was in crime and secrets?

Arla walked towards the squad car waiting near the gates.

"Arla," a voice called behind her, then Harry ran up.

She folded her arms as she turned. She could see it on his face, in the width of his eyes. He knew. No words were necessary.

"I'll get the car. Stay here."

She nodded in silence as Harry ran off again. She called out to Chris, who stood outside the squad car. He nodded, then the car drove out through the parted gates. Soon after, so did she with Harry.

"Any details?" Harry asked as he drove, eyes fixed on the road.

"Ring of stones. Single Caucasian female. Bled to death. That's all I know."

Harry swore under his breath, thumped the steering wheel.

After fifteen minutes, they were striding down the Common; the morning grass still wet with dew. Harry showed his warrant card, and they ducked under the blue and white tape. The duckboards hadn't been laid as yet, but the ring of stones, in a perverse way, formed a protective circle around the body. It was a macabre, hideous sight. The light-coloured skirt was twisted up to mid-thigh level. The body lay flat on it back, arms laid out straight. The legs were together, shoes missing. The figure was deathly white, contrasting with the green grass. The small shrine of stones was close to the head. As Arla got closer, she could see the cuts on the elbows and at the neck and ankles. The face was bone white, dark hair swept neatly underneath the head, a chillingly neat, shockingly perfect replica of the previous murder.

Except for the face.

As Arla stared closely, the first hint of familiarity jolted against her spine like a thousand volts of electricity. Then the waves of nausea lashed against her gut, and bile rose up in her throat.

She knew that face. It was Jane Crouch, the media liaison officer.

Arla gave a strangled cry and fell backwards. She bumped into Harry, whose body was rigid. He somehow managed to keep them both upright.

She didn't know how long she sagged against Harry, but through a daze of disbelief, she heard his voice, barking out commands.

Two uniformed men came running, then ran back to radio the station for reinforcements.

"You okay, Arla? Can you stand?" Harry asked.

She nodded weakly, turning her back to the scene. Her head rested against Harry's broad chest for a second or two, and then she stepped back.

"I'm going back to the car," she said, her voice unsteady. Harry's eyes never left her face, but she couldn't look at him. She couldn't look at anyone or anything. The fresh, nascent summer morning smelt like death and decay. The cooing of the birds as she walked back was harsh, ear-piercingly loud.

Once in the car, with trembling fingers, she extracted her phone. Banerjee answered on the second ring.

She explained to him what had happened.

"Oh dear. Hang on tight, Arla. I'm on my way."

She turned the phone off and dropped it on her lap. Her hands came up, cold and trembling. She rubbed her face, then stayed in that position, head hung low, hands gripping her forehead, eyes closed.

Once was a strange coincidence. Twice was proof.

She hoped the third time wouldn't happen. But deep in her heart, she knew the blood lust of serial killers. They stayed dormant for years, but when they surfaced, they were like baying hounds of hell, scouring the ends of the earth for more soft victims.

Just like Kevin Anderson, a decade ago. For two years, he shook the community in Balham and the entire country, to the core.

Arla could feel it deep in her bones. Two victims from her own workplace wasn't an anomaly. It wasn't bad luck. It was a message. Kevin had always promised vengeance, but he was behind bars. And why would he wait all these years?

A copycat killer. Arla had never faced one in her life. It seemed surreal that one had now surfaced, in a case that she had solved personally.

To her mind, Kevin either had contact with this killer, or the killer knew of Arla's role in catching Kevin.

Arla felt encased in a giant spider's web, each sticky, obnoxious tendril choking her thoughts, restricting her movements. It was suffocating. Her breaths became jerky, shallow. Her eyes bulged. All of a sudden, the car was a prison, holding her in.

She opened the door and rushed out, not knowing where she was going. She could feel the tentacles of fear wrapped around her heart, squeezing remorselessly, pushing sweat out of her skull. Bile rose in her throat again, driven by waves of nausea.

She sank down to her knees, a choking, guttural sob coming from her throat. Her head pulsed with a thick, gelatinous mesh of black anxiety. Her insides felt raw, ripped open, expunged on the calm, bountiful grass, where little daisies sprouted. This was all wrong. All messed up.

The summer was turning blood red, the blue sky besmirched by a crimson hue. Arla opened her eyes and blinked. The clumps of trees and green grass of the Common undulated before her. In the distance, a group of joggers went by slowly.

Jane Crouch had been a colleague. Arla had solved cases with her, got drunk with her in the pub. True, Jane wasn't involved in the day to day business of police work, but dealing with the media was a big part of Arla's job. Jane had been more than helpful in those situations.

Her death, in this manner, would leave scars that wouldn't heal for a long time.

And Arla couldn't stop the worst question playing over and over in her mind.

Was she responsible for Jane's death?

Should she have done more, after Debbie Jones, to make sure that everyone in the station was more aware of the threat?

Gingerly, like she was nursing a broken leg, Arla stood. She turned to see Harry standing by the car, watching her. So she hadn't run that far away. She smiled wryly to herself. She had been overcome by a strange sensation. It felt weird, that loss of control. Giving in to panic, grief. She hadn't felt like that for a while. But it wasn't an alien emotion. After Nicole's disappearance, she had visited that endless, barren marsh of grief and frustration often. That ruined, scarred landscape where she wandered alone. No one understood what it was like to lose a loved one - a sister, only five years older. And in Nicole's case, the past had come back to life in a haunting, horrible way.

Was the same thing happening again?

Arla sighed. She put one foot in front of another and forced herself to walk. Harry was observing her, but he was used to her outbursts and mood swings. It had torn them apart on more than one occasion. It was another reason she thought Harry wouldn't last, like most of the men in her life.

But Harry had, so far at least.

She walked past him, unable to look up, and he didn't offer any comment because he knew better. He simply followed her back to the crime scene.

As she got closer, Arla's mind tightened, neurons firing across synapses in their trained path. Her eyes wandered around the scene. Did the killer follow the same MO? In which case, he would've assaulted her elsewhere, then brought the body here. To Arla's mind, he wouldn't have travelled far. The victim might wake up. She might struggle. But she could be bound and gagged. Regardless, Arla felt that the killer didn't travel too far. She stopped and turned.

In that case, he would've used the same car park. She looked past Harry, who also stopped and turned, following her gaze. Then he walked up to her.

"What is it?" he asked.

Arla looked up at the hard set of his jaw, his lowered brow. Harry was suffering too, in his own way.

"The car parking lot. Is there only one road that leads up to it?"

"From what I can see, yeah." His face cleared. "I see. You think he drove up here, parked, then carried the body over?"

She nodded, and they both trudged back to the gravel parking lot. It wasn't huge, a thirty-foot square area, roughly. Arla took one end, Harry the other. After a while, they met in the middle.

"Lots of tire marks," Harry said. "Not easy to find one specific type."

"I know." Arla folded her arms across her chest, gazing down the road they'd just arrived. "We might well have trampled over valuable evidence when he arrived."

Harry shook his head. "Other cars have been, so we wouldn't get good marks, anyway. But I'll send a couple of the uniforms to have a look, take photos."

They walked back to the scene. Arla heard a car pulling up behind them and saw Banerjee getting out of his old blue VW. He hurried over, wobbling from side to side. In his light grey, creased flannel jacket and matching trousers, he looked a comical figure.

But he was all business. He pointed with a finger to the crime scene. "SOCO arrived yet?"

"Nope. On their way," Harry replied.

"Then I'll have to be careful." He stopped to look Arla once over. His eyes softened behind the glasses. "I'm sorry, Arla. Was she a friend?"

"More of a colleague than a friend. But someone I liked."

Banerjee moved his head slowly from side to side. "Sad. Okay," he straightened his shoulders. "Let's see what we can find."

Arla stayed back at the perimeter tape with Harry. Banerjee put on a white suit with surgical mask and gloves. One of the uniforms had laid down the duck planks already. Banerjee stepped over them gingerly, his examiner's bag clutched close to his chest.

The black SOC van rolled in soon after. Parmentier and his two friends hurried over. His face was set in a grim line. He nodded at Arla and Harry, but there was no wisecracking or piss-taking today. No humour to lighten the air. Arla doubted Parmentier knew Jane personally, but they worked in the same premises.

Banerjee turned and called Arla over. When she got there, he stood in front of her, blocking her view of the body partially.

"It's the same as before," he said in a steady, steely voice that matched the hardened look in his eyes. "Do you want to see?"

Arla gulped, then nodded.

Banerjee pointed at the left ankle. It was a neat drawing; a black rose rising from the bulge of the ankle bone to three or four inches. Banerjee touched it with a gloved finger.

"Indelible ink. Maybe felt tip, I don't know."

"There's a lot of ink like that, right?"

"I'm afraid so."

"Can we still send off a sample to the lab, see if there are any chemicals that stand out? And also to match the previous rose."

"Definitely," Banerjee said.

Arla was already looking at the small toes. They looked strangely white, bare compared to the dark nail polish of the other toes. She shivered and transferred her gaze to the hands. It was a similar sight.

"Lacerations in the exposed sites of the major arteries," Banerjee said. He pointed at the elbows. "Brachial artery there, external carotid at the neck." The skirt was lifted to expose the groin region. Arla could see the deep cuts on either side.

"Femoral arteries," Banerjee said. "Considering there are no signs of struggle on the ground, I would say he placed the body here, then made the lacerations."

"Time of death?" Arla asked.

"By the rectal temperature, again, similar. Between six to eight hours. So, say midnight to two in the morning."

Arla felt her jaw tighten, and her nostrils flared. A lava of rage erupted inside her, burning in her bloodstream.

CHAPTER 16

The Incident Room was strangely quiet. A somber silence hung like mist over the assembled policemen and women. It was the calm before the storm.

Arla and Harry stood on either side of the white drawing board, where the photos and details of the victims were shown. Rob, Lisa and a few others stood behind Arla.

"Someone is targeting us," Arla said. "A predator who is picking on women who are our colleagues and friends." She stared back at the faces watching her in rapt silence.

"And yes, I think this is a copycat killer. He's picking up where Kevin Anderson left off, ten years ago. I don't know if this is some twisted vengeance that Kevin has planned for me. If it is, then Kevin must be in contact with this killer. Which is unusual, as, in Category A prisons, their contacts are closely guarded."

Jason raised his voice from the front row. "They can get OPV, or official prison visitors, in addition to any family members. Can't we get a list of all OPV to Kevin Anderson in the last say, five years?"

Arla nodded. "I've just left a message for Full Sutton's governor to get in contact. As soon as he does, I will request an interview with Kevin. It's time we met."

The Incident Room was full to the brim. Men and women lined the walls, every seat was full.

Arla said, "I want all of you to be extra careful over the coming days and weeks. Especially the women, but also your families. This killer's MO seems to be single women. We know Debbie was listed in the Lonely Hearts group on Facebook and other dating websites. We're doing similar searches for Jane."

Arla held the eyes of some of the women. Many of them she knew well. Her pulse rose, drumming in her ears.

"Don't go out to meet a man you've just met in a bar, online, from an ad, Tinder, anywhere."

One woman Inspector quipped, "Shall we cut men out completely, Guv?"

Another female voice said, "Yeah, who needs them anyway."

A smattering of laughter rippled across the room, lightening the atmosphere. Arla allowed a smirk which vanished quickly.

"Joking apart, remember this guy is resourceful. He could alter his appearance or even identity." She turned to Lisa. "How are doing with the e-fit?"

"We have some eyes witnesses from the Olive Garden restaurant. Particularly the waiter who served them. I finally got hold of him. E-fit should be ready in a couple of hours."

"What was the description?"

"Tall, Caucasian, dark brown hair, long face with a prominent jaw. In his late thirties to mid-forties. He wore a black or navy blue blazer with similar coloured shirt. Jeans and dark shoes."

"Everyone, please make a note," Arla said. "SOCO have now got back to say the blood drops in Debbie's apartment matched Debbie's DNA. Anytime today, we should have the DNA results from the semen analysis." She asked Rob, "Any progress with the call data from Debbie's phone?"

"Still waiting. No sign of the phone in the common, anywhere near the body. Searched a two-mile radius yesterday."

There was a knock on the door, and the large figure of Johnson walked in. Arla had debriefed him already. He nodded at Arla and walked up to stand adjacent to her.

"Any news from the door to door?" Arla asked Warren, the uniformed Inspector.

Warren stood up to make his voice heard. "Three neighbours from her mother's apartment confirmed that she had been there at 18.30. This adds up with what Mrs. Jones said. Then Debbie left. The neighbours confirmed she had a cream-coloured, knee-length dress on. She left by walking down the road, presumably to catch the bus."

"So she didn't drive that evening," Arla said. "Which makes sense because she planned to drink."

After a pause, she said, "I also think this guy chose the Olive Garden deliberately. It doesn't have any CCTV inside, and the road that leads to it traverses the Common. But we do have footage from the CCTV outside the restaurant, right?"

Rob spoke up. "Yes, we do, and I think we might have a positive ID soon."

"Good," Arla said, relieved. "Could the media liaison team please stay back? The rest of you, get cracking. We need to know everything about Jane as well. I'm aware she was single and liked a drink or two. I think she told me she lived alone, and her brother lived somewhere in London."

Arla answered another couple of questions; then the meeting broke up.

Mike Robert, and Sarah Bloom, the two remaining media liaison guys, approached the whiteboard. Arla shook their hands, then motioned towards her office.

Harry and Lisa came in as well, and Harry shut the door. Both Mike and Sarah looked nervous.

Arla said, "Don't worry. Nothing will happen to you guys. And regarding Jane, you did nothing wrong. Tell us about what she was like yesterday."

Sarah said, "She seemed her normal self. Happy and jolly. She went out for lunch, but she didn't actually say where, or who she was meeting."

"Did you know if she was dating someone?" Arla asked.

"No. If she was, she didn't say so. And we're pretty close. Tell each other most things," Sarah gave a sad smile. Then her nostrils flared, and her eyes grew red. "I can't believe she's gone."

"Can you think of anything unusual?"

Sarah shook her head. "No. That's the funny thing. She just seemed her usual self. We talked about her brother's new son, clothes, office gossip, you know, usual stuff."

Arla said, "If she was seeing someone, it might not have been that serious yet? Maybe, that's why she didn't tell you?"

"Possibly."

Harry said, "We need to go through her laptop. If she was on any dating apps, we can track them."

"Any sign of her phone?"

"No," Harry said. "Nothing at the crime scene."

Arla said, "If she was coming back to work from lunch, she wouldn't have gone far, would she? Is there any place she visited frequently?"

Sarah pressed her lips together. "There's a couple of places we go to for lunch. You know the two cafes around the corner?"

Arla knew exactly which two she meant. Many of the staff from the station visited when they got tired of the food at the canteen, which was often.

"Angelo's does the best coffee, right?" Lisa said. Sarah looked at Lisa and nodded.

"Can you think of any other places?" Arla asked. Sarah shook her head.

Harry said, "She could have gone anywhere in that hour, Guv."

"In that case, let's broaden our search. Photos up all over Clapham High Street and ask all the shopkeepers. Don't forget the beggars; they're the most observant of everyone on the roads."

Mike had sat there without saying a word. He was in his forties and going bald. He had a thin face with pinched cheeks, and he looked more haggard than usual. Now he stood, as their meeting came to an end.

"I'll hand Jane's laptop to the lab, shall I?"

"Is it OK if we come and dust her table for fingerprints?" Harry asked. "Not that we expect to find anything."

Mike hesitated for a few seconds, which Arla found strange. But then he nodded. Arla noticed how he avoided eye contact with herself or Harry. Her brows tightened, but she managed to hide her expression. Something about Mike's attitude was off.

"Sure," Mike said, "I don't mind."

The phone on Arla's desk rang. She waved goodbye to Mike and Sarah as they filed out of the room. When she picked up the phone, it was Banerjee.

"Arla, is that you?"

"Yes, it's me. What's going on?"

"I got the semen DNA back. The semen inside Debbie Jones' body," Banerjee said. "No matches I'm afraid."

Arla sighed. "Thanks, Doc. It was worth a try, I guess."

"If I find anything else I'll let you know."

Arla hung up and relayed the information to Harry and Lisa.

Then she took out her notepad and wrote on it. "I'm calling Full Sutton's governor now. As soon as possible, I want to head up there to speak to Kevin myself. I want to take our psychologist, Jeremy Melville, with me. He's an expert on body language and lie detection. By the time I'm back, we should have Jane's forensic reports to hand and every scrap of information we can get hold of about Kevin Anderson."

She opened her mouth to speak, but a loud knock on the door stopped her. The door opened suddenly, and Rob's red, flushed face appeared.

"Guv," he said, his mouth open, "you've got to come and see this."

CHAPTER 17

The team was huddled around Rob's desk. Rob sat in the middle with his laptop open on the desk.

"Here," Rob pointed at an open Facebook page. There was a picture of Kevin Anderson's face, close up. Arla felt nauseated just looking at him. There was a slight smile on his lips, and his grey eyes crinkled at the corners, a crafty look in them.

The page was full of photos of Kevin - in the courtroom, at his house, on the street, getting handcuffed. The page had thousands of likes and endless pages of posts.

"This is the Kevin Anderson Official Fan Club Page," Rob announced, reading from the screen.

All of the posts had a photo of Kevin, either in court or posing for the cameras while handcuffed. Old newspaper photos had also made the cut. Arla blinked in surprise at the photos from a decade ago. She vaguely remembered the officers surrounding Kevin, faces with whom she had lost touch.

In all of the photos, Kevin looked up at the cameras, no beard on his cheeks, a smile on his face. He looked arrogant, cocky even. Arla remembered his easy attitude when she interviewed him the first time.

He had a natural charisma that rubbed off on people. She could see why women found it easy to talk to him and be attracted. Which made him all the more dangerous, of course. He avoided the question of why he killed the women till his fourth or fifth interview.

By that time, the evidence against him was damning. Despite that, he maintained his innocence.

Finally, he admitted he viewed women as devious. The utter garbage that poured out of his lips that day was like poison. Effectively, he sealed his own fate that day. But it didn't stop him from claiming his innocence.

When he pleaded Not Guilty in court, the gasps of surprise were audible. And neither did he ask for diminished responsibility.

Those heady days came back to Arla's mind. His eyes were riveted onto hers across the courtroom floor as she stood on the witness stand.

"Guv. Guv!" A voice said. Arla blinked and jolted back to reality.

Several faces were looking up at her. Harry was standing to one side, and she caught the look of concern in his eyes. She forced a smile on her lips.

"Sorry, I was miles away." She peered at the screen of Rob's laptop.

Rob said, "There's an admin for the page, and I've sent a join request. Let's see what happens. I had to answer three questions about Kevin Anderson. Where he was born, who he killed first, and which prison he is in now."

"This is so weird," Lisa murmured. "Stop," she told Rob. "What does the pinned post say?"

Lisa was referring to the post stuck at the top of the page. It said, Read this first.

Rob clicked on it. A Google Doc opened up with a page entitled Rules and Conditions. Each rule was numbered and went on for two pages.

Rob said, "There are three categories of membership. The top category has to prove their collection of memorabilia of Kevin by posting photos of them. Or they could have been present at the trial or become an OPV or Official Prison Visitor. OPVs are in big demand, in fact. Basically, anyone who has seen Kevin Anderson in person becomes a star in their own right."

"This is nuts," Arla said. "If the National Association for OPV got wind of this, they'd shut the site down."

"That's just it," Rob said. "No one can shut this page down. Many have tried, especially families of the victims. But it's impossible to do so."

"Look at this rule," Warren said, and Rob stopped scrolling. Warren read off the screen. "If you are attractive or cute, then post a photo of yourself with Kevin's photos. We can ask an OPV to get Kevin to sign them for us."

"And the merchandise for sale," Harry said. "Coffee mugs and T-shirts, key rings with his photo on it."

Several heads shook in silence. Arla stepped back. "OK, we can go through this and see if we recognize anyone, or of the more recent...

"Yes, there is," Rob said, cutting her off. "Sorry, I didn't show you the most recent posts. Those Twitter images found their way here as well."

"They did?"

The photos were taken from a distance, but the blue and white cordon was visible, and so was the body lying on the ground. Then the same image zoomed in, showing the body in more detail.

The caption at the top read - Is Kevin Back?

Arla felt a wave of revulsion roiling inside her guts. She felt physically sick. "Who are these people? Can we trace them?"

She was thinking aloud, but the answer was obvious. It was impossible to trace people on social media unless they made their identity known.

Rob said, "I've clicked on many of the posters, but they show very little of who they are. There are no emails, even apart from those of admin."

"How many followers does the page have?"

"More than a thousand, but that's globally. Not sure how many in the UK alone."

Arla sighed in frustration. "Well, just see how many in the UK you can track down."

Harry put his hands on his waist. "I know. Why don't some of us become followers, like Rob? Then try to become friends with some of the others. See if we can track them down that way."

"Instead of doing real police work, hang out on Facebook?" Jason said. He had just joined the group and was standing at the back.

"You got a better idea?" Harry said, clearly annoyed. Jason said nothing.

"Okay," Arla said. "Do we have the CCTV images from the Olive Garden back?"

"Yes," said a voice from behind Harry. He moved, and the diminutive form of DC Das stepped forward. She had her black hair cut short in a boyish cut. She was always serious, Arla knew, and seldom smiled or joked about, either in the office or in the pub. She was good policewoman though, and Arla liked her quiet toughness.

"Lisa and I have been through it," Das said. Lisa walked to a table, and the gathering around Rob's desk broke up. Harry, Arla and Das regrouped at Das' table.

She clicked on the keyboard till the familiar four-box screenshots appeared.

"The waiter who identified Debbie Jones said she was there with the ma, at 21:00."

Arla said, "She left her mother's at 19:30. What time did she arrive at the restaurant?"

Lisa said, "Hang on a minute." She went to her desk and came back with a notepad. She flicked a page open. "The waiter seems to think 20:30. And they left at 22:30."

Arla stroked her chin. "Banerjee puts the time of death between midnight and two in the morning. I suppose that gives him enough time to do his thing."

"If," Harry said, "we are assuming that she was dining with the killer. Her date could've taken her home and left her. She might have let someone else in and that person killed her."

"That's true," Arla agreed. "We need to keep an open mind. But he is a key suspect, and one who has not come forward, despite the murder now being reported."

Arla turned to Lisa. "Anything from the house to house on Debbie's street? Well, she lived on the High Street, so there should be plenty of people."

Harry said, "Whoever our guy is, I very much doubt he will make an appearance on a High Street he knows is full of CCTV cameras."

Arla conceded that. "That stands to reason as so far, he's been shrewd in avoiding cameras. He chose Olive Garden because it has no cameras inside. But he ignored the ones outside; I wonder why."

Das clicked on the keyboard, and one video on the top left of the screen started to run. A woman, then a couple went inside, their faces clearly visible. The camera showed a side view.

"This is her arriving," Das said.

"So she came alone?" Arla said, as Debbie ducked inside the door and disappeared from view.

"Looks like it."

"So he must've been in there already. Does a solitary man matching his image arrive before?"

"Yes," Das said, her voice gloomy. "Several. This place is a bar as well, and many people stop by for a drink. It's summer, so the footfall is heavy. If we have to isolate a tall man with dark hair, we might as well look for a needle in a haystack."

"Show me when she leaves," Arla said, putting a palm on the table and leaning forward.

The image showed Debbie and a man emerging from the same door. But they weren't alone. A group of people were leaving, and the face of the man next to Debbie was obscured.

"Stop it," Arla said. She peered closer. The man was tall and compact. He was also raising his hand to the side of his face, which could be seen as an innocent movement, to brush his hair or scratch his cheek. But Arla knew better. This guy knew exactly where the cameras were, and he was covering his face from it.

She explained it to the team. "Roll it," Arla said. The video resumed. The man lowered his hand, but all they could see by then was his back.

"Think you're clever, don't you," Arla whispered softly to herself. She looked up to see Harry staring at her with a grim look on his face. "But all clever killers get cocky at some point. That's when we grab them."

Harry nodded. "That's right, Guv."

"Ma'am," a voice said behind them. Arla turned. A PC in her uniform was standing there, looking unsure of herself. She was a young girl whom Arla hadn't seen before.

"Don't call me Ma'am," Arla said in a stern voice. "DCI Baker will do. What is it?"

"Superintendent Johnson wants you up in his office."

CHAPTER 18

"**O**h no," Johnson held his head in both his hands as he stared down at the paper. It was a print out of the report that Arla had sent him.

"Damn it. No way!" Johnson whispered vehemently, then leaned back in his high backed, red leather chair. Sunlight slanted into his face, lighting up the creases on his forehead and the grooves around his mouth. Arla often wondered how Johnson dealt with stress. He was responsible for maintaining law and order of a large part of south London. He was addicted to work, she knew that. She also knew it was a double-edged sword. She lived for her work too because she knew nothing else. But the stress was wearing her down to the bone.

She had met his wife once at a Met Force Summer Ball. She looked small next to him and mild-mannered, mousy-haired. They had two boys in senior school. Arla wondered how she put up with Johnson all these years.

"Is this really true?" Johnson said, his voice grating. A muscle jumped on his forehead, and his jaw twitched.

"How?"

"I'm working on it."

"Working?" Johnson's nostrils flared. He bit off the words as he stabbed a finger on the report. The paper rustled as his meaty finger hit it.

"I need answers, Arla. A solution. This could be the biggest shit ball to hit this station, and we need to sort this out, right now."

Anger surfaced inside her, a red haze descending over her eyes. "I can't work miracles, sir. I know your big day is approaching, and you want to look all clean and sparkling. But there's…

"Shut up," Johnson bellowed, rising to his full height. His face was purple, and a vein appeared in the centre of his forehead. He was an imposing figure, but Arla didn't step back. She wasn't scared of him. But she knew she had crossed a line. He was her superior officer after all...If only he wasn't so obnoxious at times.

"I'm sorry, sir. That came out wrong." Arla swallowed, and looked away. When she glanced at him, he was still huffing like a wounded beast.

"We're doing our best," Arla said.

Johnson turned abruptly, sending his chair skittering backwards. He shoved it out of the way and opened the window, despite the air conditioning being on. Warm, humid air flowed into the room. He gripped the window sill and stared out at the car park for a few seconds.

When he swung around to face her, his face was calmer.

"This is not about me." He pointed a finger at her. "Or you. And you know you can be more of an issue than I am."

Arla frowned. "What does that mean?"

Johnson snorted derisively. "Where do you want me to start? From punching a paedophile outside court to smashing a reporter's camera...

"Show me one detective who has a higher number of successful prosecutions in this department. You know why the Serious Crime Squad is a big deal today with all the funding it gets from the Justice Department?" It was Arla's turn to point a finger at herself. "Because of me. You know that as well as I do. *Sir*."

She stood there, chest heaving in anger. Johnson had no right to bring up old wounds.

Well, I did insult him as well, she thought to herself.

But she had nothing to feel sorry for. She had never done anything wrong. If that's what Johnson and his tick boxing bosses loved, then they could fire her. They had come close to firing her in the past. Each time, she had a narrow escape. But she couldn't be anyone other than who she was.

Damaged goods. Well, that was her lot in life. She would remain damaged, fragile, breakable like glass, but sharp like a razor when picked up, sharp enough to cut through flesh and bone.

They glared at each other for a while, all fire and brimstone. Johnson was the first to look away. Arla knew he would. He had a job to do, and he needed to pull the right strings. It's how he'd got so far in his career.

He'd also helped Arla progress in her career. Despite all the bad blood between them, he knew all about Arla's past and accepted her as she was. She couldn't forget that.

"When will you learn, Arla?" there was a note of resignation in Johnson's voice. He sat down heavily on the chair. Arla remained standing.

"Soon, my post will be vacant. If you don't get the job, then your new boss will not be as lenient as me. If you speak to him or her in that tone of voice, well, you know what's going to happen."

He was right, of course. She knew it very well. In fact, she had wondered what her options were if she didn't get Johnson's job. Look for a new posting?

To add to the mix, she didn't even know if she wanted Johnson's job. Did she want to spend the rest of her working life kissing arse and parroting the same nonsense?

"I can't keep protecting you," Johnson said quietly. "You're senior enough now to be in the big leagues. You'll be dealing with people like Assistant Commissioner Deakins. Men with real power. As you know, he's not your best friend."

"You should see the way he looks at me in the pub," Arla smiled.

Johnson barely smirked. "Joking apart. You need to watch your mouth and stop losing your temper so easily."

Again, he was right. She knew it too. But actually doing it was a different matter entirely.

"I understand, sir," she said quietly.

"What does Kevin think about all this?"

"I have a call scheduled with the Full Sutton governor - Ross Piggot. We need official clearance, and I might need your help with that."

Johnson nodded. "You got it. So we have some CCTV images of this guy but none that show his face?"

"Yes. He scopes the places out, so he knows when to hide from the cameras. We have his phone number from Debbie's call list or think we do, anyway. It's turned out to be a pay as you go. SIM card doesn't exist anymore."

Johnson grunted. "Keep looking. This guy has guts. He must know we're hot on his tail."

"I think he actually wants that. Pretty sure he's enjoying taunting us. He wants to make a name for himself like Kevin did."

Johnson sighed loudly and rubbed his face, then his hair, which was cropped close to his scalp. "We need to make sure we didn't make a mistake ten years ago, Arla. I can't figure this out. But whoever this guy is, get him as quickly as you can. How many more officers do you need?"

"Got ten so far, on top of my team. Maybe another ten?" Arla knew she was pushing it, but Johnson nodded quickly.

"No problem. I'll divert resources. This takes priority."

Arla thanked him and turned. When she had her hand on the door handle, Johnson called out.

"I know Jane Crouch was your friend..."

Arla stopped. She could tell Johnson was standing. He advanced a couple of steps but didn't come any closer.

"I'm sorry," he said. "Are you sure you're coping?

A little twig snapped and broke in the forest of fallen trees inside her heart. That's how she felt. A soul full of broken parts, discarded branches that no one wanted. A heavy weight settled at the back of her throat, cloaking the whimper that she failed to suppress.

She didn't face Johnson. After a while, she managed to speak, turning her face to the side. "She wasn't a friend. I worked with her a few times; that's all."

"Sure, I know. But still, if you can't stay focused…

"I'm fine, sir. I really am. We'll sort this out. Don't worry."

Arla opened the door and left quickly.

CHAPTER 19

S he walked past a group of uniforms who said Hi, but she ignored them. She dashed inside the bathroom on the 4th floor, surprising the female officer checking herself in the mirror. Arla got inside a cubicle, slammed the door shut and sat down on the commode.

She bent forward till her forehead touched the knees. Her head was bulging with pressure, brain swelling, skull creaking at the joints. Her purse dropped out of her pocket. She picked it up, and a photograph fell out to the floor. She picked it up.

It was of Nicole and her, two sisters with their arms around each other.

She was the dark one, while Nicole was fairer, hair aflame in the sun. Nicole was smiling at the camera, while she squinted. She was eleven, Nicole fifteen.

Yellow sunshine spilled all around them in the photo, and it flowed across the years of lost hurt and pain into this dingy old cubicle, a mellow warmth that melted the steel and bricks, seeping into the darkest corners of her being.

The black tidal wave that was hurling around her heart broke its barriers and sprang from her eyes in a saline gush. She couldn't contain it. She bit her lips and scrunched her fists, and her body heaved with silent sobs. But she didn't drop the photo. She held it gently and tucked it into her bra, where she wouldn't lose it. Her body shuddered with unspeakable emotion.

All those years ago, despite being the younger sister, she had felt guilty for letting Nicole down. Her rational mind told her she didn't - Nicole was almost an adult, confident, sure of her ways. Arla was a child compared to her. But the guilt consumed her and destroyed her life.

Seeing Jane's dead face had brought the guilt back. It was irrational. Illogical. Jane wasn't family. But guilt lay in Arla's soul like silt does at the bottom of a river bed - a constant presence.

The shaking stopped. She ripped tissue off and blew her nose. God, she must be a mess. Her small vanity case was in the office, locked in the desk drawer. Arla listened for a while, then came out. She was alone. The mirror didn't lie; her mascara was almost washed out, hair strands falling over her face. She got rid of the remaining mascara, then washed her face. She left the bathroom quickly, taking the stairs. Head lowered, she barged through the open plan office, aware of several faces looking up at her.

She locked her office door, and the phone went off almost immediately.

"DCI Baker?"

"Yes."

"This is switchboard connecting you to Ross Piggott, Governor of Full Sutton Prison. Do you copy?"

Arla was instantly alert. Prison governors had important information about their inmates, and in Category A prisons, they knew their prisoners lives inside out.

"Patch him through."

A deep male voice came down the line shortly. "Ross Piggott speaking."

Arla introduced herself. Then she explained why she was calling. Arla knew that Ross had a police background. He had been a uniformed Inspector in West Midlands Police, then applied for the

Prison Governor's fast track course, which was hard to enter and complete. Governors had a stressful job, and Arla imagined it was worse in a Category A prison.

When Ross heard what Arla had to say, he drew in a sharp breath. "A copycat killer? My goodness me." His accent had a nice Yorkshire twang, but it was modulated with softer vowels. She imagined public school and a good university education.

"All the signs seem to point in that direction."

"Yes, that's very strange."

There was a silence on the line. Arla could guess what he was thinking. What they were all wondering. Miscarriages of justice did happen, and the wrong people did get locked up. Arla knew and accepted that some of it had been down to racism in the past. But there was no chance of it in this case. She had overseen every step of the investigation, down to being present when the DNA swab was taken from Kevin Anderson's mouth. The bastard had the nerve to give her a wink when he closed his mouth. She shuddered at the memory.

No, there was no chance of this being wrong.

"The evidence is correct," Arla said quietly. "Is there any chance that Kevin could've met and influenced someone in prison? What about Official Prison Visitors?"

"OPVs go through a lengthy vetting process. Yes, Kevin did have one or two. But they were random members of the community. He has no family, as you know."

"Do you have records of these OPVs? Like camera footage."

"Yes, of course. Every meeting is video recorded and listened to live. It's impossible Kevin has met a copycat killer. Also, they are separated from Kevin by a ten-inch thick, bulletproof glass barrier. They speak through a microphone. There are always two guards on either side. It's impossible for an OPV to have any physical contact with a prisoner like Kevin."

Ross continued. "And if you want, we can email you all the images and videos of the OPV, including during their contact with Kevin. Under conditions of strict professional confidence, of course."

"Of course," Arla said, but her mind was busy elsewhere. The flimsy hope she had was dashed now. She tried a different track.

"Is Kevin a good prisoner? Does he comply with prison life?"

"I have to say, yes. We have what is known as a PIPE, or Psychologically Informed Planned Environment. Which means the dangerous prisoners have lengthy treatments like cognitive behaviour therapy or CBT and psychoanalysis, which is rarer these days. Kevin did his treatments very well. The psychiatrist was very pleased with him. Well…"

"Sorry to interrupt. What's the name of the psychiatrist?"

"Rochelle Griffiths. She runs the In-reach team, as the psychological team is called, for three Cat A prisons and secure hospitals."

Arla wrote the name down and circled it. She took down Dr. Griffiths contact details as well.

She asked, "Did Kevin speak to anyone outside on the phone?"

"Yes. He had a list of vetted contacts, only two or three as far as I can remember. His calls go through the switchboard and are recorded. Basically, every aspect of Kevin's life is monitored."

"Do you know who these contacts are?"

Ross was silent for a while, and Arla heard the clicks of a keyboard. "Here we are," Ross said in his mild Yorkshire voice. "A school friend was his most recent contact, from 6 months ago. He also spoke to three members of his fan club. I have their names but can't give them to you over the phone. You need to make an official request."

"Certainly." Arla got to her main point, finally. "I would like to interview Kevin Anderson again. With our own psychologist in attendance."

There was a silence, then Ross said quietly, "I'm afraid that won't be possible."

"Why?" Arla frowned.

"Because Kevin Anderson isn't here anymore."

CHAPTER 20

Two days ago
Full Sutton Prison
Close Supervision Unit (SCU)

Rochelle Griffiths hands trembled under the table. She gripped them together as she returned Kevin Anderson's steadfast gaze. This had been a bad idea. Kevin had wanted a one to one with her, without the presence of guards. There was an alarm around her neck, on the table, even on the underside of the chair. At the slightest hint of danger or excessive movement from Kevin, the guards would come rushing in. They were just on the other side of the door. She wasn't worried about Kevin becoming violent, but she was worried about her own reaction.

Her heart beat faster, and her breathing was rapid. She knew the basic signs of anxiety very well, and despite her best attempts, she couldn't hide them entirely.

Kevin grinned. "Not making you nervous, am I Doc?"

Of course, he would say that. But she too was skilled in dealing with men like him. It was her career, after all.

She never looked away from him. "What do you think, Kevin?" she asked in an even tone, her face impassive.

He didn't answer immediately. He tried to stare her out again, but this time, she felt more in control. It was the flat grey of his eyes. So flat, unemotional. The frank, empty eyes of a killer. But Rochelle had stared back at many killers. What was it about Kevin that made her guts roil with a strange sensation?

"You're the one who's good at thinking, Doc," Kevin said, finally.

"Everyone thinks. That's why we are human."

Kevin said nothing. Rochelle pressed on. "You went to the gym today. Did you talk to anyone?" The prison had its own gym and swimming pool.

"Yes, the trainer. Seems like a nice guy."

Rochelle was intrigued. Serial killers didn't view people the way normal individuals did. They had no understanding of relations.

"What makes you think he was nice?"

"He liked the work I'm putting in to stay fit." Kevin rolled his sleeve up slowly and showed a thick forearm. Then he did a biceps curl, the muscle rising up in a large, hard knot.

Rochelle looked from his arm back to his face. Kevin grinned. "Like that, Doc?"

"What I like is not the point. Are you enjoying the gym and interacting with the trainer?"

Kevin lowered his arm. "Why did you want to see me today?"

Rochelle stopped herself from answering and said, "It's you who wanted to see me for something important. One to one, remember?"

"Yes."

Rochelle spread her hands and raised her eyebrows. "Well?"

"Do you believe there's someone just like you in the world? I mean like an exact replica."

Rochelle was taken aback. She hadn't expected this.

"What do you mean?"

"Someone who looks like you. Thinks like you. Who is identical in every way but is not a twin. You were not born from the same womb." A shadow passed over Kevin's face, something dark and inscrutable. Rochelle didn't miss it.

"You know someone like that?" she asked, leaning forward.

"I didn't say that, Doc. I asked you." He pointed a finger at her. He had big hands, she noticed for the first time.

"Do you believe that someone like that exists?"

"Kevin, you didn't have to meet me to ask this question. I'm busy, as you know. Now if that's everything…

"Doc, wait." Kevin half rose, then a buzzer went off. The door behind Rochelle opened immediately, and a tall guard came in.

"It's okay," Rochelle told the guard. Kevin was sitting now. The guard looked around, then nodded at her and left.

Rochelle said, "I wanted to have a meeting with you to see if you were progressing. Carol says the psychoanalysis is going well. How do you feel?"

"Good," Kevin said. "She says I project the anger from dysfunctional childhood onto the women that I, you know…"

"Yes, I know. Do you think she's right?"

"Maybe," he shrugged; then his eyes narrowed. "So this is why you wanted to see me. You know Doc, in many ways, you and I are the same."

Rochelle caught her breath, and her fingers dug into her palms. But she kept her cool. "What do you mean?"

"I mean, both of us are trying to make sense of ourselves. Of this world. Of each other."

"Maybe, but in very different ways." Rochelle cleared her throat. "That's not what I want to talk about."

Kevin dipped his head, then looked up at her askance. His voice was low and throaty. "Oh, but I do. You're wearing that red nail polish again, aren't you? I saw your hands. And from your shoes, I can see your nails. Red as well."

He wasn't smiling anymore. His jaw was slack, and his flat grey eyes suddenly flashed with animosity. Anxiety stabbed at Rochelle's heart. She pressed herself back on the seat.

Kevin smiled slowly. This was a different smile; he looked like a predator eyeing his captive prey.

"You wore them for me, Doc. Didn't you?" His head shot up suddenly, and he leaned forward, eyes wide, jaw clenched. "Show me the nails. Come on, show me."

Rochelle pressed the alarm hanging from her neck, and two guards jumped inside the room. In an instant, Kevin had his arms pinned behind his back. Another guard appeared and held him down on the seat by pushing on his shoulders.

Rochelle stood hastily. She flicked back some strands of hair from her face. "Kevin, you have not made any progress. Your old instincts are still present. In fact, I think you have regressed, gone backwards. I'm going to ask the Governor to release you into a high-security prison, where you will have more intensive psychological treatments."

Kevin smiled again. "With you?"

"No," Rochelle said firmly.

*****

Rochelle submitted her report to Ross Piggott, the Governor. He looked over it and rubbed his face. "I'm sorry this happened, Rochelle. Part of me thinks I'm responsible."

"No, of course not. It was my decision to interact with him. But nothing happened." She took a deep breath. "Guess I learnt my lesson."

Ross stared at her for a while, then nodded. "Where do you want him transferred to?"

"Rampton Secure Hospital." Rampton was in Nottinghamshire, and it was one of the three ultra-secure psychiatric hospitals for severely dangerous individuals.

"No problem. I will do my recommendation with your report." Ross rose, and they shook hands. "You will carry on working here, I hope. The other inmates need your help."

"Certainly," Rochelle said.

She went to her car in the parking lot and sat down. For the first time, she had some privacy. Kevin was certainly slipping down the rabbit hole of his personality disorder again. She had to do something about it. The parking lot was adjacent to the eastern wall of Full Sutton. Six-metre high concrete walls surrounded the secure area, but the windows at the top were visible, where the inmates were held. And Rochelle knew Kevin's room faced this car park. She stared at his window and saw a figure suddenly appear in it. It was a man, who wore the same white vest that Kevin had worn at the meeting. It was impossible to be sure from this distance. Was it Kevin? It looked like him. How long had he stood there? Did he see her getting into the car?

Rochelle strained her eyes, wondering about the thoughts jostling around Kevin's head.

CHAPTER 21

Jane Crouch lived close to Stockwell tube station which meant her commute to work wouldn't be a long one, Arla thought, as she stood in front of the converted Victorian house. It was divided into three apartments, and Jane lived on the ground floor one.

One day had passed since discovering Jane's body in the Common. Arla had managed to secure a meeting with Kevin Anderson and Dr. Griffiths at Rampton, and she was meant to head up there this afternoon. The thought of meeting with Kevin Anderson again made her stomach curl up in nausea, but she had no choice. Harry would be coming as well, and though she didn't like to admit it, she felt relieved he would be around. So would Jeremy Melville, who was going to watch from behind the glass screen. Arla checked her watch. She had exactly two hours.

A white tent was erected at the entrance, and two figures in blue Tyvek suits were scraping the ground with a brush. They wore surgical masks and green latex gloves. A white police support van was parked outside with the SOCO van next to it. Arla walked towards the SOCO van, and the driver stepped out when he saw them. He opened the back door of the van after Arla showed him her warrant card. She and Harry suited up, then went inside.

The hallway had been sectioned off to make a new entrance for the ground floor apartment. It reminded Arla of where she lived. All the Victorian houses in London had been converted into smaller dwellings.

She ducked underneath the blue and white tape and entered the apartment. To her right, a large lounge looked out on the street. There was a TV in one corner with two sofas. The place was garishly lit by spotlights used by SOCO. Parmentier was on his knees, examining something on the carpet. No white lines were drawn on the floor, Arla noted with relief, which meant they hadn't found a new body here. Parmentier looked up at them and waved.

Arla looked at the mantelpiece. She picked up a framed photo of Jane with a younger man and an older couple. Her brother and parents, Arla thought. The other two photos were of Jane out in town with some friends, and another with a woman who was much older, who Arla assumed to be a grandparent.

Jane was happy and relaxed in all the photos. Arla examined the one with her friends. She thought she recognized some of them. Then she realized the person was Sarah Bloom, Jane's colleague in media liaison.

With a gloved hand, she put the framed photo into an evidence bag and passed it to Harry.

"I want the names of the other women in those photos," she told him. Harry clicked his heels together and did a mock salute. Arla rolled her eyes. Parmentier snickered from the floor.

"Have the family been in touch?" Arla asked as she walked down the room. She stopped in front of the bookcase. Jane was into her crime thrillers, it seemed. The shelves were laden with pulp thrillers written by well-known authors.

"The brother is on his way down from Essex," Harry said. "He's coming to the station later today."

Arla checked the rest of the apartment. There was a kitchen, a study which could just about fit a bed and desk in, but nothing else. A box room in all but words. The bathroom cabinet had some makeup items and a razor. The bedroom was bigger, almost as large as the lounge. Harry opened the drawers of the desk, while Arla checked out the dressing wardrobe.

"Hey, look at this," Harry said. He was holding a stack of envelopes in his hand. He picked a letter out from one of them. Arla joined him to read it.

It was clearly a love letter, handwritten in black ink. The author was clearly smitten with Jane, comparing her to a rose, then to sunset, and how he would like to move his hands through her hair.

"Jeez, he was besotted" Harry remarked. Arla turned the sheet over and read the name. It was signed by a single letter - M.

"Who's M?" Arla asked. Harry shrugged.

"Did we find her phone?"

"Not in this apartment. And not on her body in the Common. So, no."

Arla looked through the rest of the letters. There were three in total, and each one bore a similar message.

"A lost heart, pining for love," Harry said. "Seemed Jane was ignoring this guy. Well, she was a looker. Don't blame M, really."

Arla gritted her teeth. She hated the sudden stab of jealousy, then felt awful. Her eyes shut tight. Her own feelings were nothing compared to what had happened to Jane. She frowned at Harry and snatched the letters out of his hand.

"Shut up. Go and look under the bed."

"Will you join me? Under the bed, I mean."

"Harry!" She snarled, poking him viciously in the arm. He grinned.

"Be serious for once in your life." She turned away as he reached for her. Parmentier was in the next room, and his assistants could come in at any time. Harry pouted, then went down on his knees as she stepped back.

He looked under the bed and then reached inside. Arla heard a board rattling and bent down to see. Harry lifted something up and came out. He was holding a shoe box.

"A floorboard looked loose, so I lifted it. This was inside."

Arla looked at his gloved hands, holding the box. "Be careful. We need to wear a mask, ideally."

"Don't be silly," Harry said. He took the lid off slowly, and then put it on the ground. He lifted out an iPhone, one of the larger models. He tried to switch it on, but the battery had no power.

Arla held out an evidence bag, and he inserted the phone.

"This is interesting," Arla said. "Why would she hide a phone?"

"Hope it's not password protected," Harry said, standing. He brushed dust off his clothes.

Arla nodded. It was impossible to break into an iPhone that had a password. She assumed this was a phone that Jane didn't use normally. She held up the evidence bag up to the light and looked at the phone. Nothing was engraved or written on the back.

"This goes up to Cyber Crimes. But first, charge it up and see if you can download anything from it. After Parmentier finishes dusting it for prints and things, obviously."

"Obviously," Harry smirked. She ignored him and walked outside. A familiar stretch of terraced houses lined both sides of the road. Tall and once stately, now fallen into disrepair. But they fetched a healthy price, being so close to the tube station.

Two women walked by on the opposite pavement, pushing prams. They were barely women, just above school age, and they wore hoop earrings and tracksuit bottoms, which was like a uniform in the council estates. Arla looked to the end of the road, where it curved around a bend. Sure enough, a grey-coloured council apartment block stuck up into the sky like a fat finger.

Both teenage mothers smoked as they talked. A baby threw a toy out of the pram, and one of the mothers bent to retrieve it.

Arla crossed the road and walked up to them.

"Excuse me."

They stopped and faced her. "DCI Baker, London Met." Arla showed them her warrant card. They leaned forward to peer at it, then checked Arla out with interest.

Arla asked, "A woman called Jane Crouch lived in that house," she pointed. "Do you live around here?"

One of the girls bent her hip and raised her eyebrows. "You a copper, yeah?"

"I just showed you my ID, didn't I?"

Neither of them replied for a while. One wore a pink Kappa tracksuit jacket with a silver trim down the arm and sides. The boiling heat didn't seem to affect her. The other wore a shoulders bare tank top, showing her navel with a ring in it.

Tank top asked, "What happened in there?"

"A crime has been committed, and a police investigation is on its way. It involves the woman who lived there. Do you live in that estate?" Arla gestured towards the council block.

Pink tracksuit said, "No, we don't. We live in one of these houses, down the road."

"Have you seen anything unusual in front of this house or anywhere on the road?"

They remained silent and looked at each other. Arla said, "What are your names?"

"Sharon." Tank top chewed on a bubblegum and moved the pram when the baby inside it cried.

"Tracy," said pink tracksuit.

The baby in Sharon's pram had stopped crying. Arla said, "Anything you can tell us would be very useful."

Tracy said, "I seen a man standing here, watching her house last week. He moved on when I saw him. I only remember that because I seen him the week before as well, innit?"

Arla flipped open her notepad. "What did he look like?"

"Tall, broad shoulders, with dark hair."

"White or black? How old?"

"White guy. Age, dunno, old guy, like."

Arla sighed. "Can you be more specific?"

Tracy made a clicking sound with her tongue against her cheek. It was the universal south London, street way of showing impatience. Common amongst Caribbean people, all races had adopted it as their expression of irritation.

"I seen him as well," Sharon said. "Forties maybe? Older guy."

"What was he wearing?"

"Dark top and jeans."

"Half sleeve? Any ink on his arms?"

"Nah, full sleeve."

"Shoes?"

"I don't know, man. What is this, twenty questions?" Sharon frowned.

"Was he doing anything, taking photos or writing something down?"

Sharon said, "Nah, he just stood there. When he saw me an' Trace, he moved on, like." Her eyes grew wider suddenly. "Oh my gosh, he done somethin' to her, innit? That's why you're here, innit?"

Tracy cocked her head back and pointed a finger at Sharon. "See, I told you though. I told you though, right?"

"Told her what, Tracy?" Arla said. "Talk to me."

The girls looked at each other and shrugged again. Tracy said, "At night, we seen her a couple of times, being dropped off by men. Different men, each time."

Sharon said, "And the one time, she was arguing with this bloke, innit?"

"Did these men match the guy you saw watching her house?"

Both girls shook their heads. Tracy said, "She liked men, she did. Never knew her, like. But I could tell. She enjoyed it."

Arla asked, "So all the men you saw were different?"

"The drop offs were at night, so we couldn't see them, right?" Sharon said, giving her pram a push as the baby squealed. "But the man she was arguing with was in the late afternoon. I think he knocked on her door, and she told him to fuck off."

"And you're sure this man didn't look like the one watching her house?"

Sharon blew out her cheeks, then shook her head. Tracy was nodding.

Tracy said, "Nah. The guy watching her house was good lookin' but kinda creepy, innit? Creeped me, anyways."

"Yeah same," Sharon agreed.

Arla said, "Both of you have been very helpful. If I send a sergeant to take a statement from you, is that okay?"

Sharon narrowed her eyes. "You ain't gonna make trouble for us, right?"

"Not at all. This has nothing to do you. All you're doing is submitting a statement."

Arla said goodbye and the two girls pushed their prams off, turning to look at the white tent erected outside their house.

Harry was waiting by the car. "Witness?"

Arla couldn't hide her excitement. "Think so. Tall, white guy with dark hair. Dark top and jeans. Sound familiar?"

Harry shrugged. "Not much to go by. But the basic description matches the man with Debbie at Olive Garden."

Arla folded her hands across her chest and looked at the house. She pursed her lips together. Harry was watching her.

She said, "I didn't know. She was into blokes. I mean, heavily into them."

Harry raised his eyebrows, and the chestnut brown eyes twinkled. "Really?"

"Yup. The neighbours saw her with three different men. We need to ask more neighbours, though, so the house to house needs to start ASAP."

Harry asked, "Did you know this about her?"

"Nope. I knew she was single. So she must've been dating. We need to get into her phone, Harry."

He walked over to the car and pulled the door open for her. He indicated with a flourish of his arms. "Your carriage awaits."

Arla shook her head as she climbed inside. "You forgot the uniform and the salute."

"Oh, I know you want to see me in a uniform," he smirked as she pulled the door shut.

"Beyond annoying," Arla grumbled to herself.

CHAPTER 22

The man watched the detective's drive away. He was sitting in a parked car on the opposite side of the road. He had seen the female detective and her tall sidekick arrive. He saw her cross the road and speak to the two slappers who lived in a council-owned house down the street. He should've been more careful about those slappers. It was a mistake to walk past Jane's house when she was at work. He had no doubt that Arla Baker would've asked them plenty of questions. And they had probably described him. He glanced at the house where the two teenage mothers lived. He could make an example out of them. Then he thought of the babies.

Their children.

The blue sky suddenly vanished like a switch had been flicked. It was replaced by black space, and the bone cold bareness of a cold winter, the shearing whistle of an icy wind as it penetrated the gaps in worn windows.

The children.

He remembered holding hands with another boy in the darkness. The cold turned their hands blue, toes numb. There had been no heating in the house for two days. There wasn't much food either, and they were forced to eat mouldy crumbs of bread from the fridge. Hunger gnawed in their bellies. Wallpaper peeled off the walls. They hugged each other for warmth, for some comfort.

Downstairs, they could hear the sound of a bottle breaking, and the crash as something fell in the kitchen. There was silence; then they heard footsteps. They stopped in the hallway; then the first stair creaked as someone climbed.

"He's coming," the younger boy said, clutching the other tightly.

The other boy was silent. "What shall we do?" the little boy asked again, his voice breaking.

The footsteps came all the way up, then stopped at the landing. There was a sudden crash which made them both jump. The man had just kicked a door open. The boys knew he was looking for them. He was drunk and angry. He wanted to beat someone up.

The floorboards creaked, then they could hear him outside the door.

The little boy was holding the other tightly. Tears ran down his eyes. "What shall we do?" he whimpered.

The blaring horn of a truck pierced the dense miasma of his terror-filled memories. He jerked awake, the blinding sunlight like a slap to his retina. He smelled the cheap leather of the seats, the diesel fumes and dust from the open windows. Wide-eyed, he looked around, breathing fast. Then he remembered where he was. Leaning forward, he rested his head on the steering wheel. His mouth opened, and he licked dry lips.

He didn't like the visions. He wanted to forget that life, but every now and then, he couldn't stop it. Thinking about those babies, that's what did it.

He saw two figures in blue Tyvek suits come out of the house and load something into the van. His thoughts turned to Arla Baker. She was prettier than he had imagined. A hard, angular face, sharp nose, big mouth. He had checked her with his binoculars, sitting in the car. Strands of dark hair fell over the small forehead. Her cheeks were sunken like she hadn't eaten for days. Somehow, the probing angles of her face worked and made her pretty. In his eyes anyway.

He smiled as he thought of her. A hunger grew inside him, heating his blood. It was time to get to know her better.

CHAPTER 23

There was a crowd around Lisa's desk when Arla and Harry walked into the office. Arla cleared her throat, and the throng parted for her. She thanked them and leaned over Lisa's shoulder, staring at the open laptop.

"Oh shit," Arla whispered. She was staring at FB page with a photo of a figure in the Common. The white SOCO tent was visible, as was a couple of uniform officers. The officers' faces were clearly visible.

"This is illegal," Arla fumed. "Is this that fan page?"

"Yup," Lisa said. "The KA Fan Club." She scrolled down the page. Arla felt sick. Several photos of Jane's body, all taken from a distance, filled the screen.

"Hang on," Arla said, pointing to a post. "How do they know the nails are missing?"

"I thought that too," Lisa said. "How do they even know these murders have the same MO?"

Arla exhaled, a knot of stress contracting in her stomach. "We have a leak. This is great. Just great."

She swung on her heels to face the group of around ten officers who had gathered around the table. Arla didn't pull any punches. "Who did this?" she asked plainly. "Who leaked word to this website? Or even worse, to some scumbag reporter?"

She met the eyes of each person. Warren, Das, Rob, all of them looked her in the eyes and shrugged. Jason walked over, and Arla noticed him lean in, listening.

Arla dropped her voice. "I know sometimes reporters can offer good money for information. But this is your career. I need to submit a report to Johnson. As you know, the London Met has extensive contacts in the Media. If anyone spoke to the media, the time to come clean is now."

Silence. A few more detectives strolled up to the huddle, sensing something was happening.

Arla repeated her question again. Only blank stares met her eyes.

Jason asked, "What about the coroner's office, Arla? What if he sold information?"

"Banerjee has done this for years. He has no reason to. His accomplice is also trustworthy, but it's a good point, Jason. Worth checking out."

Lisa said, "Guv, it gets worse. Look at this."

She scrolled down the page. There was a post called The Planning of a Murder. It had hundreds of likes and emojis. Arla read the first few lines, a sickness spreading inside her.

"First, you identify them by their needs. They could be lonely. Needing someone. Or they could be outgoing, always in search of excitement. Be patient. Follow them around. Learn their routine. When all the preparation is done, don't rush at the final stage. Don't make mistakes that beginners do…"

Harry had one hand on the desk, brows creased as he read from the screen. "This is a manual of how to be a serial killer."

He straightened, at a loss for words, unusually for him. Arla was still reading.

"He's taunting us." She gripped her forehead. "Right, that's it, Harry. Contact Facebook's UK HQ and ask for this site to be shut down. If necessary, contact the Home Office as well. We might need an official request. I'm going to speak to Johnson about this now, so he can get the Commissioners to throw their weight behind it."

Harry tapped his watch. "Train leaves Kings Cross in one hour."

Arla asked. "Okay. Get busy then. Did you drop Jane's phone to cybercrime?"

"Yes."

The phone rang on Lisa's desk. She answered, then gave it to Arla. "It's Parmentier. He wants you."

Arla answered. Parmentier said, "You're a hard detective to get hold of."

"Spare me the chit chat. What do you want?"

"Found a big book. On her shelf, on the lowest rung but hidden behind a stack of magazines. Pages were cut out in the middle, and a flash drive was hidden in the middle."

Arla remembered the bookshelf, rising to halfway up the ceiling, full of crime thriller books.

"A flash drive?"

"Yup. I've dusted it for prints. Would you like to see it?"

"Can you check the contents and get back to DI Lisa Moran?"

"No worries."

"By the way, I forgot to put this in my report yesterday. We found the same boot prints at the second murder scene."

"Great. What about fingerprints?"

"Nothing on IDENT-1, sorry."

"Good work, Frank. Keep it up. Email me the new reports ASAP." Arla hung up.

Someone called out, "Jeremy Melville's here."

Arla waved at the long-haired, casually dressed psychologist as he came into view.

"I'm off to give Johnson the latest," she said. "When I'm back, we head out to King's Cross Station." She looked at the detectives and uniformed officers facing her. "You guys need to hold the fort. Make sure the killer doesn't strike again. But most importantly," Arla paused, making sure she had everyone's attention. "Look after each other. No female officer out on patrol tonight, on her own? Got that?"

Several heads nodded, and there was a muttered chorus of Yes, Guv.

"Good," sighed Arla. "Now I have to face the Commander again. Wish me luck. All I bring him is bad news."

CHAPTER 24

It was raining all of a sudden, and thunder flashed in the sky. A jagged white line split the invisible night sky into two before vanishing itself. The booming sound was lost in the steady drum of pelting rain.

"Nicole," Arla pulled at her sister's sleeve. "It's late. Don't go out now. Or let me come with you." Nicole had makeup on, lipstick a loud red. She wore a black mini skirt with black tights and matching leather jacket.

"Stay here, Arla," she admonished. "I'll be back tomorrow morning."

"No." She clung to Nicole's jacket, but Nicole was stronger. She got herself free, then Arla grabbed her again. Anger flashed across Nicole's features. She was sixteen and more than a head taller than Arla.

"Let me go, now."

"No, I want to come with you. I…" Arla's words were lost as a shadow loomed behind Nicole. Huge arms spread from its sides and they enclosed upon Nicole. Lightning flashed again, this time so close it scorched the ground beneath Arla's feet. Thunder boomed like a giant drumbeat in her ears, and she was flung backwards.

"No! Nicole, NO!" Arla screamed, getting to her feet. Nicole was waving her hands at her, shouting something, but the black shape was dragging her away.

"Arla," a voice whispered in her ear. She felt the shake more than she heard the voice. Her eyes flew open. Harry's face was inches from hers. She was moving, and it took her a split second to realize she was on the train. Waning sunlight was slanting in from the window. Arla put two hands on the seat and sat up straight.

"You okay?" Harry asked.

She passed a hand down her face. "Sorry. Must've fallen asleep. Where are we?" She looked out the window. The train was slowing.

"Close to Nottingham. Sure you're alright?"

"Yeah." She frowned. "Just a bad dream that's all." Luckily, Jeremy wasn't sitting with them. Arla asked Harry where he was.

"Four seats behind us."

"Good," Arla yawned. Her dream was recurrent, repressive. She had learnt to live with it. But she was glad for the sleep. The last two nights she had tossed and turned, then climbed on top of Harry. Which meant he hadn't slept much either. She squinted at him.

"Did you sleep?"

He yawned too. "Not as much as you." He pointed outside the window. "Look."

Tall blocks of flats were appearing, and the rail lines proliferated, rusty bars on which stolid old carriages rested, going nowhere. Cargo trains and discarded old junk motors. The spire of a cathedral appeared, rising like a needle into the azure sky.

The train pulled into the platform, and the three of them alighted. They had to catch a connecting train to Retford, which was closer to Woodbeck, the village outside which Rampton was located. In an hour's time, they were in a Toyota Prius speeding down a one lane A road.

Inside Rampton, they had to submit their warrant cards and IDs and then waited while they were checked. It took longer than Arla expected.

Finally, they were called for security. The Governor of Rampton was a portly man called Jason Beasley. Arla had spoken to him briefly, and he had agreed to arrange a meeting with Kevin and Dr. Griffiths.

The receptionist took them to the security door. "Governor Beasley will see you on the other side," she said.

Ross Piggott hadn't lied when he said security was tighter than in an airport. First, each one of them had to go inside a cubicle like a passport photo booth. There, Arla had to sit in a dark chamber with her face pressed to a glass surface. A laser sharp blue light beam swivelled around twice, and her iris scan was taken. This would serve as one of her biometric identity features when she next attended.

She also had to do a thumb scan and fingerprint. All three of these, along with her photos, height and weight, were now her biometric "passport." However, she had her passport with her and a gas bill, but in the future, these would be eschewed in favour of all the tests she had done now.

While the others went through the same routine, Arla had to step into the women's segregated zone. A chubby security woman with a stern face and buzz cut blonde hair gave her the hardest pat down she ever had.

"Spread your legs please," the woman barked. Arla had to hold onto the sides of the cubicle while another security guard watched on, hands on her hips. Then she had to remove her shoes, socks and leave her phone and hairpins in a locker. She was asked about her bra liner and informed it would be checked when she went through the X-ray scanner. She assured them it was a normal bra, bought on the high street. Off Primark, on Tooting Broadway, to be precise. Her phone, pager, warrant card, two pens - all of it was confiscated, to be returned when she left. Visitors were not allowed to have pens or paper inside, never mind a phone or any other gadget.

When she finally emerged at the other end, she was impatient for the ordeal to be over. But it wasn't. All of them were fitted with a buzzer, and Jeremy's buzzer went off just as they cleared security. Three guards rushed up and searched Jeremy again. Thankfully, he didn't have to through the scanner again.

Governor Beasley was waiting for them at his office. He shook Arla's hands first. "Sorry you had to go through that. But this is a high-security hospital for a reason."

"Feels like a prison, not a hospital," Arla said.

"Indeed it is," Beasley nodded, as they all sat down. Arla brought him up to speed on the cases. Beasley listened carefully, hands crossed on his lap.

"How long has Kevin been here for?" Arla asked. "Ross Piggott mentioned he had left only a couple of days ago."

"One day, to be precise. But he was admitted here initially before transferring to Full Sutton. Dangerous individuals like him always do. So we know him, from about eight years ago."

"How does he seem to you?"

Beasley shrugged. "I've only met him once. Seems calm, but who knows? Ross said he had malignant urges again, as Dr. Griffiths calls them. She thinks his severe PD is coming back."

"Personality Disorder?"

"Yes."

"Is Dr. Griffiths here?"

Beasley checked the watch. It was almost five pm. "She's finishing up at another hospital, then will drive down. You can interview Kevin in the meanwhile."

There was a moment's silence. Then Beasley said, "Ready when you are."

CHAPTER 25

Arla rose, feeling the staccato beats of her heart knocking against her ribs. She nodded, then followed Beasley, the others falling in step behind her. She tried to keep her mind blank as she walked down the brightly lit corridor but failed. She had dreaded this moment. Despite the fact that she had spent her life hunting down men like Kevin Anderson, she despised speaking to them. More often than not, she lost her cool. What would happen today?

Only time would tell.

Harry, Jeremy and Beasley went inside the inspection chamber. Harry held her eyes as the door closed, and she could see from the set of his mouth he was tense, apprehensive. She was shown into the room by a burly guard, who took up position behind her on the wall. Then Kevin came in, hands cuffed, accompanied by another guard. The guard took the handcuffs off and made him sit down opposite Arla.

She stared at him in morbid fascination. He hadn't changed much. Prison life must be agreeing with him. He looked fit and toned, and if anything, had bulked up with muscle. His grey eyes stared back at her with frank interest. His close cut black hair had some white on the sides. There was a hint of mirth in his eyes, which touched his lips as well. Arla didn't like it.

"Well, well," Kevin drawled after a while. "We meet again, Inspector Baker. Oh, wait. Are you a higher ranking officer now? Seeing you caught me and all?"

"I am, actually. Detective Chief Inspector now. But not because I caught you, Kevin. I caught many others, too."

"But none like me?"

"Not far off from you."

"There you go. Knew I was special."

The fact that she was sitting here speaking so casually to a brutal serial killer seemed surreal to Arla. Kevin had a relaxed and easy attitude, but she remained vigilant. She suspected he was acting casual on purpose, to draw her in, lower her guard.

"Do you know why I'm here, Kevin?"

He shook his head slowly, but Arla noted the hint of a sardonic smile remained on his lips. It was ever so faint but present, palpable. It bothered her a great deal.

She decided to test the waters. "Are you sure you don't know why I'm here?"

"You want me to guess, Inspector Baker?"

They watched each other for a few seconds. Arla's mind whirred with possibilities. Kevin had, of course, been told she was going to visit. He was prepared. If she had expected any emotions from him – anger, sadness, she was getting nothing. Maybe that was his preparation.

"No, I don't want you to guess." She decided not to waste further time. It wouldn't benefit either of them.

"Two women have died recently. The way they were killed is very similar to what you did, ten years ago."

Kevin watched her in silence. The hint of smile was now gone, replaced by a slight narrowing in the corner of his eyes.

Arla said, "The dead women look similar to your victims. Dark hair, brown eyes, medium height."

"What about the nails?"

Arla stared at him for a while. He seemed more animated now, that was for sure. "Taken," she said slowly. "From the small fingers of each limb."

Again, she paused. Kevin's eyelids flickered, then stabilized. Arla said, "Do you know anything about these murders, Kevin?"

His face remained flat. He shook his head slowly.

"Are you sure?" Arla asked.

The hint of a grin appeared again. This time, it stayed. If anything, it was broader.

"What?" Arla asked. She fought the churn in her guts. She felt like she understood him, which was weird. Very weird. She couldn't shake off the feeling he was acting. Like he had known, all along, what she had come about. But that was impossible. Arla blinked. She didn't want to overthink this. Kevin had barely any contact with the outside world. What little contact he had was carefully monitored. No, there was no way he had known. He did now, but only because she had told him. And she suspected he would milk it for all he was worth.

"You're fishing, Inspector. In very deep waters, I might add."

"What do you mean?"

His jaw slackened, and his mouth grew tighter. "Don't you know what I mean?"

Something rustled at the corner of Arla's mind; like a mouse scurrying around the corner. She didn't frown. But her pulse speeded up. There was a shift in the air between them all of a sudden, and she knew they both felt it.

She said, "I'm not here to play games, Kevin. So why don't you tell me? What do you mean by deep waters."

"I guess you'll find out," he said.

"Are you saying you know nothing about these murders?"

"Look where I am, Inspector. How could I?"

Arla was tempted to ask him about his fan club. She knew that Cat A prisoners weren't allowed access to the internet, but they could read newspapers. They couldn't email, and emails from relatives had to be printed out and then given to prisoners to read.

"Just answer the question, please," Arla said.

"No," Kevin said softly. "I know nothing about them."

The hint of a grin appeared on his lips, and his eyes hooded slightly.

Was he doing that just to get to me? Arla wondered. *Because he knows I'm worried. Otherwise, I wouldn't be here.*

But she decided to leave it alone. She couldn't let Kevin get under her skin. He was trying, that much was plain to see.

"Is this why you're here, Inspector? To ask me about these new cases?"

"Why else would I be here?"

There was that maddening hint of a smile again. This time, it vanished quickly, like he didn't want to upset her too much.

Is he playing me?

Arla's jaw flexed, and she couldn't stop the sudden flame of anger in her veins. Her nostrils flared before she quickly got back in control. Anger flared in her too easily. It was her weakness. But she couldn't let that influence things.

"I don't know," Kevin said. "You came to see me, remember? How will I know what *else* you might be here for?"

Arla didn't miss the emphasis on else. She narrowed her eyes. "What are you trying to say, Kevin?"

He sat back in his chair, flexed his shoulders. The shoulders were wide, his neck muscles rippled.

"Nothing, Inspector. Nothing at all."

Arla changed track. "Your psychiatrist, Dr. Griffiths, thinks that you've regressed. What do you think?"

Kevin blinked a couple of times. Maybe the change of topic bothered him. Eventually, he said, "I don't know why she thinks that."

"You tried to grab her hand to see her nails. Didn't you, Kevin?"

He didn't reply, and this time she saw his jaw move, and he swallowed. He tried to keep his face impassive, but there was subtle movement in his cheeks, eyebrows.

"Did you think she was wearing them for you, Kevin?"

He flexed his jaw and stared back at her stonily. Arla let it go. She didn't want to fluster him too much. It defeated the objective of getting information out of him. But it seemed there wasn't much he had to share, in any case.

She asked, "These new murders, how do they make you feel?"

Kevin smirked. "Are you the doc now, Inspector?"

"Can you answer the question, please?" Arla asked.

"It was meant to happen. No one can stop fate, Inspector." His gaze was dead calm. Eyes riveted on hers. With an effort, Arla kept her calm.

"What are you talking about, Kevin?"

CHAPTER 26

He had known. Sooner or later, it would happen. That Inspector Baker would come up to see Kevin. It was only by keeping a close eye on her coming and goings at the station that he had known what she was up to.

His phone rang. He answered when he saw who it was.

"Are you up there?" the female voice on the line said.

"Yes, I am. Thanks for letting me know." He paused, then said, "The police are panicking now, aren't they? I told you they would."

"Of course. I would too if I was the police." Both of them laughed.

Then his voice dropped, and he grew serious. "We have to be careful about the Facebook site. Can't give too much away on it. You need to watch that side of things."

"I will. We don't want to put Kevin under unnecessary stress, do we?"

His jaw tightened. "No, but that's exactly what is happening. This Inspector coming up here is a nuisance. I hope Kevin is coping. Why was he transferred here anyway?"

"The transfer from that prison to here would only happen on the recommendation of a psychiatrist."

"Dr. Griffiths," he whispered. "I saw her name on the website. Is that the right person?"

"Yes."

He nodded eagerly. "Excellent. It's time I paid her a visit."

"You don't have to," the woman said.

"Really? Why?"

"Because she's on her way to Rampton. She's scheduled to meet with Arla Baker today."

*****

Dr. Rochelle Griffiths got inside her black Mazda sports model. She was half an hour early, but it would take her almost that time to get to Rampton from the Category B prison in Shorehampton, near Mansfield. She was looking forward to meeting Arla Baker. The woman who had caught Kevin Anderson. Rochelle had always admired police officers who hunted killers. They had to be persistent, patient and dedicated. Besides, it would be nice to meet a senior police officer who was also a woman.

She showed her ID at the security barrier. The bar lifted, and she drove through. The drive to Woodbeck, the village in which Rampton hospital was situated, was a scenic but quiet route. She had travelled the road before and barely a car passed by.

Soon, she was speeding along the B412, yellow fields of wheat undulating in a breeze around her. In the distance, rolling hills danced along the horizon, rising and falling in rhythm, it seemed, to her radio music. A small crossroads came up, two dirt tracks from the farms on either side meeting on the road. It was a place where tractors crossed. She slowed when she saw the sign.

Rochelle didn't expect the blue car that sped out from the dirt track on the left. She had slowed down, but from sixty to about forty. She slammed on the brakes as the car stopped on the road, and swerved her steering wheel wildly to the right. To the left lay an open divet, and if she fell in that, her accident might be fatal.

Tires screeched on asphalt, and her eyes bulged with fear. The blue car grew bigger in her windscreen, as her Mazda skidded on the road, the back fishtailing as she struggled for control. For a brief second, her terror-struck eyes caught the image of a man sitting in the driver's seat, perfectly still, as her panic ascended, threatening to overcome her. In the blink of an eye, the Mazda slammed into a wooden fence on the left of the road, airbag blowing up in her face.

Pain mushroomed in her head and neck as she was jolted forward, then back, only the seatbelt preventing her from going through the windscreen. Then she stopped moving. The engine was still ticking over, a sharp whine interfering with its low growl.

Through a haze of pain and nausea, she heard another sound. It was her door clicking open. Her eyes were blurred, misty. The ache in her skull felt like someone was drilling into it. She could vaguely make out the legs of a man standing on the road. Then he kneeled.

"You put Kevin back in the hospital," a voice said. It came from the figure on its haunches now. Mouth open and panting, she looked at him.

He moved so quickly, it took her by surprise. A hand encircled her throat, and his face was close all of a sudden, so close she could barely see him, apart from his lips, and the fetid breath from his nostrils.

The hand grew tighter around her neck, and she couldn't breathe. A croaking, gagging sound came from her throat. He whispered something to her, in almost a tender voice. Then she heard what he said, and fear lurched inside her anew.

"What colour nail polish are you wearing today? Will you tell me or do I have to look?"

She wanted to see his face, but the pain in her head was like tiny shards of lightning bolts, and she couldn't breathe. Her eyes dimmed, and nausea rose in her throat.

Before she passed out, she saw a movement streak across her windscreen.

"Hey, you!" a gruff voice called out.

Instantly, the pressure on her throat eased.

CHAPTER 27

Rochelle lurched forward, saliva drooling from her mouth. A dull ache filled every part of her head, but the buzzing noise was subsiding. When she moved, she cried out in pain. Her left leg seemed stuck underneath the steering. Her left arm felt heavy, and when she tried to lift it, a white hot bolt of pain shot down her shoulder. She winced, her neck dropping forward.

She felt hands reach over her. She shrieked in alarm.

"Easy, love, easy," the mellow tones of a deep Yorkshire accent floated into her ears. Rochelle shrunk back in her seat, rigid with fear. A bearded, older man, his face wrinkled with lines from being out in the sun too much, was leaning over her. She could smell the humid sweat lifting from his body. A click sounded, and he moved away. He pulled the seatbelt away from her, and with one meaty hand, stabilised her left shoulder.

"Are you okay, love?"

Rochelle squeezed her eyes shut, then opened them. The buzzing and nausea were almost gone now. She could see the farmer's red nose, his weather-beaten craggy face. A startling pair of blue eyes looked out from his tanned features.

"Yes, I think so," she said, wincing as she tried to move her left hip.

"Wait, let me help you."

The farmer assisted her in getting out of the car, then to stand. But she could. Her legs took her weight, and after a few rotations, she could move her left shoulder. It was all in working order.

"You had a close shave there, chuck," the farmer said. "And that guy." He shook his head. "Was he mad? He attacked you, didn't he?"

"Yes." Rochelle was starting to get her bearings back. The windscreen of the Mazda had a crack in it. The left side of the car was dented, resting against the fence. Thankfully the fence was sturdy enough to take the car's weight. Rochelle put a hand on the roof of her beloved sports car and felt a wave of dizziness engulf her. Her hand moved to her head.

"Sit back down, love," the farmer said, opening the car door for her. "Let me call the police. I'm going to fetch some water for you."

Rochelle nodded weakly and sat down on the driver's seat again, legs stretched outside in the sunshine.

It took an hour, but the police came, took a statement, then dropped her off at Rampton. She called the medical officer on duty, and he came down to put a dressing on the graze on her forehead and also put her left shoulder in a sling. Rochelle knew she didn't need an X-ray, as she had no broken bones. Her fingers and limbs all worked fine. But the pains would be worse tomorrow.

She had to go through security and eventually was shown into Governor Beasley's office. He hurried around the corner of his table and took her right hand in his.

"Goodness me, Rochelle, I heard. How ghastly!"

They sat down, and she told him what happened.

Beasley frowned. "So he was waiting for you?"

Rochelle rubbed her forehead with her good hand. She had been to the bathroom, and her face was a total mess, but she still had her handbag with her. All she could do is fix some blusher up and straighten her hair.

"I have to think he did, yes. The way he blocked the road, he must've known it was me."

The eyebrows on Beasley's forehead were getting knotted tighter. "Hang on. That means someone is watching you."

Rochelle closed her eyes and leaned back on the chair. She felt exhausted all of a sudden. "I guess that's right. How would he have known where I would be, otherwise?"

"This is dangerous. Who on earth could it be?"

Their eyes met and locked. Both knew they did dangerous jobs. The number of evil, sick minds they had dealt with over the years were considerable. But most of them were in prison and would be for life. There was almost no chance any would be let out. But their friends and relatives were another matter. It was one of the reasons why these prisoners had such limited contact with the outside world. They were charismatic men. They could influence people and engage them enough to make the whole world think that they were victims.

"I don't know who it could be," Rochelle said softly. "But I think we need to start with the OPV list and the voicemail contacts he has."

"Consider it done," Beasley said thoughtfully. "But there are hundreds, if not thousands of others on this website. Kevin Anderson's own fan club. Have you seen it?"

"No."

Beasley took out his phone and sat down next to Rochelle. When she saw the screen, her mouth fell open. Rapidly, she scrolled down.

"My gosh, there's so many."

"Yes," Beasley said, taking his phone back. "You can imagine now what a challenge we face. Any of them could be the psycho who's coming after you."

"Who told you about this site?"

"The officers from down south. The ones investigating the copycat murders. The ones I told you about."

"Oh, I see. Where are they?"

Just then, there was a knock on the door.

CHAPTER 28

The guard strode in front and was the first to reach the end of the corridor where the Governor's room was situated. Arla noted the armed guard at the mouth of the corridor as well. The Governor had his own security detail.

The guard held the door open, and the three of them filed in. Arla saw a woman sat opposite the table from Governor Beasley. She was a dyed blonde, pretty, but looking worse for wear with a white dressing on her left forehead and her left arm in a sling.

Beasley stood and did the introductions. Rochelle Griffiths stood and approached Arla. She stuck out her right hand.

"Heard a lot about you, DCI Baker," she said.

"Arla, please." They shook hands. Rochelle's lips moved in a tired, tight smile. The corner of her eyes had crow's feet wrinkles. Arla didn't miss the fresh bruise on her left jaw, and her eyes moved down to her legs, where two more bruises were evident on the shins.

"What happened to you?" Arla asked.

"Shall we all sit down," Beasley said. They followed his instructions. There were just enough chairs for all four of them. Beasley remained standing. When he spoke, his voice was grave.

"Rochelle has just been ambushed, for want of a better word." He told them what happened. When he got to the attacker trying to strangle Rochelle, she interrupted and took over.

"He opened the door and must've watched me for a while," she said, taking a deep breath. Her eyes went to the floor and remained there.

"He asked me what colour nail polish I was wearing, and I remember the way he spoke," she shivered visibly. "His voice dropped, almost a whisper…" Rochelle stopped speaking and closed her eyes.

Arla's mind was in turmoil again. She couldn't help but make connections, and she didn't like the picture that emerged. Kevin had mentioned Rochelle's nails the last time she interviewed him. Now, another man had almost killed her and wanted to see her nails as well. The case for a copy cat killer was now almost watertight, but a killer who travelled up and down the country to terrorise his victims? That was new and deeply disturbing.

Had the killer followed them all the way up north? But how did they know where Arla was headed or where Rochelle would be?

The silence was thick with the musings of five minds. It was Harry who broke the silence.

"This person, whoever he or she is is more dangerous than we thought. What is important now, before we try to decipher who he is, is to ensure that we secure our staff." He glanced at Arla.

She said, "Harry's right. We have two deaths in my station in south London, and we are on red alert. The last thing we wanted to see was this." She flexed her jaw, sudden anger making her nostrils flare. "It's like he knows where to hurt us. He's following us, well me, around, and choosing to strike individuals around me."

Harry said quietly, "I don't think this is about you, Guv."

Beasley nodded. "He's right, Arla. This psycho would be doing this stuff, even if you weren't involved."

Arla shook her head. "I don't think so. He chose our station for a reason. Because I work there." She looked at Rochelle. "I'm not saying that he attacked Rochelle because she was about to see me. Given how well-resourced this guy is, I wouldn't be surprised if he knew that Rochelle was Kevin's psychiatrist."

Beasley gave a deep sigh. "It's ridiculous to even think about it. Information within our institutions goes nowhere, as you can imagine. All our staff are sworn to secrecy and are aware they will lose their jobs if there are any leaks. But I suppose Rochelle's details are public."

Rochelle cleared her throat. "That's true. I work in a secure hospital and cat A prisons only, but you only have to search for the

In-reach teams, as the psychological teams are called these days, and look for the lead psychiatrist. I'm the one who's working here at the moment."

Arla said, "That doesn't mean he can find out your exact routine though."

"No," Rochelle said. She had sea green eyes, and they settled on Arla.

Arla knew what it felt like to be threatened. She was used to it, but she knew Rochelle wouldn't be. The psychiatrist was being brave and putting up a front. Her eyes were a fraction wider, breathing just a little faster. The muscles on her neck contracted around the windpipe.

"Don't worry," Arla said softly. "Whoever this is, we'll catch him or her. But the more important thing right now is that we get you safe." She turned to Beasley. "I could speak to the Chief Constable of West Midlands police, or even better, get my boss to speak to him. A bodyguard for Rochelle is necessary for the next few days."

Rochelle shook her head. "No, really, that's too much."

Beasley said, "I think that's very sensible, actually. We would all feel very foolish if something happened to you, Rochelle."

Rochelle's lips were pressed together tightly, and her jaw clenched. Her nostrils flared. "I can't believe this is happening," she whispered.

"Have you never been threatened by one of your patient's before?" Arla asked gently.

Rochelle swallowed and composed herself before she spoke. "I have, yes. Been spat at, called names. But nothing like this."

"This is well-planned and coordinated," Arla said. "But the weakness also lies there." She looked at everyone in the room. "When Rochelle left Woodville Hospital today, she was either followed, or her attacker was informed about her route."

Beasley said, "It wouldn't be anyone inside Woodville. It's a secure hospital."

Harry said, "But it could be a person who's been following Rochelle around. He knows what her car looks like and where she lives." He turned to her. "Did you sleep in your own house last night?"

Rochelle nodded. "Yes. I live in a village near Mansfield."

Harry continued. "Like you said, Governor Beasley, it's not hard to get Rochelle's details as they are on the prison and hospital websites. From there, it's a matter of surveillance."

Arla was lost in the mists of her mind, only half listening to Harry. A shape was taking form through the mist, vague and indistinct but certainly present.

She asked Rochelle, "You interviewed Kevin when he was first admitted here, ten years ago?"

Rochelle shook her head. The discussions were having a strong impact on her. Her chest seemed to be caved in, and she shrank back on the chair, looking smaller. She held her left arm in a sling gingerly across her chest, like a wounded bird.

"No, I didn't. Another team did. I've been looking after him recently."

"Have you seen his original crime scenes?"

Rochelle looked interested. A light shone in her eyes, and her chin lifted. "Can't say I have. To be honest, I've always wanted to."

Arla pressed on. "And the recent copy cat killer's crime scenes as well. We could use a psychiatrist's evaluation."

Jeremy Melville spoke mildly. "You need a psychiatrist after the person is arrested. A psychologist can provide you with a lot of information from the killer's suggested profile."

A ripple of humour spread across the room. Arla said, "No one's trying to take your place, Jeremy. But given that Rochelle knows Kevin so well, she might find something interesting when she sees all the evidence we have gathered so far."

Rochelle was nodding. "I agree. When I took over Kevin's case, I always wished I was involved from the beginning."

Arla looked at Rochelle and smiled. "Would you like to come down to London for a few days?"

*****

Governor Beasley stood by the long window in his office, watching the two cars leave the car park. One was a taxi, carrying Inspector Baker and her team back to the train station. The other was Rochelle Griffiths, being driven back by a member of his security staff. He watched both cars drive down to the large fountain in the middle of the long drive that led up to the hospital. The cars headed down the road till they crossed the gates, then turned in the same direction. The police car that had brought Rochelle here followed behind them.

Beasley watched the empty drive for a few seconds, then turned to his desk and picked up the phone. He spoke on the phone briefly, then strode out of his room. Wherever the Governor went within the hospital, his guard followed. The man sitting at the end of the corridor stood as Beasley approached. With his guard, Beasley approached the Close Supervision Unit or CSU, where Rampton's most dangerous criminals were kept.

He stared at the camera on the wall, then leaned closer for an iris scan. The blue line passed across his eyes; then a lock clicked on the door. Beasley depressed the handle and entered the room.

"Stay here," he told the guard.

Kevin Anderson was already seated at the table. He was on his own. Beasley sat down opposite him. The two men stared at each other for a while, then Beasley smiled. Kevin returned it.

"Well, how did that go?" Beasley asked.

"Quite well, I think."

"Good," Beasley said. "Very good."

CHAPTER 29

He stared down at his shaking hands. Things were getting out of control. He needed to be more careful.

That farmer…not only had he seen his face, but he had also taken the registration number of the hire car. He had to drive into the nearest woods, douse the vehicle with gasoline and set fire to it. Then it had been a long hike down country lanes, staying away from the larger roads. He stole a motorbike at a village and ditched that five miles outside Nottingham. Now, he was on the train back to London. He watched the countryside zip past the window.

That had been a close shave. He wasn't out of danger yet. The train station had cameras ,and so did the train. He had got into the train as quickly as he could, then kept the hood of his top pulled low over his head, and the sunglasses on. E-fit photos of himself would now be circulating in the west midlands, as well as London. The trap was closing in, as he had expected. As he watched the countryside slip by, he thought of the years that had flown by so quickly. Time never stood still. Like running water, the days had trickled through his hands. He had to wait for his chance. Now it had arrived.

He would make Arla Baker pay. He knew what was going through her mind now. She was going nuts trying to second guess him. She was clever, and he respected that. He had no doubt their paths would cross soon. It filled him with anticipation. Taunting her with clues but staying out of reach was proving to be more enjoyable than he had imagined. He smiled wolfishly, scratching the stubble on his chin. This was what he lived for. The chase. The game. The women he had killed so far were just pawns. He was getting closer to the queen now. That was his ultimate prize, his great denouement. When he captured her, the world would sit up and take notice.

But the debacle near Rampton proved one thing with crystal clarity. He couldn't let his excitement get the better of him. He should've killed that old farmer. He knew it. But he had no way of knowing if the farmer had called the police already. He couldn't afford to waste time.

"Ticket please," A voice said from his left. He was at the end seat, slouched against the window. He moved his head slightly and caught sight of the ticket inspector. He produced his ticket quickly. The inspector stamped it and returned the stub to him, then moved on. He heaved a sigh of relief.

His phone beeped. The number on the screen was a familiar one.

"Are you okay?" An anxious voice asked him.

"Yes. Yes I am. Where are you?" He whispered.

"I'm fine, don't worry. Headed back down to London. So are you, I hope?"

"Good," he said, relieved. "I think we need to lay low for a while. Time for more surveillance, and less action. For a few days anyway."

"I was going to suggest that. Keep an eye on the greater prize."

"Get a new pay as you go phone when you get to London. Leave the number for me on the email. I'll get back to you." They used an email address from which neither answered any emails, just sent each other confidential information. They could log in from anywhere.

"See you back in London," he repeated. "Wait till you hear from me."

CHAPTER 30

The alarm went off next to Arla's ears like a banshee wail. Instantly awake, she flailed with her right arm, trying to locate the source of the noise. Harry grumbled next to her. She'd wanted to be on her own, but he insisted on staying over, to guard her, if nothing else.

Her skinny right arm finally made contact with the offending object. The shrill noise ceased, and it had served its purpose. Arla moved Harry's heavy arm, draped over her tummy. He held on tighter, and she had to slap it twice for him to let her go.

"What's the time?" he mumbled.

"Five past six," Arla mumbled in a matching somnolent voice. Her bottom slipped off the bed, onto the carpet. She padded her way to the bathroom, wincing when she turned the light on. It was too bright. She tied her hair up in a bun, put a shower cap on, then stepped into the shower.

*****

An hour later, Arla was sitting in the canteen, sipping scalding hot coffee. The wooden chairs and rickety tables were empty. The coffee was rancid, from the vending machine in the corner. The canteen staff were evidently not paid well enough to attend at 7 am. It made her cross. An email had circulated recently informing everyone of the budget cuts. There was hardly any cooking staff left to operate the canteen these days. With police teams working overnight, that was a shame.

At least the heating was on, Arla thought as she swallowed another mouthful of the muddy liquid. Grimacing, she turned the page of the report Lisa Moran had left in her pigeon hole.

The Cyber Crime Unit had worked wonders and managed to download photos from Jane Crouch's second and hidden phone.

Arla was going through the colored prints. Several of them were explicit images. Jane lying in bed, hands tied to the bedpost, black blindfold wrapped around her head. Her legs were spread, and she was wearing nothing but a G string. In the next photo, Jane had her mouth open, and an erect penis was in view. It was clear the man took the photo, looking down.

More photos followed of Jane in various positions. Arla flipped through them, surprise resounding through her. If anything, Jane had been an average mild-mannered person. She was sociable but never the life and soul of the party.

"It's always the quiet ones," Arla muttered to herself. She stopped at the next photo. This was an image of the man. It was of his back specifically. Most of the photos were black and white, including this one. He was naked and was standing with his hands by his side. Obscured by his body, a woman lay on the bed in front of him. Arla couldn't see the face but guessed it was Jane. This photo was taken with a timer, she surmised, or to make things more complex, by another person.

Three uniformed sergeants came into the room, and Arla recognized Warren and Darren.

"Guv, you're back," Warren's face split into a smile. Darren shook hands with her. Darren was a good policeman, and he had been pivotal last year when Arla had to track down a killer threatening the Secretary of State.

"Lisa was saying she needs to speak to you," Warren said, sitting down with his coffee. He sipped and grimaced like Arla had. She couldn't help grinning.

"Like petrol, right?"

"Yes, but I ain't no car engine."

Darren got up. "I'm going to get a delivery from Angelo's. What does everyone want?"

"Hey that should be me," Arla said. She took out her purse and gave Darren a twenty pound note. "Get coffee for all of us, please."

"Thanks, boss," Darren said, taking the money. He took orders from everyone and left.

Arla turned to Warren. "Anything happen while I was gone?"

He shook his head. "We did what you said. All the female detectives, uniforms, secretaries, all were monitored. We're all safe."

"Thank goodness," Arla breathed easy. She had frantically checked her phone all of yesterday, while she was up north. No urgent messages had come through, but it was a relief to hear it from Warren.

Darren came in, with Harry helping him to carry the tray of coffees. Lisa and Rob followed shortly after. Proper coffee in hand, they regrouped in Arla's office.

Arla spread the photos out on the table and picked up the nude man's image.

"What can you see?" she asked. Four pairs of eyes scanned the image.

"Nice muscles on his back," Lisa ventured.

"Look at his right hand. Closely."

Harry was the first to comment. "He's got a bracelet around his wrist. The kind some men wear. Or used to wear."

"Celtic tribesmen used to wear them," Rob said. Everyone stared at him. "What?" Rob asked. He pulled on his shirt collar, which was damp with sweat.

"Assuming he's not Braveheart," Arla said drily, "I'd like to see a magnified image of that bracelet. Today, please. This is a man who obviously played elaborate sex games with Jane, some of which involved elements of sadism." She pointed at some of the photos. She didn't miss the light dancing in Harry's eyes as he grinned at her. Arla averted her face from Harry's lecherous eyes quickly, trying in vain to fight the warmth creeping up her neck.

"What else?" Arla cleared her throat.

"Possible tattoo," Harry said again. "On his right torso. Only partly visible."

"Correct. Given that only the bracelet won't be covered by his clothes, I suggest we circulate magnified images among the staff. As you can see, his build and hair colour matches the description of our suspect."

Lisa asked, "You really think he could be our killer, Guv?"

"He's definitely a suspect. Jane went to some lengths to hide this. Was she trying to hide it from him?" Arla shrugged at her own question. "Notice how in the two photos we see him in, it's only of his back, and he's naked. This is unidentifiable. This bracelet is our only clue."

Arla sat down on her chair and swivelled across the floor. She opened the drawers of her filing cabinet.

"Briefing in Incident Room please, in half an hour. We have Dr. Rochelle Griffiths coming down from Rampton Hospital, and we need to make absolutely sure nothing happens to her." Arla told Lisa and Rob what happened to Rochelle.

"Jesus," Rob whispered. "How far will this guy go?"

CHAPTER 31

Rochelle Griffiths arrived with a uniformed sergeant from the West Midlands Police. Arla was waiting for her and wasted no time in introducing her to the detectives and also to Johnson.

Rochelle still had her left arm in a sling, and although she had fixed herself up nicely, Arla could see her wincing subtly whenever she moved. She had a lucky escape, Arla thought and should recover soon. The mental scars, she wasn't so sure of.

"Can I see the evidence you have gathered so far?" Rochelle asked. "By that, I mean the pathological evidence."

"Of course," Arla said. "Rob will show you around."

When Rochelle left, Arla sat down in her office and shut the door. She opened up the case reports that she had written, along with the notes left by SOCO and Pathology. Something about the MO was bothering her. She felt like she had overlooked something.

Arla had to work backwards, which was routine in her line of work. She started with where the body was found. To lay the body down there and then to slice the major arteries in those places, the murderer had to be sure of what he was doing. Firstly, the body had to be still. Almost passed out.

No. She tapped a pen on the desk. Not almost passed out, totally passed out. Why? Because the body had to be transported in the car. He couldn't risk the victim waking up en route. She could scream the place down once the boot was opened. Bruises in the victim's faces meant they were hit, but would those hits be powerful enough to kill them?

Arla didn't think so. More importantly, it wasn't the killer's MO to murder them just by assaulting. He wanted them to bleed to death slowly like Kevin had done.

Hence, this guy did something to the women when he first encountered them. If he assaulted them suddenly, they would fight back. Sure, this guy was stronger, but the victims were young, physically fit women.

Arla picked up the phone. She asked switchboard to put her through to Banerjee's office.

"Well, well, if it isn't my favourite detective inspector. Have I got news for you, by the way."

"You do?" Arla answered with a smile she knew Banerjee would hear over the phone. "I have a question for you, but I'll wait till I hear what you have to say."

The older pathologist's voice dropped an octave. "It's not good news I'm afraid. But I suspect it's news that you were waiting for."

He paused, and Arla said impatiently, "Go on then Doc. Sooner the better."

"The sperm found inside Jane Crouch has no DNA match from the database. Sorry, Arla."

Arla digested the news in silence. Banerjee was right, of course; she had expected this. But to hear it from his mouth was depressing. A numbness spread in her mind, fighting with the neurons that were spiking all over the place.

Eventually, she asked, "Which brings me to what I was going to ask you. Did the toxicology reports come back? Any other drugs in their bodies?"

"Tox reports always run late but let me check. Can you hold on?"

Banerjee returned after two minutes. Arla whiled the time by checking her emails, putting the phone on speaker mode.

"Oh, dearie me," the Pathologist exclaimed.

"What?"

"Guess what I just found. High concentrations of flunitrazepam in the bloodstream of both victims. Do you know what that is?"

Arla frowned, a distant memory hitting her. "That's related to Valium, right?"

"Exactly. It's the date rape drug. Rohypnol. Can be injected or taken as a tablet."

Arla felt excitement twist in her guts. "And it can be added to drinks as well."

"Correct. Either as a crushed powder, in which form it can also be snorted. But I should bring one thing to your attention. This Rohypnol is highly concentrated. Which means it was purified in a lab. In turn, that means it was probably designed for medical use."

Arla bit her lower lip, thinking. "Can we track it down?"

"Probably. Not sure. I need to ask the lab if they can do it."

"That would be a big favour, Doc. So you think the women had their drinks spiked?"

"Well, I didn't see any needle puncture marks in their skin. So yes, probably."

"Thanks, Doc. Let me know what the lab says about the source of the Rohypnol."

Arla hung up. She pushed her chair back, turned, and put her feet up on the window sill. A shaft of light fell on her face through the open blinds, reaching inside the corridors of her mind. A path was visible, but she couldn't as yet see the beginning or the end.

This killer had drugged the women. That's how he overcame them, and that's why they didn't fight back when he cut their arteries. Her lips curled upward in anger. But the bastard still had to beat them up.

She stood and pulled the blinds up. Sunlight flooded the room with brightness. Arla twisted the old handle on the window and opened the sash. A sultry breeze escaped between the blocks of council houses, bearing diesel fumes and the sighs of a million lungs trapped in this cement and steel jailhouse of a city. Heat was turning England yellow and parched, dreams turning into dusty decay, rising into the vacuum of a gasoline-coloured sky, ephemeral like the morning dew.

The wind ruffled her hair, spoke in her ears of the masses outside, walking, living, talking, hurting. And she thought of Nicole, lost out there, gone for so long, leaving her so alone. Pain pierced her soul like a laser beam of light, carving a crack down her middle. Arla closed her eyes, fighting the pressure building behind them.

CHAPTER 32

There was a knock on the door, and Lisa poked her head in. Arla waved her into the room.

"You alright, Guv?" Lisa asked.

"Yes, fine," Arla said, wiping her nose with a tissue. "Got some hay fever, that's all."

The door opened again, and this time, Harry's lanky frame filled the frame. He shut the door behind him. Arla tried not to look at him. Both Lisa and Harry knew all about her. She didn't need their sympathy.

Lisa said, "We got hold of Jane Crouch's work laptop. Her emails are usual work-related stuff. But her web browsing shows up interesting material." Lisa turned to Harry.

Harry lowered himself on a chair. "Just got the report back from Cybercrime. Jane was a fan of Facebook. She didn't browse it at work normally. But she slipped up once or twice. She clicked on ads for sex toys and bondage clothes."

Arla shrugged. "We kind of knew she was into kinky sex. Anything else?"

"Her colleague, Sarah Bloom, wanted to talk to you," Lisa said. "She wouldn't say what it was about."

"Okay," Arla said, "Get her now. Harry, can you stay please."

Lisa left, and there was a knock on the door. Sarah Bloom walked in, on her own. She sat down opposite Arla and glanced from her to Harry. He got up and locked the door.

"You wanted to speak to me?" Arla asked.

Sarah stared at Arla for a while, then her eyelids flickered. Her Adam's apple bobbed up and down, and she looked away. Her lower lip trembled.

"It's been hard," she said in a strangled whisper. "Very hard since what happened to Jane."

Arla felt sorry for her. Sarah had worked with Jane, so, of course, she would be affected.

"I know," Arla said. "It's been hard on all of us. Were you close to her?"

"Kind of. Jane was a strange person, in some ways. The more you got to know her, the more you realized you didn't."

"What do you mean?"

"I always got the feeling she kept one side of herself shielded away. Like, I told her about my boyfriend, but she never spoke about her relationships. She was single when this happened, or at least that's what she told me."

Harry said, "You think she was lying to you?"

"I don't know. That's just what I mean. Jane was nice, easy to talk to, but you could never tell with her."

Arla leaned forward and crossed her hands on the desk. "Sarah, what are you trying to tell us?"

Sarah swallowed and glanced around the room like she was looking for something. Then her eyes settled on Arla.

"I'm not sure if this is important."

"Go on."

"I once saw her and Mike Robert have an argument."

Arla tensed. "Mike Robert, your boss in media liaison?"

"Yes."

Harry and Arla exchanged a glance. He asked, "What do you mean by an argument?"

"It wasn't in the office. I was out for a smoke, walking around the Common at lunchtime. It was quiet, and I like doing that. I heard some voices and saw a couple arguing under the shade of a big willow tree. It was clear they were trying to hide, but I heard their voices."

"And then?"

"They didn't see me. I got closer, and then recognised them."

Arla asked, "Did they see you?"

"No."

"This is very important, Sarah. Did you hear what they were talking about?"

"Only when Jane was raising her voice. She was saying – I can't do this anymore. What you're doing is not right. She was shaking her hands in his face; they were clearly having a massive argument."

"And what was Mike Robert doing?"

"He was pleading with her. Trying to calm her down. But then he pointed a finger at her and kept jabbing it in her face, almost."

The room in the air was thick with tension. Arla's eyes were riveted on Sarah's.

"How far were you?"

"There's a path around the trees. I was say, about twenty or thirty feet away."

"Are you sure you recognised them correctly?"

"I'm positive. Jane was wearing her pink cardigan and knee-length brown skirt. Mike had his blue striped shirt on and dark trousers. I'm sure it was them."

"Did they see you?"

"No."

"Where in the Common was this?"

"On the south side, near the A3."

Where Jane's body was found, Arla thought, a sickening feeling spreading inside her gut. She glanced at Harry and saw the hard glitter in his eyes.

Harry asked, "You never saw anything between them in the office?"

"No. They obviously kept it very well hidden."

"And Mike hasn't been any different to you?"

"No. But..." Sarah paused before continuing. "He does have a temper. He can have fits of anger. One day, he began to shout because this reporter wouldn't listen to him. He yelled at the guy, then threw his phone at the wall."

Arla sat back in her seat. The silence was an oppressive, heavy weight between them. A clock ticked on the wall.

"Who was in the office then?"

"Both Jane and myself. Mike stormed off, slamming the door. Jane and I just shrugged and carried on."

"You were used to this behavior?"

Sarah sighed. "It happened every now and then, yes."

Arla let the moment settle. Sarah took the time to wipe her nose, dab at her eyes.

Harry said, "You know what this means, Sarah, don't you?"

Sarah bowed her head. "Yes. I need to give a statement. I might even be called to give evidence. That's why I thought about it before I came to you. I'm sorry I took so long."

Arla crossed the table and sat down next to Sarah. "You did the right thing. Don't worry. Now, where's Mike?"

"I don't know. He didn't turn up to work today."

CHAPTER 33

Mike Robert leaned against the massive Oak tree in the Common, the white SOCO tent visible in the mid-distance. His breath was ragged, a thin film of sweat on his forehead. He still remembered their last night together. Passionate and wild. That evening, they had another argument, and she was always at her best when she got angry.

She had found out. She knew. But Mike had never thought it would end in this way. His head hung down on his neck.

What had he done?

He had tried to keep it a secret from her. If she found out, it would all come to a crashing end. It was ironic, actually. It came to an end anyway, an inevitable, inglorious rupture. His nails dug into the bark of the tree.

When this had started, he knew it was going to end one way. He couldn't trust his urges any more than he could stop breathing and live. They ruled his life. He liked the domination, and yes, even the violence. He couldn't lie to himself. Lying had got him here.

Mike knew he was in a dangerous place. That Detective Arla Baker would soon put something together. He had tried his best to be normal when they last spoke, but with her, you could never be sure. The woman was reputed to have eyes in the back of her head.

Anger surfaced inside him, bubbling like hot lava in his veins. He wouldn't let Arla Baker rule his life. Catch and treat him like a common criminal. No, he was destined for better things in life. For the time being, he had to escape. There was too much heat down here.

Since Jane's death, he had seen a change in Sarah's attitude. Did she suspect anything? He had always kept it cool with Jane in the office. But there was always a chance…that's why he had stayed off work today. And for the last two days, he'd also kept a close eye on what Inspector Baker was up to.

So far, Mike hadn't seen any surveillance around his house. But that didn't mean it hadn't started. He knew how cops worked. Let him loose, wait for him to make a mistake, then catch him red-handed.

Had they found Jane's phone already? The one they took photos on. Thoughts of their time together came flooding back to him. His mouth opened as his sweaty forehead leaned against the coarse trunk of the tree.

If the cops had found that phone, then Mike knew his game was up. He cursed, then kicked the tree with his shoe. Well, he wasn't going to go quietly. He was a master of manipulation. He would drive that bitch Arla mad, running circles around her.

His carefully layered plans were coming unraveled, but he still had some tricks up his sleeve. He made mistakes with Jane that he didn't with Debbie. But even thinking about Debbie filled his mind with remorse. Not on the same scale as Jane. But it affected him deeply, still.

Debbie had been younger blood, fresher, softer, more pliant. While Jane had been the sexy siren, Debbie was the virginal flower. Well, not quite the virgin, but the comparison still stood.

He had been more careful with Debbie. Built walls around his communication with her and made sure he met her mostly at home.

His phone rang, jerking his mind back from the murky past. It was her. He backed away from the tree, casting one last look at the white tent. He wouldn't be coming here again.

"Hello?" he answered.

"Where are you?" her voice was lowered. In the background, he heard a train whistle.

"In the Common. Leaving now."

"Good. We need to meet up. This has gone too far now."

"Yes, I agree. But don't meet at our place. I feel the cops are onto me. Don't ask how I know. I just do."

"What shall we do then?"

Mike thought for a while. "I have a plan. Listen to me carefully."

CHAPTER 34

Arla stood in the middle of Mike Robert's office. The drawers of the desk were pulled out, and all the contents had been removed by SOCO. One of Parmentier's men was dusting the table top for prints. Another SOCO officer had his tripod up and was taking photos of the office as if it were a crime scene. Arla felt strange watching them. It felt unreal this was happening in her own station. A few hundred yards from her own office.

Mike's work laptop had been seized already, and Cyber Crime was dealing with it. No phone was found in the office.

Harry appeared at the doorway and beckoned Arla outside.

"We got something on the CCTV outside Debbie Jones' house. DC Das has them on her screen. I think you need to see it."

Arla followed Harry down to the detective's room on the ground floor. Lisa and Rob stood on either side of a seated Pamela Das. She glanced up at Arla when she arrived and nodded at her.

"Here, Guv," Das said, indicating a box on the screen. She clicked on the top left, and the box enlarged to fill the whole screen.

Das clicked a few more times, then moved a pen-shaped cursor over the box. She made a white circle with the pen. The circle showed a man's face on the busy high street.

"This is Balham High Street," Das explained. "Outside Debbie Jones' apartment, above the betting shop." She put a white dot where the apartment was. "Now watch."

The man with the white circle on his head began to move, along with the other people on the street. The man turned left and disappeared into a door, right below Debbie's apartment.

"He's headed up to her place," Das said. She fast forwarded the roll to one hour later. The man emerged from Debbie's apartment and headed down the street. He was facing the cameras, and Das put a circle around his head again. Then, she magnified the image.

Arla breathed in sharply. A pulse slammed against her eardrums. The face belonged to Mike Roberts.

He was also dark-haired, wide-shouldered, tall. The same physical profile as the man who had left the Olive Garden restaurant with Debbie.

She asked, "Can you get the films from the restaurant up? Where the suspect was seen with Debbie?"

Das clicked some more and got the images rolling. When she came to the part where Debbie was leaving with the suspect, Arla said, "Slow it down."

The man's face wasn't visible, as this time he had a hand up, ostensibly to brush his hair, but a movement that effectively blocked any visual of his face.

"Damn," Arla whispered. But the build and physique were the same. She straightened and found Harry's intense eyes. They widened a fraction when she nodded slowly.

Arla said, "Take Mike's photo and show it to the restaurant staff. Right now. I need an ID by tonight."

She turned to Lisa and Rob. "Did we get the magnified images from Jane's photos? Of the man with his back to the camera?"

Lisa rushed over to her desk and flipped open her laptop. She called back. "Yes, Guv, I got them."

She sat down and located the files, then enlarged them on the screen. Arla and Harry came over. A magnified image of the bracelet on the man's right wrist was visible. So was the letter M carved on it.

Harry and Arla looked at each other. Harry said, "Remember the letter in Jane's desk? The one signed M? The love letter."

Arla's mind was spluttering and blinking, travelling at the rate of a thousand knots. Synapses joined, new avenues of light were spreading tentacles around her brain. Her mouth was dry, and the pressure building in her chest was immense. She sat down heavily on a vacant chair. All the dots were now getting joined in, the minute pieces of the jigsaw, and a ghastly picture was emerging.

She leaned forward, clutching her head. Her forehead felt hot, like the wires in her brain were melting after a short circuit.

It all made sense now. From the beginning, when the photos of Debbie's body were circulated on Twitter to how the killer had always stayed one step ahead.

Arla felt a hand on her shoulder. She looked up to see Harry. He was holding a phone to his ear and speaking on it.

"Sarah, this is DI Mehta. I needed to ask you something." Harry glanced down to make sure Arla was listening. He moved his hand away.

"Please think about this carefully. Did Mike Roberts wear a bracelet on his right wrist?"

There was silence as Harry listened. Arla saw the lines on his forehead clear suddenly, and his jaw become lax, and she knew. She knew.

"Did it have the letter M engraved on it?" Harry asked. He nodded once. "Thank you, Sarah. Please stay indoors today. If you hear from Mike, let us know immediately and don't contact him under any circumstance."

Harry put the phone in his pocket. Everyone had gathered around them, and they were all staring at him. For once, Harry, the smooth operator, seemed at a loss for words. He squeezed his eyes shut, then cleared his throat.

"Sarah saw Mike's bracelet a couple of times. He even bragged about it in the pub once, how women loved it. And yes, he did have the initial M engraved on it."

CHAPTER 35

Mike lived on Great Dover Street; a few stops down from Stockwell. Mike got off the bus, one stop away, and started walking. He had decided against taking the tube. It was harder to get away from the tube if he was pursued. His baseball cap was pulled low over his head, and he had his shades on. The sun burned his neck as he walked swiftly, keeping to the shadows. Mike knew where the CCTV cameras were. It was impossible to hide from them, but by keeping his face down and hands thrust in his pockets, he could avoid easy recognition.

He stopped at the corner of his street, pretending to tie his shoelaces. A few pedestrians walked past, including one of the mothers with a pram. Those two welfare witches who walked up and down like they had nothing better to do. One of them gave him an interested look, and he bowed his head down quickly. They sauntered slowly past. Mike cursed, then got up and moved. He had to move. He didn't want the teenage mums to identify him.

He barely turned the corner when he halted abruptly. A police squad van and a support vehicle were parked outside his house. It was a small terraced house, two up, two down. SOCO officers in blue Tyvek suits were putting up a tent. Mike's blood turned to ice. His heart jackhammered against his ribs, and he was suddenly short of breath.

So, it was happening. They were onto him. A door opened opposite him, and one of the neighbours poked out her head, staring at the police. Mrs. Morgan, the old Welsh lady, and gossip of the street. Mike moved quickly. If he was seen now, it was all over. He crossed the street and kept walking till he came to a crossroads. He turned left and went around in a circle, coming to the main road that led to the other end of his street.

He crossed the road, keeping well away from his street and stood at a bus stop. He wasn't as close now, but the SOCO guys and the two uniform officers standing on either side of his front door were clearly visible.

A black BMW that looked suspiciously like an unmarked CID car turned the corner from his end, heading up to his house. He caught the front passenger's face as the window was lowered.

Arla Baker.

Driven by that lanky gimp who followed her everywhere. He was sure they were banging each other. Couldn't anyone else see that?

He watched Arla jump out of the car and strut up towards his house. Her heeled shoes made her look taller. Her movements were brisk, and she looked around her like a hunter looking for prey.

"I'll make you pay for this," Mike whispered softly.

Arla and Harry were speaking to the SOCO officers. Mike wanted to know if they had smashed down his front door, but he knew the detectives had an assortment of keys they could use to gain entry as well. Either way, damage to the front door was the least of his worries. But his laptop was in there. So was his spare phone, locked in a safe. They would confiscate all of it.

Anger boiled inside him, and when he exhaled, his breath was hotter than the afternoon sun. Mike took out his phone and called an Uber. He waited impatiently for it to arrive. Luckily, at that time, the detectives stayed inside his house. He flagged the Uber down and tapped on the driver's window to lower the glass.

"I'll give you fifty quid extra if you stay here and follow a car for me."

The driver hesitated. Mike said, "I'm an undercover cop." He showed the driver his ID, putting his fingers over the portion that had his job title. The driver would only see Clapham Police Station, London Met, in big letters.

"I'll make it seventy-five," Mike said.

The guy nodded. Mike got in the back seat. "Turn the car around, Wait for my signal."

As Mike had expected, Arla didn't stay at the scene for long. The black BMW nosed out of the street. Mike tapped the driver on the shoulder.

"Follow that car."

The BMW drove all the way to the Clapham Station. Mike ordered the driver to carry on past the station. He got off at the next block. He knew a spot opposite the rear car park, where a large oak tree rose above a bus station. He could see the black BMW parked near the back entrance of the station, and Arla's office two floors above it. He stared hard and was rewarded by a flash of sunlight from the glass on the window. A pasty-coloured, well-tanned hand opened the window. It was Arla. She stood there, in plain view, watching the skyline.

"I got you in my sights now, you bitch," Mike muttered. "There's nowhere for you to hide."

CHAPTER 36

Arla's desk phone rang, making her jump. She was lost in her own world, knots loosening in the warm heat as she stood in the sunlight. She answered, and the little relaxation she was feeling went down like a lead balloon.

"I'm coming to your office," Johnson barked. "Got something to show you."

He was knocking on her door barely a minute later, then striding in without waiting for an answer. His face was red, eyes grim, jaw set in a tight line. He had a load of newspapers under his arm. Without a word, he spread the papers on Arla's desk. They were a collection of tabloids and national broadsheets. Arla's heart sank as she read the headlines.

Return of the Nail Collector.

Police bamboozled as copy-cat killer terrorises London.

Twin murders rock Clapham, police have no answers.

"Who?" Johnson thundered. "Who is leaking news to the media?"

Before Arla could answer, he snatched one of the tabloids and opened an inner page. He read out loud.

"Sources close to the London Met say….." he turned another page, "Anonymous sources say the police are searching, but there are no hard clues as yet."

Johnson threw the paper down in disgust, making Arla flinch back as it landed close to her.

"Who the hell are these sources?" Johnson growled. He kicked one of the chairs out of his way and began pacing the room.

"Sir, we do have a lead. A very strong one, in fact. SOCO are inside the house of a suspect…"

Johnson stopped pacing. "Who?"

When he heard, Johnson's face lost its rigidness. His eyes enlarged, pulled upward by his bushy eyebrows.

"What? Mike the media liaison officer?"

"Yes, sir."

Johnson's mouth dropped open, and he made no effort to shut it. "But that's impossible. He...

"He worked with the second victim. I mean, Jane." It still felt odd referring to Jane Crouch as a victim. Arla pointed at the newspapers on her desk. "And the sources these reporters keep referring to? Who better than our own MLO?"

Arla laid out the whole story of Jane's involvement with Mike. Johnson sat down on a chair opposite Arla.

"What did you see at Mike's house?"

"We got his laptop. He didn't have a hidden phone that I could find, unlike at Jane's house. I'll send a team back inside once SOCO have cleared out."

"Yes. We need to search the house properly."

"If anything, it was quite neat and clean. He looked after the place well, unless he had a cleaner coming in to look after the place. Small, but well-kept garden too.."

"If you think he's our guy, then turn the place upside down."

"Sure, sir. But we need to tread carefully as well. Mike knows the system better than any suspect. The fact that he didn't turn up to work and wasn't at home makes me wonder if he knows we're onto him."

"Quite possibly, if he's as devious as you think he is." Johnson shook his head. "Jesus, who would've thought." He looked up at Arla. "Where do you think he is?"

"We don't know. I've checked his file already. No close family. He has a sister in Australia, but she rarely visits. Everyone he worked with knows to let us know if he makes contact. And Sarah, the other MLO, is under surveillance with a uniform team on guard."

"A whole team to guard Sarah?"

"Think about it, sir. Who would he come after next if he suspected someone ratting on him?"

Johnson stared back at Arla stonily. She realized he was offended by her tone. She opened her mouth to change the topic quickly, but a sharp rap on the door, followed by Harry entering, stopped her.

Harry's face was flushed. "Cyber Crime just came back. They got into his laptop. He was into filming his love life. He was also a member of several websites where BDSM was practiced."

Harry left, and Arla followed with Johnson. Cora, one of the analysts from the lab, was sitting at Harry's desk with a laptop. The team had gathered around her. When Cora played a video, Arla saw a wide angle, 180-degree view of a bedroom where two men were practicing bondage with a woman. One of the men was recognisable as Mike, and both were naked.

Cora switched the view to a bedroom where a couple were having sex, again with the same wide angle view.

"These are hidden cameras, I think," Cora said. "They're the size of a fifty pence coin, but raised like a ball shape. They can be hidden almost anywhere, and from the angle, it's clear they were at an elevation."

Arla thought of the photos she had found on Jane's phone. Then she thought of Jane's bedroom. The bedroom this video was shot in looked uncannily similar. From the look on Harry's face, he too had seen the resemblance.

Lisa said, "Guv, he was into violent porn. Vile stuff really, where the man literally beats up the woman in the name of sex. I've got a list of the websites he was in."

Cora started playing another video, and Arla looked away, unable to watch. She caught Johnson's stare.

"Sir, I need authority to call the Home Office and put a ban on his passport. I also need all airports, train stations and ports to have his details and arrest him on sight. This will need a major incident response."

"I'll handle it," Johnson said, grim determination on his face. "Put out an all points bulletin to stop him on the roads as well. Did he have a car?"

"Not registered with DVLA. I guess not, in that case. But I have a feeling he couldn't have gone far. Hopefully, we can get to him soon."

She turned to Harry. "Set up the incident room, please. We need to debrief everyone."

CHAPTER 37

It was close to eight pm when Arla finished speaking to the British Transport Police's Commissioner. She put the phone down and threw her head back, massaging her eyes. The whole afternoon and evening had been an endless barrage of phone calls and meetings. Arla's throat was parched, and her head felt like it was submerged underwater.

She was at Harry's desk. Swinging the chair around, she put her feet up on a chair. Beneath the giant map of London, divided by the undulating blue line of the Thames, eight detectives were still making phone calls and chasing up leads. Harry entered, and behind him came two uniformed constables with packs of pizza. A muted cheer went up from the desks. Pizza was handed out in plastic paper plates.

Arla had paid Harry to get the pizza, and several voices shouted out to thank her.

"Least I could do," Arla said, standing, still massaging her neck. "Thanks for staying behind."

Harry placed a bowl of chicken Caesar salad in front of her. He sat down, chomping on a slice of pizza. Arla wasn't hungry. She stared at the salad, then pushed it away.

Harry said, "If you don't eat now, you won't sleep later."

"Really, Dr. Mehta?" Arla rolled her eyes.

Harry swallowed noisily, then slurped some coke from a can, much to her distaste. The man was a brute. She hated the noise he made while eating. Also, no matter how much he ate, it didn't stick on him.

She said, "If you put as much energy into this case as you do into food, we might've caught him already."

Harry lowered his brows. "Take that back," he growled. "And eat something. You can't live on caffeine."

"Better than living on cigarettes, like you."

She got up and walked to the whiteboard next to the large map. Mike's photo was next to Jane and Debbie's, with a list of his address and contact details.

"He came to work yesterday, Sarah told us, and we saw him on the station cameras," Arla said, addressing the team. "We also know he left early. Any clues on where he might have gone?"

Lisa wiped her mouth with a tissue. "We're still going through CCTV on his street. But his phone data has come back already. All the calls he made were to unknown numbers. Not on our databases, I mean."

"The key thing is," Arla said, "to see if we can link him with what happened up north. Did he carry out the attack on Rochelle?"

"But he was *here*, at the station," PC Das said. "We know that."

"Yes, but he also left early in the afternoon, about the same time I left for Kings Cross to take the train up North. How do we know he didn't follow us?"

Harry said, "Time to look at CCTV in Kings Cross then. Gosh, that will take a while. Big place."

Arla stifled a yawn. "I know it's been a long day. Tomorrow, we start digging into camera footage from Kings Cross, with fresh eyes. While we're at it, check out the cameras around the station as well. Who knows if he could be hiding out here?"

Harry said, "By the way, I got an email while getting pizza. SOCO found hair strands in both Debbie and Jane's house. Their own DNA was found in them, of course. But also at least three others. They could be from friends. Or Mike's."

"Good work. We have CCTV confirming Mike went to Debbie's place already and having his DNA on her carpet really seals the deal. He was there, now the question is what he did with her."

Everyone was quiet for a while, and the sound of jaws moving busily was all that was audible. Then Lisa called out from her table.

"I got Mike leaving the premises at 12:00. That's almost the same time you guys left for Kings Cross, right?"

Arla walked over to her table, Harry joining her. Lisa had the camera footage up on her screen. She scrolled through them, then stopped at one where a man was leaving through the large sliding doors of the main entrance, but it showed his back. Seconds later, another camera outside showed it was Mike Roberts. The camera showed him walking off in the direction of the main road and Clapham High Street.

"So, he left at that time," Harry said. "Doesn't mean he was following us to Kings Cross."

"Quite," Arla said. "That's why we need to check the cameras up there as well. I'll make a call to the northeast section. But tomorrow morning."

Arla picked up a piece of pizza and bit into it, despite the fact that she wasn't hungry. It tasted like food, and her tummy rumbled, making her realise how famished she was. Odd that she didn't feel the hunger. Might have something to do with the endless cups of coffee she had today. She sat down with her Caesar's salad and stuck some of it in her mouth.

Rob came over and sat next to her. He put down two sheets of paper on the table. They were phone call logs, and Rob had circled some numbers with an ink pen.

"Both victims called this number several times in the last four weeks. No other number is recorded as frequently as this one. Given that neither victim knew each other, that's suspicious, right?"

Arla drank some mineral water. "And it's not Mike's number?"

Rob shook his head. "Nope, Guv, sorry. But that's not to say he wasn't using a pay as you go number for something like this."

Harry was poking around in his laptop. "I got a positive ID for Mike in front of Jane Crouch's house," he said. "Just got the images back."

Arla rose and walked over to him. She rubbed her eyes then squinted at the laptop. "That's one good thing about Jane's house. She lived on a big road, and we have eyes."

Harry stood, and PC Das, who, like Lisa, was a whizz kid with computers, occupied his seat. She clicked on the screen till a magnified image showed a man and a woman facing each other on the road, quite clearly having an argument. It was Mike and Jane, that much was obvious.

Arla went to the whiteboard and ticked off the points on her fingers.

"So, we have Mike going into Debbie's apartment the night before her murder. He matches the physical description of the man who met Debbie in the Olive Garden restaurant. Did we get any feedback from the waiter who gave us the initial statement?"

Warren raised his hand. "Yes, I showed him Mike's photo. He said it could be him but wasn't 100%."

"If we get Mike, we could do a lineup," Arla said. "He went to Debbie's apartment a few times in the last month, is that right?" She directed her question to PC Das, who nodded.

"As far as I have been able to look back, yes. But it will take me a while longer to see if it's more than the three times I've seen so far."

"Don't worry, that's enough to satisfy a jury. Shame we can't find a phone for Debbie. There's nothing in her laptop?"

Lisa said, "Nothing like what we found in Jane and Mike's, no."

Arla continued. "So Mike knew Debbie well, and she obviously trusted him if he was coming and going from her apartment. Which means he had the means. Motive is not critical in this case. Mike loved violent sex, and he clearly acted out those urges as the videos on his laptop show."

Harry said softly, "And if they were in the restaurant, and then out in the Common, he also had the opportunity."

"Exactly. With Jane, we have plenty of evidence already. His motive is stronger this time, as he was angry with her. All we have

164

to do now is find him. What I want to know, however, is how he became a fan of Kevin Anderson. Is he on that website for Kevin? The one with all his admirers."

Rob said, "Guv, if he's on it, he's using a fake name. Everyone does it."

Arla shook her head. "It'd make sense. But he can't fake it for long. I have a feeling he's on the run and will slip up soon."

CHAPTER 38

S ome of the team went to the pub for a nightcap. Arla knew one would turn into two, and it was a slippery slope. She walked with them to the pub, but then walked off to the tube stop. Harry offered to drive her back, the familiar twinkle in his eye.

"No," she said, glancing at the others. Lisa and PC Das were chatting away, while the men had ordered a round. "I'm knackered. All I want to do is sleep."

"Yeah, me too."

She raised her eyebrows, and they both grinned. His chestnut eyes danced, and his sexy lips were parted suggestively. But she meant what she said. Her bones felt so heavy; she was barely able to walk.

"Let me drive you back, at least," Harry said. "Before I have a drink."

Arla gestured at the others. "Not while the others are here. I don't want gossip."

"I'm coming back soon enough. Come on; you look shattered."

In the end, Harry won. It was easier anyway, than the ten-minute walk to the Clapham Common tube stop. Her apartment, a ground floor two bed in a typical terraced Victorian conversion, was within spitting distance of Tooting Broadway tube. Harry got there in ten minutes, the traffic flowing easily at this time of the night.

Arla got out and leaned over his open window. She looked around, then kissed him quickly.

"Sure you don't want me to come in?" Harry asked. "I could give you a back massage."

"I'm sure," Arla smiled tiredly. "See you early tomorrow. Get a good night's rest."

It was warm still, the asphalt baking from the relentless sun, the heat held in a cage of noxious traffic fumes, and grid iron cement and glass blocks. Arla stifled a yawn as she watched the BMW's red lights glimmer brightly, then vanish from sight as it turned left at the top of the road.

Her street was suddenly very quiet. It was past ten pm, and the natural ambient sound of traffic, rising and falling like sea waves on a shore, was muted. Arla looked up at the black night sky. The stars were milky dull, and so far, their faint glow useless. It always struck her as strange that the same stars were spread all over the morning sky, but invisible.

It was how she lived, half her broken life in the shadow of dark sorrow, and the other half restless, relentless in its fire and fury. She'd always miss Nicole and a mother she'd never known. To her, they were like the missing stars in her heart-shaped sky, they came out at night to shine on her and then vanished as the stars did in the morning.

She remembered a story she used to read with Nicole when they were young, maybe ten or eleven years old. In the story, a little girl gazed at a star every night, till one night the star fell off the sky. It dropped right below her window. The girl ran down to the street and brought the star inside. She repaired its broken body. Then she hid the star under her pillow and then under her bed. The adults never found out. But slowly the star began to lose its light. It told the little girl, if you don't let me go, I will die here. Please let me go. The little girl was very sad, but what could she do? She didn't want her dear star to die.

So, that night, when her parents were in bed, she opened the window and let her healed star fly away. I will come and see you, the star told her. And whenever you look up into the sky, you can see me.

Nicole loved that story so much; she used to read it out loud till both of them knew every word by heart.

Arla was leaning against the fence of a house, and the sky and clouds blurred in her eyes. Saline drops spilled over and wet her cheeks. It had been so many years, but the pain was like an iron cloak she had to wear every day. It stayed on, under her clothes, beneath her underwear, an integral part of her body and soul. Often, it made her angry. Bitter. But mostly, the sadness was overwhelming. She led a double life. As a policewoman, her mind worked overtime. It was all hurly-burly, movement and kinetic heat. But when she had a moment to herself or her mind was vacant, she had no escape from the pain.

She knew her father suffered the same way. He kept to himself, slowly withering away like the star in the story, alone in his high-rise apartment in Battersea. Arla saw him every now and then. A shrunken, wasted man. But also her only blood link, her last remaining strand in the rich latticework of a lost family life. And she could remember happy days she once had with her dad and grandmother. Her mother, she had never known. Till she discovered her, in the most gruesome way possible.

Arla shivered, a sudden chill making her skin break out in goose pimples, despite the warm weather. She wiped her cheeks, glancing around hastily. She was acutely self-conscious now, having lost herself for a few seconds. Normally, she had these moments in the privacy of her home. Arla stood and walked down the road, her low heels clicking on the pavement. The sound was loud in the stillness.

She got to her front door and noticed the security light didn't come on. She sighed. It was on the blink again. Light bulbs popped often in her apartment; she really had to get the landlord to do a rewiring. She fumbled for keys in her bag. She couldn't find them. She turned to face the street light, and knelt, lowering her bag to the ground. A dark shape suddenly appeared in front of her. Arla screamed and fell backwards. The shape flashed past her, then stopped. It was her neighbor's cat. Its green eyes gleamed at her, the black fur standing up. Arla felt foolish. She rooted round in her bag and finally found the keys. She opened the door and stepped inside.

She flicked the light switch on, but it didn't work. The hallway remained dark, and she could barely see.

"Great," she fumed. Taking out her iPhone, Arla shone the flashlight around. The white walls reflected the dome of light, revealing an empty hallway. The mirror shone the light back at her. She moved it down quickly and walked to the cabinet on the side wall where the circuit board was located. The door creaked loudly when she opened it. Arla bent on one knee and looked at the board. As she had thought, the main switch had tripped and was in the off position. She reached out and flicked the switch up.

Nothing happened.

She heard a creak on the floorboard. Hairs stood up on the back of her neck, and a silent scream gripped her throat.

She was up swiftly, turning on her heels, slamming back against the cabinet. Wildly, she jerked her phone around. The flashlight revealed three closed doors, one for the lounge and the other two for the bedrooms. She always left them closed. To her left lay the open door to the kitchen. Faint light spilled in through the kitchen windows at the back. The kitchen had a back door, which she always kept locked. It was a tiny, cramped kitchen, just enough space for two adults to squeeze in between the cooker and cabinets.

Arla moved, and the floorboards creaked again. This time, it was her own feet. Is that what she heard?

She shook her head. Her nerves were so frayed they might just snap altogether. Time for her to get a grip. She didn't understand why the circuit board wasn't working, but there might be an explanation. Maybe upstairs had their electricity shut down as well. Or maybe it was the fuse for the circuit board that had gone.

Arla shoved it to the back of her mind. She knew the electrics here were dodgy. No reason to let it rile her so much. She opened the lounge door. It was black as a tomb inside. She dropped the blinds before she left. But through the cracks, a few dribbles of light came through. Her eyes were getting used to the dark now. Arla groped for the switch on the wall and flicked it on. Nothing again. Anger flared inside her. How was she supposed to live without any lights? She had the landlord's number. Time to give the idiot a dressing down.

She fumbled her way to the windows and lifted the blinds. The streetlights sent yellow shafts of tepid light inside. She was still barely able to see but could now make out the sofa, shelves, TV. Her fingers trailed around the base of the window sill. She locked the windows before she left as well. In fact, she never opened the street side windows, only her back bedroom window.

Her fingers felt the latch on the sill. It was in the open position. Fear shot through her like a geyser bursting upwards. She looked down and felt it again. There was no doubt. The window had been forced open.

She heard the floorboard creak again, and she whirled around, heart jackhammering against her ribs, shivers cascading on her skin.

A figure, coated in darkness, entered the room. It was a man, tall, wide-shouldered. Arla's nails dug into her palms. A strangled sound came from her throat. The window ledge was digging into her spine. She couldn't go any further back.

"Who…who are you?" she whispered.

CHAPTER 39

The figure moved in her direction, and Arla moved sideways. The streetlight slanted into the man's body, but his face was lost in darkness. But Arla could guess from his body shape.

"Mike? Is that you?"

The figure didn't speak. One of his large hands was illuminated, the veins on it standing up. He clenched and unclenched it. Arla could see his chest rise and fall. He moved again and so did she. Her sideways movement was ineffective, as it only brought her closer to him. She could go the other way, but there was no escape.

But Arla had a plan. She was inching closer to her bookshelf.

"Mike, I know it's you," Arla said, her voice cracking. She hated that. She wanted to sound confident, in control, not reveal the panic spasming through her like an earthquake.

"It doesn't have to end like this, Mike. I have friends coming around tonight. In ten minutes, they're gonna be here. You can't escape Mike. Do you hear me?"

Still, the figure approached her in silence. Briefly, his face was revealed in the stripes of the streetlamp glow. It was too quick to identify him. Arla fought the fear that was rising from her toes, freezing her legs into solid blocks of ice. Somehow, she had to keep moving. She had to make him talk.

"Kevin Anderson doesn't care about you, Mike."

That made him stop. Arla shifted further along. She was now within touching distance of her bookshelf.

"I saw him, remember? When you followed us up North. I spoke to him about you. He doesn't give a damn about you, Mike."

Finally, he spoke. His voice was low, guttural. "I don't know what you're talking about."

"Didn't you hear what I said? Kevin does not care. Everything you're doing is in vain."

"You destroyed me, you evil bitch," Mike whispered. "There was no need for this. We were all doing fine."

Arla felt a wave of nausea stir in her guts. Was he talking about his victims when he said we?

"Mike, listen to me. In ten minutes, you'll be under arrest. If you come in with me, I'll try to get you the best deal for cooperating with us. You'll get a lighter sentence. You know how it works, don't you?" She put a plea in her words like she was speaking to a child. She knew that serial killers saw the world in a simplistic, black and white way.

She had her back to the bookshelf, and her body was shielding her hands. She reached behind her and her finger encircled the narrow stem of the heavy brass flower vase. It was a gift from Harry, and it was empty. It weighed more than a big hammer, and Harry had joked how it might help her knock out a burglar.

If only he knew. She missed him now. Cursed herself for not letting him stay.

Mike shuffled closer. There was a sofa between them now and not much else. If he lunged for her, he wouldn't catch her, but neither could she escape. The only positive was the apparent lack of weapons in his hands. But he might have something in his pocket.

She took her phone out. "Here look, you can call them yourself." She made the screen active, then pressed down the green button twice, knowing it would call Harry. She held out the phone to him.

"It's ringing," Arla said.

"What?" Mike snarled. He advanced, and Arla lobbed the phone at him. Mike cursed and went to catch the phone. It landed on his feet, and he bent down. Arla seized her opportunity.

In a lightning quick movement, she jumped over the sofa by levering one foot on the handle. Her right hand held the heavy vase. She grunted as she reared over Mike, both hands now gripping the vase hard. He realized his mistake at the last microsecond and tried to stumble backwards. But Arla was on to him already, her body supple with running and yoga. She brought the vase down over his head as hard as she could, her hands jarring with the impact as it crashed on his head.

Mike slumped, and Arla fell to the side of the sofa, then slid down to the floor. She could feel Mike's hand trying to grope for her, but he was flailing. She kicked his hands away and scrambled past him. She got to the door when she felt him behind her. He shouted, a strangled, rough sound that was primitive, raw. He lurched for her, but she dodged him, falling to the floor on the hallway. He slumped against the doorframe, dizzied by the blow to his head. Arla sprinted for the front door. She reached it with Mike close on her heels. She felt his hands on her back as she opened the door.

Then she slipped out into the warm night, murky light from the street lamp spilling around her. She ran to the road, then glanced behind. Mike had a hand to his head. Blood was spilling down over his forehead, through his fingers, covering one side of his face. He looked ghastly, demonic in the light, like a Frankenstein who had just emerged from her apartment.

"Mike, stop this. Now," she called out. But she knew he wouldn't listen. He stumbled towards her, and Arla ran. She was faster than him and reached the top of her road without incident. She could see him coming up. There was a phone box, and she got inside it, and feverishly stabbed 999.

She called for the police, and when switchboard answered, she didn't even let them speak.

"This is DCI Arla Baker. Major violent crime ongoing in Tooting Broadway. My life is threatened by a dangerous individual." She gave the address quickly. She could see down her road but couldn't see Mike anymore. Where was he hiding?

Arla did a 360 survey. A car went past her, then another. She could see the lights of the tube station, and a few people milling around. She called Harry's number and waited impatiently for it to ring. She stared down her road, straining her eyes to see where Mike was. Shadows fell between the streetlights, and her eyes couldn't detect any movement.

Harry's number was engaged. Arla slammed the phone down, then lifted it again. She had to call her dad.

The door of the phone booth opened suddenly. A long hand thrust inside, and a sweaty, heavy body, reeking of sweat, crushed her against the phone. Arla felt thick fingers encircle her throat, and the pressure was immense, bone crushing. It made her gag.

"Thought you could escape me?" A voice whispered in her ear.

CHAPTER 40

Harry was clutching the phone to his ear tightly. His eyebrows were hooked tightly against each other, and he kept flexing his jaw. Arla's number rang out again. He stared at his phone, a rumble of anxiety echoing deep inside his heart.

He had answered when the phone rang, only to hear a strange voice, then a thud. He couldn't tell if the voice was Arla's or someone else. It sounded deep…could it belong to a man? Harry rang for a third time, and it rang out again. He'd just got back home to his house in Earlsfield and was getting changed. He put his jeans back on and rushed out the door.

He had two pints now and was legally over the limit. But something weird was happening. He would only rest easy when he had Arla in his sights. He got into his car, dialing the station as he drove. He hadn't returned the BMW to the carpool, which was lucky. It just meant he couldn't afford to get breathalysed if he got stopped.

To hell with that.

Harry turned the siren on full blast and floored the accelerator. He took bends faster than he had learnt in the obstacle driving course as a junior detective. The BMW's wheels screeched and complained, the car jolted and shook under his hands. But Harry drove on, skillfully avoiding the traffic when he jumped lights.

He approached Tooting High Street at more than sixty miles an hour and screamed past the intersection. At this time of the night, it was empty. Then he saw the flashing blue lights. Right at the mouth of Arla's street. Fear sparked inside him, and his hands shook. Briefly, his eyes could make out two uniformed officers leaning over a figure lying on the pavement. Harry pulled over and jumped out, leaving the engine running.

"DI Mehta, Clapham," Harry shouted, flashing his warrant card. "What's going on?"

One of the officers leaning over the body turned to him. "We got a 999 call for a major violent incident."

Harry could see a man's body sprawled against the phone booth. He seemed out cold. But there was another body, and he could only see the legs. He leaned forward to look between the officers. It was Arla. Her face was so white it seemed bleached of blood.

"No," Harry cried out and shoved the two officer's away. They resisted him but couldn't hold him back.

"I know her, damn you," Harry panted, "She's my boss." He took his face close to hers and felt relief wash over him when he saw the chest rise and fall. A quick feel of the jugular told him her circulation was strong. But she was unconscious. He patted her cheeks lightly, feeling a hot pressure growing behind his eyes.

"Arla. Arla!" His voice submerged under a heavy weight pressing at the back of his throat. The uniformed officers were telling him something, but their voices were lost in the high-pitched whine of the ambulance siren as it pulled up next to them.

*****

It was half past midnight. Harry watched as the blue-uniformed nurse bent over Arla and took a sample of blood from the intravenous line on her left elbow. Arla was sedated. Her eyes were shut. She had woken up briefly, but the sedation put her to sleep again quickly. Harry had pleaded with the doctors admitting her for a private room, but none was available. They were in a general ward of the hospital. At least it was female only. The curtains were pulled around the bed. Harry sat at the foot of the bed on a chair, hands folded under his chin. He rose as the nurse began to leave.

"What did her blood results show?"

"I'm sorry, but I don't know. Please wait for the doctors to arrive."

"Where are they?"

"It's very busy down in A/E, sir. Lots of admissions. I'm afraid you'll have to wait."

The African lady looked at Harry's anxious face, and her features softened. "Look, she's going to be fine. She's just in shock, that's all. There are no broken bones, no head trauma apart from a bump."

"Thank you," Harry said. Not knowing was the worst part and to hear it from the nurse's mouth was reassuring.

"Do you know when she'll wake up?"

"She's had IV diazepam, so she'll sleep for a while. Best for her to rest."

Harry scratched his stubble and stared at Arla.

The nurse said, "Why don't you get a coffee or something? There's a drinks machine at the end of the ward."

She smiled and walked away, her footsteps padding down the hallway. The sound of soft snoring came from one of the beds, and all of them had their wrap around curtains drawn to afford some privacy. Harry looked at the red digits on the machine next to Arla's head. Green and yellow lines squiggled on a black monitor. A clip was attached to Arla's finger, from where a wire snaked into the machine. A drip stand held an upside-down sac of fluid, which Harry was told contained Normal Saline, whatever that meant. It was feeding into the venflon on Arla's elbow, the entry point of the IV line.

His heart twisted in its bony cage. It was sad seeing Arla like this. She was always running around, doing things. Now she seemed so till, so quiet. He shook his head once and felt the rage rising within him like a tidal wave. That idiot would get what he deserved.

For now, he had to be strong for Arla. He went to the drinks machine and made himself a cappuccino. It was even more rancid than the coffee at the station, which was saying something. Harry dropped the cup into a bin and dialed Lisa and Rob's number. He left messages on their phones, then texts as well. He debated whether to inform Johnson but then decided against it. He would know in the morning in any case. But he did leave a text for Banerjee.

Then he filled up a cup of Bovril from the drinks machine, a kind of soup-based liquid. It tasted like beef broth and was much nicer than the coffee. He sat back down at the bedside. He put the cup on the floor, then reached out and touched her fingers. They felt cold, lifeless. Harry could feel the weight in his neck again, making it hard for him to swallow. He rubbed her hand, making it warm.

"Come on, Arla. Come on," he whispered.

Voices came down the corridor, very low. A man and a woman appeared, both with stethoscopes around their necks, and a bleep machine stuck on their belts. Harry stood. The doctors smiled at Harry, and the woman, who was younger, picked up a chart stuck on a clipboard at the end of the bed and shone a torchlight on it. Then she came closer to Arla.

The man addressed Harry. "Hi, I'm on the on-call medical registrar for tonight. My name is Andy Durkin."

Harry introduced himself. They didn't shake hands. Dr. Durkin asked, "What relation are you to the patient?"

"Work colleague," Harry answered promptly. The doctor gave Harry a look, sizing up his answer. Then he nodded.

"Is there any next of kin that needs to be informed?"

"She has a father. I have his name and address. I will notify him if you wish."

"Please. That needs to happen ASAP."

Harry didn't miss the undertone of urgency. He frowned. "Is she in any danger?"

"No, but…"

"But what?"

"Shock can do strange things to people. They can either become hysterical or become almost comatose. Your colleague was disturbed when she woke up, and she was screaming."

"I know," Harry replied wearily. "I was here."

"That's why we had to sedate her. But it's very light sedation. She should wake up soon."

"That's good."

"Yes, of course, but we need consent to treat her. If she doesn't have the capacity to consent, then her next of kin, or relative with power of attorney, has to consent on her behalf. Do you understand?"

Light dawned in Harry's mind. "You need permission to treat her."

"Yes, and it's a big issue. We cannot force any treatment on her. She has the right to refuse treatment. But if she is flailing around, then for her own interest, we have to treat her. But not if she has the capacity to refuse treatment."

This was all new to Harry, and frankly bewildering at one in the morning. The doctor saw the confusion in his face.

"Don't worry. Let's wait till she wakes up. See if you can get her father to call back. She hasn't suffered any major trauma, just some cuts and bruises. As for the mental effects of the shock, I'm not so sure. Only time will tell."

Harry said, "She's a tough cookie. She's been through similar situations in the past. However, she's never passed out before. That's what bothers me."

The female doctor came and whispered in her boss's ears. Dr. Durkin nodded, and the woman left.

Harry said, "What did the blood results show?"

"Nothing. They were all normal." Dr. Durkin appraised Harry. "You could go home now. If she wakes up...

"No," Harry said firmly. "I'll stay here till she does."

CHAPTER 41

It was like being in a boat, eyes closed. The swelling currents rose and fell, an ocean of black waves. Impenetrable, total darkness, the kind that is enclosing, ensconcing, even suffocating. But Arla wasn't suffocating. She was breathing. That much she could tell because the waves moved with every breath. She couldn't tell which senses were working. There was no smell in this inky sea, no wind, no vision. The waves were almost silent; she only heard a whisper like dragging her fingers across water.

The boat jolted. Arla winced. Her hands gripped the sides of the boat harder. If she got pushed over…fear scalded her like burning water. Her breaths came faster; the waves became choppier. The boat was jolted again; its serene rhythm suddenly disrupted. Arla felt something on her face, was it splashing water? A crack appeared in the darkness above her, with a sound like paper being ripped.

A ray of dazzling white light pierced the granite blackness. Unlike normal light, it did nothing to dispel the gloom. But it hurt her eyes. She cried out, moved her head. Wherever she went, the hideous ray of light followed, like a white laser beam, burning her eyes. The boat was going berserk now, moving sideways, then in a circle, making her dizzy.

Arla moaned and felt sharp tingles prickle her hands and feet. Like she was touching, walking on barbed wire. She started to thrash around. The boat went under a wave, and now she felt water splash on her face. Panic gripped her. She couldn't sink. She couldn't sink.

"Help! Help," she screamed. She felt a pressure on her arms, then on her shoulders, then on her legs. She was sinking again, going down, falling into the depths of an endless abyss. A cold trickle of water went up her left elbow. It moved up and up, flooding into her brain. The last thing she remembered was Mike Robert's scarred face, his mouth wide open like he was trying to swallow her whole.

Then the white laser light vanished, and the total blackness came back to claim her.

*****

Arla didn't know how long had passed, but she felt movement. At first, it seemed the ground beneath her was moving. Then she realized it was her upper body. She saw that face again, blood pouring down one side, clutching the left eye, right arm reaching out for her. She gasped, and her eyes flew open.

Daylight. Morning. White wall. Where was she?

Arla twisted her head. The first thing she saw was Harry. For once, he had stubble on his face. His eyes had bags under them, and his eyelids drooped. But light flared in his chestnut browns as he stared at her. Next to her, she saw the shorter, chubby figure of Lisa Moran. Lisa's mouth opened wide.

"Arla," a cracked, dry voice said next to her. She turned her head. An old man, his forehead marked with deep lines, cheeks sagging with weight, was leaning over her. He sat back down, his dark eyes wide, pensive.

"Dad?" Arla said.

Timothy Baker nodded slowly. "Yes, it's me." His eyes scanned her face anxiously. "Are you alright, darling?"

For no reason, tears sprang to her eyes and trickled down her sides. She blinked and tried to lift her arms to wipe them. She felt stupid; there was no reason to cry. Or maybe it was seeing her Dad after a long time. She didn't know, but it was embarrassing. Especially with Lisa watching. Her right arm felt heavy, and she saw a black cloth wrapped around her bicep. A blood pressure cuff. Over her head, a machine bleeped.

Her father gripped her shoulder gently. He didn't say anything.

All of it came back to Arla in a flash. It was like a switch turning on inside, flooding her mind with clarity. Coming back home, discovering...

She dug her palms into the bedsheet and sat up in bed. The machine above her went crazy, emitting a series of beeping noises.

"What happened?" Arla asked Harry, who had moved towards her. "Tell me."

Harry said, "Lie down. You need to rest."

She wanted to caress the stubble on his cheeks because she had never seen so much emotion in his face. His eyes were brimming full, liquid, and if she didn't know better, she could think Harry was close to tears. He sank down on one knee, looking down at the bed. She felt like ruffling the hair on his head.

"Please," Harry said. He wouldn't look up at her, which was odd. Well that's what he was. An oddball. She desperately wanted to touch him but couldn't with her Dad and Lisa present.

"Just tell me what happened."

The curtains were flung apart with a grating sound, and the tall, slender figure of an African woman in a dark blue uniform appeared. Her uniform was short-sleeved, and the sleeves had white rings at the end. Her hair was tied up in dreadlocks, and she was very beautiful. Arla gaped at her stern face.

"All awake now, I see," The nurse said. She smiled suddenly, showing white teeth. Harry stood to make way for her, and her Dad leaned back. The nurse pressed some buttons ,and the beeping stopped.

"How long have I been here for?" Arla asked to all of them. The nurse answered first.

"Since last night. It's now half past two in the afternoon. You slept for most of it but kept waking up."

"I did?"

"Uh-huh."

Arla stared down at the blood pressure cuff on her hand, then at the bandage on the left hand, holding the venflon in place. She glanced from Lisa, Harry to the nurse.

"I need to get to work. There's a lot to do."

"Not so fast," the nurse said, steel creeping into her voice. "The doctor's need to review you before you can be discharged."

"Where are they?"

"Doing their rounds. They'll be here at some point."

"I don't have time to waste." She looked at Harry. "Where is Mike Roberts?"

"In custody, Arla. He's not going anywhere. Please listen to the nurse."

Arla tore off the Velcro that attached the blood pressure cuff to her arm. She started picking at the bandage that held the venflon.

"I wouldn't do that if I were you," the nurse warned in a loud voice. Arla didn't listen. She tugged till the bandage ripped off her skin. Then she pulled the IV line out. Blood poured down her right hand, but she staunched the flow by pressing on it with the bedsheet.

"What are you doing?" the nurse demanded. She leaned down to help Arla. She took out a roll of wool, clamped it over her hand, then tore off some Mepore bandage and tied it around.

"Thank you," Arla said. She swung her legs off the bed, fighting the dizziness that threatened to overcome her. Her Dad stood as well, reaching out to grab her shoulder. The world swayed in front of her eyes, then corrected itself. The light was crisp, every detail around her visible. She felt rested, strong. Her head was light, airy. Maybe this is what she had needed. A break from chasing this case relentlessly.

"Where are my clothes?" she asked the nurse.

"Listen, you cannot leave like this. You-

"Yes I can," Arla interrupted her. "There's no law to say I have to stay here unless I'm under arrest."

The nurse shook her head and sighed, irritation etched on her face. "Then you have to sign a self-discharge form."

"Please get one. And my clothes please."

The nurse looked at Harry. "Your friend here can get it. It's in the lockers." She lifted her chin and walked out of the room. The scene had caught the attention of a few patients. An old woman opposite was sitting up in bed, curlers in her hair, lipstick in hand. She was watching with interest.

"Nothing to see here," Arla called out to her. She turned to Harry. "Please get my clothes, Harry. That's an order."

Harry puffed out his chest. "What are you doing? Is this really necessary? I told you Mike Roberts is under custody. We got him. It's over."

She gazed at him calmly. "I'll be the judge of that Harry; I'm the SIO. Now, please get my clothes."

Harry flexed his jaw, flared his nostrils. Their stares met and emitted sparks for a few seconds, then he turned on his heels and left. Arla turned towards Lisa. She smiled.

"Thanks for coming, Lisa."

"No worries, Guv. We were all worried. You did well to hold him off. What an arsehole."

"It's done now, Lisa. Now time to wrap it up." She sat down and focused on her Dad. Discreetly, Lisa left the cubicle.

Arla stared at her father, neither speaking for a while.

"I don't want to see you like this," Timothy said quietly. "I think your job's becoming too dangerous."

Arla shook her head. "No. I can deal with it. Don't worry. This was a one-off. It won't happen again."

"Happened last time as well. When Harry's sister got into trouble. Remember?"

Arla looked down at her hands, folded tightly on her lap. "Not now, Dad. Okay?"

When she looked at him, she saw the same fractured, broken eyes she saw in the mirror. But his was worse. They spoke of a grief that had hollowed him out inside, leaving only a shell of a man. His dark grey eyes had the vacant, lost look that some people had, whose faces spoke of the losses they had lived with.

"I can't do it again, Arla. Not with you. Please." His voice broke.

His gnarled hand came to rest over hers. The palm was soft on her skin. After a few seconds, she put her other hand over his.

Arla swallowed, memories and visions like the colours of a forgotten rainbow in her mind. Tarnished, rusty, but still a rainbow. Still worth keeping.

"It'll be alright," she whispered. "I promise."

CHAPTER 42

Arla saw the shoes appear under the curtains. They belonged to Harry. He stood there in silence. Timothy removed his hands from Arla's.

"Come in," Arla said. Harry didn't pull the curtains apart. He stepped inside, glancing at Arla, then at Timothy. Arla's clothes were stacked in his arms. He put them on the bed.

Timothy stood. "I better go." He looked at Arla one last time. "Please look after yourself. I did get your phone call last night. But I was sleeping then."

"I know," Arla said.

"Call me again. Anytime. Next time, I'll be up," he smiled wanly. Sadness and frustration conflicted into that familiar quagmire of emotion inside Arla. She leaned forward and hugged her father, who was stiff at first but then held her tightly. He nodded at her once, then shook hands with Harry.

"At least I was up when you called," Timothy said to Harry.

"I guess we're all up now," Harry said. He raised his eyebrows at Arla. "And raring to go as well, it seems."

"Yes," Arla said. Hunger was gnawing in her guts. She couldn't remember the last time she'd eaten. In fact, she couldn't remember the last time she'd felt hunger.

"Now stand outside please while I get dressed." Her Dad had stepped outside already. Harry looked at her slowly up and down, a slow smirk spreading across his face. She felt heat touch her cheeks.

Harry's smile faded. "I'm worried you're rushing into things. I think you should rest either here or at home, at least for today."

"Outside," she hissed. "Now."

She still had her underwear on, which was a relief. She got dressed in the old clothes, which stank. She needed a shower and change before she went anywhere.

Arla dressed quickly. There was no mirror, but her phone still had some battery left, miraculously. Her dark hair was clumpy and in knots. Even trying to straighten it with her fingers was a pain. She did the best she could and came out of the cubicle. She took a deep breath, smelling the hospital antiseptic. It was strange being here. The windows were open, and yellow sunlight suffused the beds close to it. She could see the brown rack of buildings and chimney stacks stretching out below the windows. A faint sound of traffic floated in. The old woman was staring at her again, checking her out head to toe. Arla waved goodbye to her.

At the ward desk, the nurse confronted them. Lisa was leaning against the wall, and she stood straight when she caught sight of Arla and Harry.

Arla could see the nurse's name badge clearly now. Her name was Mandy.

"So you're going then, are you?" Mandy put her hands on her hips, not hiding her displeasure.

"Yes. I know you're doing your job, but I'm doing mine as well. Trust me, I'm fine."

"That's not what you were last night," Mandy said stiffly. "And another day's rest would've done you the world of good."

"Have you got the self-discharge form?" Arla asked impatiently. Mandy glared at her, then held the form out. Arla took it from her, spreading it on the counter. She signed it briskly, then held it out to Mandy.

She nodded at Harry. "Let's go."

*****

Lisa and Arla walked ahead, Harry trailing behind them. Lisa nudged her.

"Harry stayed the night here."

Arla didn't know that. A warmth spread over her body, like a summer sea wave on a beach. She blinked and raised her eyebrows. "He did?"

Lisa nodded. "He didn't tell me. I found out from the nurse, Mandy."

Arla feigned surprise. "I wasn't aware."

"Guess he really cares about you, Guv." Lisa gave Arla a meaningful look. A coy smile played at the corner of her lips.

Arla frowned, then looked away quickly. "Think he was just doing his job. That's all."

"Pretty sure staying the whole night in hospital for his injured boss is not in his job description, Guv."

Arla shrugged. "What can I say? Sometimes, he gets carried away. I'm sure he'd do it for you as well."

Lisa still had the hint of a knowing grin on her face. "I really don't think so. Men only do that for a special person."

"Oh shut up, Lisa," Arla said, trying in vain to halt the bloom of heat spreading up her neck.

"Shut up about what?" Harry asked.

Great. The big oaf had caught up again. If only he hadn't stayed overnight. Typical of Harry to mess things up, she thought with an inward grin.

"Nothing," Arla sighed. "Nothing."

They had reached the elevator doors, and they got in. There were others inside the lift, and Arla was thankful for the silence with which they got to the ground floor.

Lisa drove off in her own car, and Harry took Arla back to Tooting. She was feeling better till the car drove down the grimy streets. Boarded up shop windows, bearded bums in torn jackets begging on street corners. Summer had driven the masses onto the streets, skimpily dressed young people frolicked with sleek-suited business types. The high streets were heaving with people. London's usual senseless mix of affluence with pockets of depravity.

As the car got closer to Tooting, a peculiar knot tightened inside her gut. The windows were up, and the air conditioning was humming, but the heat from outside seemed to seep in through the windows. As she stared at the faces of strangers who looked back at her, the mothers standing with prams, the young men walking in groups, beads of moisture arrived on her forehead.

She felt her heart cannon against her ribs, the sound loud in her ears. Her hands were tight fists, by her side.

"Shall we stop to pick up some food? What do you fancy?" Harry asked.

"Nothing. Just get me home."

She could feel Harry glance over at her. She ignored him, staring out the window, wishing the sidewalks were empty, the compressed buildings were gone, flown away into the sky, leaving only solitude. She closed her eyes and sank back into the seat.

When she looked again, Harry was turning into her street. Briefly, the red telephone booth on the corner flashed past her. A cold fist curled around her heart. That's where Mike had tried to strangle her. If the cops hadn't arrived on time...

CHAPTER 43

The moment came back to her like a slap across the face. The wild look in his dark eyes, the stench of sweat and blood. His left eye, closed where the blood had clotted around it. She had kicked and punched him, but he managed to drag her out of the booth. She had kneed him in the groin, and his hands had come off her neck. But before she could run away, he caught her vest and didn't let go. She was pulled down to the ground. She could see his bloated, angry face rising above her like a nightmare, vein throbbing in the middle of his forehead. His hands reached for her again, and that's when she felt her vision blurring, her head suddenly light and spinning away into nothingness. She vaguely remembered the flashing blue lights, the sharp note of a siren, before everything faded into oblivion.

The car was parked. Arla felt her collar damp with sweat, breath flirting with a heaviness in her chest, unable to dislodge the pressure.

"Hey," Harry said softly.

Arla was staring at the bright yellow potted dahlias on her neighbour's garden. Old Mrs. Corbyn. She lived alone, and those flowers were her pride and joy. They were blooming with summer. Her eyes flicked to her front door. Blue and white tape, in a single line, was dragged across the door.

"SOCO have already been. It's okay to go inside. They should've removed the tape," Harry said. When she didn't reply, he reached for her hand. She moved it away. Harry's hand froze in mid-air, then pulled back.

They were silent for a while. Harry had killed the engine already, and now he wound the window down.

Sultry air, reeking of diesel fumes, and the oil-heavy batter of fried food drifted in through the window. Arla wished she didn't have to breathe it. She didn't want to be here. Inside the hospital, in that cold, clinical bed, surrounded by her Dad, Lisa and Harry, she had felt cocooned, safe. Refreshed even, after a long rest.

Now she felt like she was coming apart, one bolt at a time, leaving her exposed. She had this inexplicable urge to wrap her arms around, draw her knees up, involute into herself like the spirals of a sandstorm, whirl her way, fade into the desert that opened up inside her. Where she could hide from everyone, even herself.

"If you don't want to go in, I can get your stuff, and you can come to mine. To get showered and changed, I mean." Harry muttered.

Arla closed her eyes. All the bravado she had in the hospital had suddenly run dry like a riverbed in dry heat. The heat outside seemed full of hot barbs that might burn her skin. She wanted to stay here, in the air-conditioned cool, and not go anywhere. But she also knew that wasn't possible.

Arla fluttered her eyelids. Her jaw flexed. This was stupid. Idiotic. She was acting like a bloody teenager, not a hardened police officer. She ignored the emptiness stretching inside her heart and swallowed the weight in her throat.

"No. It's okay. I can go inside myself." Out of habit, she patted the pocket of her coat. Then she remembered how she had run out of the house.

"Here," Harry held out his hand. Her key chain dangled from his thumb and forefinger.

"Thanks," she said. Their eyes met briefly before she could look away. The world she could hide away from, but not Harry. He knew her too well.

She got out, blinking in the heat. One of the west Indian women who lived opposite Arla was putting out the trash. She put a hand on her ample hip and stared at Arla.

Arla crossed the road. Harry followed her. She stood still for a few seconds, staring at the blue and white tape. A sight that was so familiar, but yet so strange on her own door. For some reason, she didn't want to touch it. On the other hand, she wanted to tear it down with a hammer. But her hands wouldn't emerge from their pockets. Despite the heat, her fingers were numb with cold.

Wordlessly, Harry reached around her, and his hands ripped off the tape.

"Keys?" he asked, holding out his hand.

"I can do it," Arla said, trying to keep the tremor out of her voice. *What the hell was the matter with her? Why was she feeling like this?*

She put the key in the lock and heard the bolt slide open. She entered. The hallway was exactly the same. She checked out the walls, the cabinet at the end, where she had knelt to examine the circuit board. A faint smell of dust and furniture, like always. Heart thudding, Arla stepped in. Harry shut the door behind her.

That made it worse. The noise from the street, the heat was all suddenly replaced by a cold silence. Arla glanced around like she was seeing the place for the first time. She stepped forward, then opened the lounge door. She let the door fall open. Sunlight spilled into the room where she had been assaulted the night before. From where she had barely escaped with her life intact. Where she had bludgeoned Mike on the head.

The sofa was still at an angle; the coffee table still overturned. Arla took a deep breath and walked inside. She lifted the coffee table, helped by Harry. Together, they pushed the sofa back to its original position.

She walked to her bedroom, ignoring the tiny spare bedroom, which also acted as her study. Her heart pumped faster as she pushed the door open. Did Mike hide in this room? She stepped inside. Her clothes were on the floor. The desk was turned over. The bedsheets were ripped off the mattress and lay on the floor. The dresser doors were open, and her clothes, shoes, everything lay in a heap.

Arla cried out, the sound a primal, raw grunting in her throat. Waves of nausea flooded her gut, and she fell to her knees, retching. Her mouth opened, and a thin stream of mucus trailed from her mouth.

Harry was next to her instantly. His hands hooked around her armpits, and he lifted her up, holding her limp body against his. Somehow, he walked her backwards, into the kitchen. He rested her on a chair, then got her a glass of water.

Arla covered her face in her hands and knelt on the table. The pressure on her chest had built to the point of bursting. Her ribs creaked, and sickness lurched inside her stomach. She stood, brushed past Harry and heaved on the sink. Mucus and bile rose from her stomach. She gripped the sides of the counter and retched again, till nothing else was left to come up.

She slumped to the floor. Her stomach burned with acid, spreading to her bloodstream, igniting a vortex of rage and bitterness that consumed her like wildfire. She screamed, eyes watering, and kicked out at nothing. She banged her futile heels on the floor, then knelt and hit the floor with her fists. The floorboards shook as she pounded the ground.

"Stop," Harry said, arms around her again, holding her back before she could do more damage to herself. But she had done this many time in her life. She didn't need Harry to hold her back. She didn't need anyone. Anger throbbed inside her like loud music inside a car. It filled her up, rage blasting against her eardrums. She used it to push away the panic and anxiety, the helplessness and fear.

It's what she had done all her life. Fight one feeling with another. Force out the poison by lacerating the poisoned limb. Only numbness remained and the parched earth of raw emotions, too hot to tread on. Well, she had lived like that for a long time.

It was who she was.

If Mike Roberts or any other fucker thought they could get one over her, they could think again. She would take all of them down, one by one.

"Come on," Harry said, but she moved away from him. She held onto the kitchen counter for support and lifted herself.

Harry blocked her way. Her eyes were hazy with tears, and she brushed them away angrily. The stubble on Harry's cheeks was unfamiliar, and his swirling brown eyes were deep with hurt. She couldn't bear to look at him.

"I told you, didn't I? Let me get your stuff, put it in a bag, and then I'll bring it out to you." He leaned closer to her. "Just get your personal stuff from the bathroom. I'll do the rest."

"No," she said firmly, lifting her chin.

She walked past his long frame. Taking a deep breath and wiping her eyes and nose, she stepped inside the mess of her bedroom. She scooped up clothes and put them inside the dresser. She stood on the bed and pulled out a traveller's bag. Harry was right in one respect. She didn't want to stay here tonight. Maybe tomorrow she'd feel better, and move back in. But not tonight. Neither did she want to use the bathroom here. For some reason, the thought of being naked in the shower made her feel vulnerable.

She didn't want to stay with Harry, but he was the safest bet, and a darn sight cheaper than a hotel.

Arla gritted her teeth and went about the grim task of sorting her clothes out. She put most in the dresser, her chest heaving, nausea curdling inside her guts as she arranged dresses back on the hangers. Underwear back in their drawers. The feeling of being violated returned, stronger than ever. She wanted to kick, hit, hurt someone, even herself. She worked at a furious pace, trying to keep her own thoughts at bay. Actions drowned out the sparks flaring across her neurons.

The mind could be her own worst enemy, if she let it. She knew that very well.

When she finished, she was sweating, but the room was neater than before. Harry helped to put the desk back up straight. The chair had a broken leg; she couldn't do anything about that.

Harry took the two bags she had packed and headed out to the car. Arla locked up and came out into the sunshine. Mrs. Corbyn was outside, tending to her flowers.

"Are you alright dear?" she called out to Arla. "I saw the police here this morning. What was that about?"

"Nothing," Arla said. "Nothing at all."

CHAPTER 44

Arla wouldn't admit it, but she was glad Harry was here. His apartment wasn't far, and she had stayed the night there before. By the time she had showered, dressed and changed, she was feeling close to normal again.

Her appetite had reared up in the hospital, but she didn't feel like eating anymore. Harry ate fish and chips for lunch and had a portion for her. She refused and picked at some chips while he wolfed his food down.

They left for the station soon after. Arla checked her messages while Harry drove. Her father had called several times. She sent him a quick text to say she was fine and wanted to be left alone. When Harry parked at the station, she felt a flutter of nerves. Everyone knew about her. She recalled the sympathetic glances she used to receive when she was suspended once, for punching a paedophile outside court.

This was worse, more personal. Harry stopped outside the entrance and pulled out a packet of cigarettes. He lit up and took a deep drag, throwing his head back. It seemed like he needed that smoke.

Arla felt bad. If it wasn't for him, she would be worse off by several degrees. She got closer.

"Thank you. For staying over last night. And for everything else."

He didn't reply, filling his lungs with smoke again. Then he glanced at her and smiled.

"Anytime."

She gave his hand a quick squeeze, glancing around. Then she felt stupid. How long could she hide their relationship? Didn't Lisa know already?

If anyone suspected, she'd rather it was Lisa and no one else. Maybe it was time to have a deeper chat with her.

"I'll make it up to you," Arla whispered. She eyed the cigarette, wondering if she should have a drag. She had quit for several years now, but every now and then felt the urge. She squashed it but waited for Harry to finish his smoke.

"It's you who suffered," Harry said. When he looked at her, his eyes were blazing. "That bastard will pay for this."

Arla's fingers brushed Harry's and then curled around his. His large, strong hand felt warm, reassuring.

"He's sick," Arla whispered. "Don't worry about him. But you came through for me, Harry. I owe you."

His eyebrows furrowed in the middle, and a look of pain flashed across his now smoothly shaven cheeks. He looked like the old Harry, sharp-jawed and big boned, but the corners of his eyes drooped in defeat.

"I wasn't there. I'm sorry."

It was her turn to console him. "You couldn't have been. In fact, it's my fault for not letting you stay with me. You would've scared that bugger off."

Harry took one last, long drag, then crushed the cigarette on the ashtray stuck on the wall. He blew out smoke in a fragrant breath.

"I would've scared him off," he remarked, rolling his shoulders. Arla squeezed his hand, and they grinned at each other.

"Did you inform Johnson?" Arla asked as they walked down the rear corridor.

"Yes, of course. Hasn't he called you?"

Arla shook her head. "But he did leave a couple of texts. I rang him from the car; he didn't answer."

Arla steeled herself before she walked into the open plan office. Harry walked in behind her. Heads turned, and she heard the murmurs from a few desks as she walked past. Harry went to his table, and Arla went straight to her office and shut the door. She took her coat off and took out the laptop. The phone on her desk rang, and she answered.

"Good to have you back, Arla," Johnson said in a quiet voice. "I'm sorry about what happened."

"We got him, sir. That's what matters."

"But you shouldn't have suffered. You've won admiration from the whole force for your bravery. This will go a long way towards furthering your career; I can assure you of that."

"Thank you, sir."

"Will you please come up and see me in half an hour?"

"Of course."

Arla hung up, then picked up the phone again. She called her team into the office.

Lisa, Rob, Das and Harry congregated in her office. Arla brushed the sympathetic murmurings aside but thanked them.

She asked the question whose answer she needed urgently. "Where is he?"

Lisa said, "In the Cellar." The Custody Chamber, where the Clapham Police station had their overnight detention cells, was in the basement. Johnson had once joked it was their wine cellar. The name had stuck.

"I want to see him," Arla said. She looked at Harry. "Arrange one of the Interrogation Rooms. Does he have a solicitor yet?"

"No," Harry said firmly, "and yes. You can't see him, but he does have a lawyer. Pinstriped arrogant cock. Our old friend, Wilmshurst."

Arla groaned. The veteran defence lawyer had been a thorn in their side for many years. Although, she doubted even Wilmshurst would have much of a case against GBH (Grievous Bodily Harm) in Mike's case.

She focused on Harry. "Call his lawyer. I want to interrogate Mike."

Harry shook his head. "I don't think so. He obviously has a fixation on you. After the assault…

"That's an order, Harry. I mean it."

Harry stared back at her. "You might want to see Johnson before you do it."

Arla's conviction faltered. "What do you mean?"

"Orders from above. He wants to see you before you go anywhere near Mike."

"What?" Arla stood, frowning. "After what he did, I would've thought at least I could interrogate and then charge him."

"That's just it, Guv," Lisa said. "If you do, it will be an emotional issue. You know what defence lawyers are like, especially Wilmshurst. What if he poked holes in your statement in court?"

Harry continued. "You know better than me, Arla. Best not to be the victim as well as the prosecuting police officer."

Arla stared at them in disbelief. She saved her sharpest glare for Harry.

"Fine! I'll go and see him myself." Arla strode for the door, ignoring Harry, who called out to her.

She pulled her door open and came to an abrupt stop. Johnson stood there, wearing his uniform, arms folded across his massive chest.

CHAPTER 45

"May I have a word?" Johnson said quietly. Arla nodded. This was important enough for Johnson to come down from his office. She had to obey.

Johnson walked in and glanced around the room. "Everybody out. Not you, DI Mehta."

Harry shut the door. Johnson sat down opposite Arla, and Harry perched on the window ledge behind Arla.

Johnson said, "I'm on my way to HQ, so thought I'd drop by. In fact, one of the things I have to discuss in HQ is this case. How we never had a clue Mike could be the main suspect."

Arla frowned. An uneasiness reared up in the back of her mind. "We did sir. When Sarah Bloom gave her statement, we knew he was the main suspect."

"It points to a serious security breach, Arla, as you well know. We had a suspected serial killer working right under our noses. The Commissioners want answers."

He let his statement float in the air for a while, letting its importance sink in. "And then they want a quick prosecution."

"Of course."

"A prosecution where you aren't involved."

Arla stood, her face flushed. "What? That's absurd. He comes into my house, almost kills me, and now I can't prosecute him?" She leaned forward, pointing a finger at Johnson.

"How would you feel if he did that to your wife? Would you sit there and let someone else handle it?"

"Sit down, DCI Baker, before I reprimand you officially." Johnson's voice had the rumble of thunder.

"Arla," Harry said from behind. "Listen to him."

Beads of sweat trickled down the back of her neck, itched on her hair roots. Rage had blossomed in her chest, colouring everything red. But she came to her senses. Nostrils flaring, she slumped down on her chair.

"If my family was attacked, I wouldn't be allowed to be the SIO in the case, unless there were exceptional circumstances," Johnson said, watching Arla carefully. "I know you're angry about this. But consider this: what if the lawyer blew holes in your case? They'll know your record. Your visits to the psychiatrist."

In not as many words, Lisa had said the same thing to her. It made sense, even in her current emotional torpor. She didn't want Mike to get away because some slick lawyer made the jury believe otherwise. Her punch to the paedophile's face was well-known to the Independent Office for Police Conduct or IOPC. It amazed her that she lived in a society where vermin like him could complain about her, but that was life. In addition, she had depression and mood swings, which had taken her to the Occupational Health psychiatrist's office more than once.

Johnson said, "Therefore, it is imperative that we have another SIO in this case." He lifted both hands as Arla began to protest. "Now hear me out. Please."

"I'm not saying you can't be involved in the case. You can. As DCI, you even have direct authority over the SIO."

Arla raised her eyebrows. Her tightly clenched jaw relaxed. "I do?"

"Yes. These are my orders from above, Arla. I must say they make sense as well. Once again, you have my full support, as long as you obey the orders."

"I will, sir, of course. This has been one hell of an ordeal, as you can see."

Johnson's voice became softer. "I know. That's why, if you cooperate, you can do as you like."

"I promise I will."

Johnson gave her one of his rare smiles. He twirled the cap in his hands. "Excellent."

Arla clasped her hands together on the desk. She smiled back at Johnson. "On one condition, sir."

Johnson's smile faded. His eyebrows lowered. "What's that?"

"I choose the SIO."

Johnson opened and closed his mouth. "You...but why?"

"You just said as DCI I can have direct authority over the SIO. Correct?"

"Yes, but..."

Arla said, "You want me to help the new SIO, don't you, sir? Make sure the investigation is progressing in the right direction?"

"Yes, I do."

"Then why don't you let me choose the SIO?"

Johnson stared at Arla, his mouth open. He blinked several times. He wanted Arla's cooperation, but he also wanted to please his bosses. Arla smothered her grin. Her domineering boss was caught in a pickle.

Johnson glared at Arla, his eyes hard and glittering. Arla held his eyes. She knew Johnson's mind was running through hoops, seeking a way to put her down, but also ensure the case went to court quickly. Johnson rubbed his jaw and sighed.

"Okay," he said in a resigned voice. "Who do you want to be the SIO?"

Arla didn't turn her head, but she hooked a thumb behind her. "DI Mehta."

CHAPTER 46

Rampton High Security Hospital
Nottinghamshire

Governor Beasley stood with his hands folded behind his back. He saw the dark blue Ford Titanium come down the long drive that led to the hospital's main gate. From his vantage point; he saw Rochelle Griffiths sitting in the back passenger seat, driven by security personnel. She didn't drive anymore, and he couldn't blame her. The car passed under his window and turned the corner for the large car park to the west side.

Beasley continued staring at the long drive, and the green hedge that formed parallel lines on either side. His mind moved in an equally linear direction, as it often did. The path led straight into more death and destruction. He took a deep breath and let it go. Maybe things had gone too far. It was time to put an end to this.

There was a knock on the door, and he asked them to come in.

Rochelle was shown in by a guard. The sling was off her left elbow, and she wasn't limping anymore when she walked. She had light make up on, and her hair was cut shorter at the shoulder and fixed with hairspray. She still looked lovely, Beasley thought, a woman with a certain presence. He wondered why she had gone into medicine when she had the looks and glamour of a model.

"So good to see you," he said, shaking her hand. Now that he was close up, she could see the lines in the corners of her eyes, the slightly drooped eyelids. She looked tired.

"Arm feels better?" Beasley asked.

"Almost," she said, with a wispy smile that vanished quickly. "I still keep looking out my window every night."

"Is the police squad car not outside your house?"

"They patrol, going past every hour or so. I don't see them all the time. It's better than nothing, I guess."

"I can put one of my men outside, if you wish." Beasley wondered why he hadn't thought of that before. If anything, that was a better option. He would always be aware of Rochelle's whereabouts.

"No, it's fine. It's getting easier, I think."

Beasley looked at her questioningly, but she wouldn't elaborate. Her neck moved gracefully to the left, staring out the window at the sunshine over green fields. The grounds inside the Hospital were large, partly to ensure that if convicts escaped, they could be captured. Guards with dogs patrolled the perimeter twenty-four hours.

Beasley asked, "Have you heard about what happened to DCI Baker? The policewoman who came up to see Kevin."

A frown creased the smooth expanse of Rochelle's forehead. "No. What happened?"

Beasley sighed. "It seems our search for the copy cat killer is over."

Rochelle leaned forward and raised her voice. "What?"

Beasley inspected her carefully, wondering how much he should divulge. In the end, he went for the truth. She was friendly with Arla Baker. If she rang her, she'd know in any case.

"Johnson, DCI Baker's boss, rang me this morning." Beasley proceeded to tell Rochelle the whole story.

Rochelle's mouth opened in shock. "She was assaulted? In her own home?"

"Yes," Beasley maintained a grim expression. "And the suspect worked as a media liaison officer in that police station. He was having an affair with the second victim. Can you believe it?"

Rochelle was at a loss for words. She stared at Johnson, shaking her head.

Beasley said, "DCI Baker is alright, thank god. She had to spend the night in hospital though."

"Are they sure it's the same person that killed the other two women?"

"Yes. He matches the description, and they have CCTV footage of him going up into their homes. An eye witness has reported seeing him having an argument with the second victim. They found letters he wrote to her. His laptop has videos of violent pornography. This guy was disturbed."

Rochelle digested this in silence. Then she asked, "And his connection with Kevin?"

"They're working on that right now. You know the websites that are devoted to Kevin? His Fanclubs, so to speak? Well, they think he's a member, with a fake name."

Rochelle nodded. "That would make perfect sense. It's not uncommon for a serial killer to have fans who would kill for him, as you know. It's a scary world."

"Indeed, and that's why I'm glad they got this guy."

Rochelle asked softly, "Does Kevin know?"

Beasley appraised her for a while. "He doesn't have any contact with the outside world, and I haven't told him. Therefore, no."

Rochelle pursed her lips. "I wonder how he'll take it. However, it wasn't anything to do with him. But men like him have egos. Arla told him about the copy cat killings. I worry that would've boosted his twisted sense of achievement, if you know what I mean."

Beasley nodded. "I do."

"It fits in with his regression. You know, when we had to move him here, from Full Sutton." Rochelle frowned. "And now, I wonder what his reaction will be."

"He was making progress with you, wasn't he?"

"It took some time, but yes, he was. This environment makes him calmer, I think. He was more on edge in Full Sutton."

Beasley grunted. "They all say that. Here they have a swimming pool, gym, even unisex discos. What's not to like?"

"Regardless, he was, I mean is, improving. It's just this deadly lunatic who's running around." Rochelle heaved a big sigh. "I'm just glad they've caught him now."

She bent her head, and her lips pursed. "Actually, I think telling Kevin that this guy is under lock and key might be a sobering experience for him. Even if Kevin's ego is boosted, I can use that to show him crime doesn't pay, and punishment will follow."

Beasley nodded without speaking. Rochelle asked, "Can I see him, in that case?"

He stared at her for a while, then nodded. "Would you mind waiting here for a second? I need to inform my staff."

Rochelle looked surprised. "You can't do that from here?" Her eyes fell on the phone on his desk.

"Our secure line is undergoing work today. I'll be back in a moment."

Beasley rose and walked out of the room, leaving Rochelle on her own. The guard at the corner rose when he saw his boss, but Beasley waved him to sit back down.

Beasley went to a covered phone on the wall. He dialed a number that was known only to him.

"Yes it's me," he said. "Get Kevin on the phone."

CHAPTER 47

The Incident Room was only half full, but Arla ensured she had everyone's attention. The whiteboard behind her had the photos of both victims and Mike Robert.

"I guess you've heard by now what happened," she said, and the hubbub in the room died down. Jason Beauregard came in and took his place at the back against a printer.

"Don't worry about me, I'm fine," Arla said with a grin. She felt anything but fine inside, and the grin on her face was forced. A cheer went up in the room.

"However, I'm not the SIO anymore. DI Mehta is taking over from me."

Several voices began to mutter in the ensuing silence. Arla caught the frown on Jason's face. Without a doubt, he was pissed off at not being the new SIO. She addressed the assembled staff.

"Please give DI Mehta the support he needs." She moved, and Harry took her place.

"The suspect is in custody as you know," Harry said. "He is charged with GBH, but the real charge, of course, is the murder of these two victims. I know this is a distressing case for many of you because it involves one of our own. But it is what it is. We still need more background on Mike, his past history, as well as that of his friends. Let's build as strong a case as we can."

Harry gave some more directions, written out by Arla in advance, and the meeting broke up.

Das strolled over. She was looking radiant with a bright yellow flower in her hair and a red and yellow dress.

"Look at you," Arla remarked.

Das grinned. "Sun's out, so I thought I might as well." She sat down next to Arla. "Remember you told me to look through cold cases up north, similar to Kevin's MO?"

Arla had asked Das to do some digging after what happened to Rochelle. She was instantly intrigued. "Yes?"

"As it turns out, there was a murder in Stockport, near Manchester, about five years ago. The MO wasn't similar to Kevin's murders, but there was an eerie link to our current killer's methods."

Arla frowned. "In what way?"

Das spread a photocopied newspaper article. It was the Mansfield Daily News, a local newspaper, dated from 11 July 2014.

"Here," Das said. "It says the body of a young woman was found with her throat slit. She had cuts on other parts of her body as well. No nails were removed from her fingers. But she did have a ring of pebbles circling her body and also a triangle of stones by her head."

Arla's eyes widened. Das stopped, and they looked at each other. Breathing quicker, Arla said, "Did they prosecute anyone?"

"No, Guv. There are still enquiries, but no one's been caught."

"Was Mike up there at the time? Have you looked?"

"He's always lived down south, according to the electoral rolls. His CV backs that up. Mike worked as a journalist before he joined us. He was born in Dorking and stayed down south all his life."

"But he could have travelled up north and done this," Arla mused.

"Possibly."

"Get back to the Manchester Forces. Ask them to open a file on the case and send us all the documents and witness statements."

"Yes, Guv."

Harry was hanging around, listening. "That puts a new angle. But I need to interview Mike now." He stood.

"Can I watch from the viewing chamber?" Arla asked.

Harry lifted his eyebrows and walked off. She followed. They went downstairs, where two thick iron gates led them down a narrow corridor to the basement.

The Custody Sergeant on Duty looked at their warrant cards and wrote down their names on a clipboard. Then he unlocked the grilled steel door that led to the cells. He stopped outside one. Before he could reach for the metal door, Parmentier stepped out. He shook Arla's hand.

"Sorry to hear about what happened. Sure you're alright?" His habitual irony was replaced by frank concern.

"If you're not taking the piss," Arla replied, "then I must be."

Parmentier grinned. "Well, I'm glad you are, anyway. Plenty of bad people out there for you to still catch."

His smiled faded. "I hope you get this one too." He held up what looked like a flat exercise book and two vials. The vials were inside a zipped plastic bag that had the letters "DNA Evidence", printed on them in bold letters.

"Just took his prints and a DNA swab. Be interesting to see if we have a match with the DNA from the victim's bodies."

"Exactly what I was going to suggest," Arla said. "Please put them in as an urgent. It's Tuesday, so the database should have plenty of time."

The National DNA Database took 48 hours to send a reply and quicker if they found a match. Arla said, "And can you let Banerjee know? I'll catch up with him later."

"Back today and already giving orders?" Parmentier raised his eyebrows.

Harry said, "And she's not even the SIO anymore. I am."

"Yes, but you take orders from me. Just remember that."

It was nice being back in the usual swing of things. It gave her a cloak of normality, beneath which she could hide. Inward, she was worried about crossing that door and seeing Mike again.

Parmentier took his leave. Harry glanced at her. "You don't have to come in. Stay in the viewing chamber, and you can watch Lisa and myself interview him."

Arla stared at the closed door with the grill at eye height. She wanted to face him, look into his eyes. But what Harry said also made sense. She was just getting back on her feet. She didn't want to slip down into the nightmare again. The state of her bedroom flashed before her eyes. Arla blew out her cheeks.

"Okay. I'll get Jeremy Melville as well. I need him, sorry, *you* need him to check Mike is telling the truth."

CHAPTER 48

Arla stood by the window of the viewing chamber as Mike walked in. His hair was disheveled, falling over his eyes. On the left scalp, his hair was partly shaved where he had stitches. A white plaster covered the stitches.

He had a week's stubble on his cheeks. His hands were cuffed, and he was brought in by a white-shirted custody officer. He wore scruffy jeans and a blue T-shirt. Mike looked at the glass box, and his eyes met Arla's. Her heart jumped in her mouth. His lips bent lower in a grimace as he continued staring. Arla knew he couldn't possibly see her. But it was still unnerving. The officer pushed him and Mike sat down. Then he turned his head to stare at Arla again.

Harry and Lisa followed with the pinstriped suited solicitor, Mr. Wilmshurst. After they sat down, a speaker above Arla's head crackled into life. She walked to the table and turned the volume from the dashboard of the audio machine.

It was strange watching them go through the motions. She should be sitting where Harry was. With an effort, she shrugged her feelings away.

"Identify yourself for the recorder," Harry instructed Mike. He did so. Harry took Mike through the usual questions of where he was at the time and date of the murders.

"I was at work," Mike said. When the question was repeated, Mike gave the same answer. He was calm as he said it. He was either acting extremely well or telling the truth.

"Debbie Jones and Jane Crouch, did you know them?"

Mike hesitated, then spoke. "Jane Crouch worked with me, so yes, I did."

"They called your phone number the night before they both died," Harry said. He opened an envelope next to him and took out Mike's phone log. The numbers of Debbie and Jane had been circled. He pushed the paper towards Mike, who leant forward to look at it, a frown on his face.

"So, they called me. You don't get calls from women, Inspector?" Mike smiled, but it seemed more like a snarl.

Harry showed him photos of the victims as they were found in the Common. Mike rocked backwards on the seat, his mouth open.

"Why are you showing me these photos?" His voice was very different now. It was loud, angry.

"You knew both these women, Mike."

Mike glared at Harry. "What if I did?"

Harry paused, and Arla knew what was on his mind. *Mike was not denying that he knew the victims.*

Suddenly, Mike stood, pushing his chair back. Wilmshurst stood as well, pressing on his arm. Mike yelled out. "So you think I killed them, do you?"

Wilmshurst was leaning into Mike, speaking in his ears. Mike's chest rose and fell with deep breaths, and he was clearly agitated. But he nodded eventually and sat back down.

Harry said, "Are you denying that you killed these women?"

"Yes, of course, I am," Mike yelled again, and again, his lawyer spoke to him.

"Keep your voice down," Harry said sternly. "I won't say that again."

Wilmshurst kept talking in Mike's ear for a while. Mike was having trouble calming down.

Harry said, "How well did you know Debbie Jones, the first victim?"

Mike closed his eyes and hung his head. He didn't reply for several seconds. When he did, it was a strangled whisper. "I'm sorry. I'm sorry." He kept repeating himself.

"Sorry for what?" Harry asked.

"About what happened to them."

"Do you know what happened to them?"

"I check the news like everyone else. And I know things as I work in the station. Apart from that, no, I don't."

"Did you have a relationship with Debbie Jones?"

A brief, hushed conversation with his lawyer followed. Then Mike said, "Yes. We met a few times. It was a casual fling. Nothing else."

"And Jane Crouch?"

At the mention of Jane's name, Mike's head hung down. His face was creased with pain, and his eyes were shut tight.

"Can you answer the question please?" Lisa asked.

Keeping his head bent, Mike nodded. "Yes," he mumbled, eyes still closed. "Oh, Jane." He covered his face in his hands, and his body shook with sobs.

Arla stepped back from the glass, her brain whirring, clicking. Mike was emotional, but that could happen with some killers. They got attached to their victims in a weird, twisted way. Mike could be that type. Arla got the distinct impression he was letting it all out.

The reverse of what she had expected him to do.

Harry glanced at the glass for a second or two before looking away. *Yes, me too, Harry, she thought silently.*

"Tell us about your relationship with Jane."

Wilmshurst and Mike had another chat. Mike was handed some tissue by Lisa. He blew his nose and dried his eyes. Then he stared at Harry.

"I loved her. There you go. Happy now?"

"How long were you seeing her?"

"We worked together, so I saw her every day. It went on for almost a year."

"Were you seeing Debbie and Jane at the same time?" Lisa asked.

Mike bit his lower lip. He glanced at Wilmshurst, who nodded.

"Yes," Mike said. His face was downcast again, and his fingers moved constantly on his lap.

Harry asked, "Were there any others?"

"What do you mean?"

"Did you have any other women you dated concurrently?"

Mike swallowed and looked around. After another hushed chat with the lawyer, he admitted, "I had two or three women on the go, yes. But Jane was the one I loved. I always told her that. But she found out about the other women. It put a strain on our relationship."

"Were you angry with Jane, Mike?" Harry asked. "After she found out?"

"Yes. She was too. She threatened to leave me."

"And you didn't want that."

Mike shook his head. Harry leaned forward. "Did you kill Jane so she would always be yours? If you couldn't have her, then neither could anyone else, right? Is that what you did, Mike?"

Mike's mouth opened again, and a deep frown spasmed across his face. His cheeks reddened again, and a vein started throbbing in his forehead.

"No," he shouted. "Why do you keep asking me that?"

Wilmshurst intervened in his crisp public school accent. "I must say I object to this manner of questioning, Inspector. My client has already answered your question. Can we move on please?"

Harry and Lisa exchanged a glance. Harry looked down at his notebook, picked up a pen and scribbled something. Then he circled. He tapped the pen on paper as if preparing himself for the next question.

"What about Arla Baker?"

CHAPTER 49

As Arla stared through the glass box, she felt a cold fist curl inside her guts. Mike twisted his hands in his laps and tapped one foot against the chair. His chest rose and fell rapidly. For a while he said nothing, staring at Harry.

"That bitch!" Mike said venomously.

Wilmshurst leaned towards him again. In one sense, Arla was enjoying the veteran lawyer's discomfort. W, as he was known, had landed a difficult client. One who was making no bones about his feelings. In the same breath, Arla was growing increasingly uneasy.

How could someone as emotional as Mike plan these elaborate murders?

"Can you explain what you mean?" Harry said in a steady voice. He was calm, but Arla could see the stiffness in his spine, the hard jut of his chin. He gripped the pen tightly in his hand. Harry was angry. She caught Lisa giving him an anxious glance.

Mike swore again. "She brought it on me. As if what I did was so wrong!"

"What did you do?"

"Is sleeping with more than one woman a crime? Since when?" Mike bared his teeth, panting through his lips.

"But when both Debbie and Jane died," Mike broke off and clutched his forehead. He remained like that for a few seconds, struggling to speak.

"When they both died, I knew I would become a suspect. I knew someone like Arla would put two and two together and come up with five."

Lisa touched Harry's sleeve and took over. *Well done, Lisa, Arla thought.*

Lisa cleared her throat. "Can you clarify what you mean?"

"If the police looked hard enough, they would find clues about me and the women. I knew that. It's not like I hid my identity when I met them. Then you guys would come after me."

Mike paused, then continued. "When Arla took over the case, it was a matter of time. She's like a dog with a bone, that woman. Persistent to a fault."

"So?" Lisa asked.

"So?!" Mike gnashed his teeth together and leaned forward. "So she raided my house, didn't she? Turned it upside down. Made me homeless! Destroyed my reputation, my livelihood! And you sit here calmly and...." Mike broke off, shaking his head. "I have nowhere to live. No job to go to. I'm a bloody fugitive. And it's all her fault."

There was silence for a while. Arla saw Harry shift in his seat. A muscle was flexing in his jaw. Lisa had seen it too. She touched Harry's arm again, and he turned to look at her. He nodded, then exhaled. So did Arla. Harry was doing well to keep his cool. It made her glad suddenly that she wasn't facing Mike.

Lisa asked, "Is that why you attacked Arla Baker?"

Mike didn't answer immediately. Wilmshurst whispered in his ear again, for a long time. Mike listened carefully.

Lisa changed her question. "Where did you get her keys from?"

Mike glanced at Wilmshurst, who inclined his head a fraction.

"I jumped over the back fence. Broke into the window of her bedroom and climbed in. Before that, I had cut the wires feeding the circuit box."

"Hence the alarm didn't go off," Lisa said. "And the lights didn't work."

There was a short silence. Harry spoke softly. "What did you expect to get out of this, Mike?"

Mike's face twisted as if he was in pain. "I didn't want to hurt her. Honestly, I didn't. I had a few drinks beforehand. Guess I went out of control."

Lisa said, "You attacked her in her house, then chased her up the street to the phone box where you assaulted her again. Do you still claim you didn't mean to hurt her?"

Mike covered his head in his hands. His fingertips blanched white as he gripped his head tightly. He mumbled something incoherent.

Lisa said, "Did you want to subdue DCI Baker the way you did the other women?" She picked up the A4 brown envelope next to her and shook out some photos. "These are photos that Jane Crouch had taken. Also present are photos from your laptop. You engage in violent and abusive sexual practices, don't you, Mike?"

Mike removed his hands. He glanced at the photos that Harry spread out on the table.

Wilmshurst said, "My client is aware of these photos. The terms violent and abusive are judgmental and pejorative. Where did you come up with those words?"

Harry said, "The photos show such practices. There are no other words to describe them."

Mike removed his hands. His face was white like he'd seen a ghost. He licked his lips. When he spoke, his voice was dry, cracked.

"I only wanted to scare Arla, okay? Like I said, things got out of hand."

"My client was drinking heavily at the time. He wasn't in control of his actions," Wilmshurst said crisply.

Harry frowned. "Don't tell me. Next, you're going to claim diminished responsibility."

Wilmshurst shrugged his pinstriped suited shoulders. "It's certainly a consideration."

Harry put a finger on the photos and focused on Mike, who was still looking shocked.

"What about these? What about the arguments you had with Jane? Were you drunk all the time, Mike? Is that your defence?"

Mike leaned forward, putting his head in his hands again. He made a keening noise from his throat, a sharp, plaintive sound.

His eyes were red, blurry with tears when he looked up. "No. No. For a hundred time, NO!" he said. "I did have sex with them. But I didn't kill them. I never killed anyone. And I wanted to teach Arla a lesson. Not kill her!"

He shouted the last words out, then hung his head and wept. Arla had seen enough. She left the room, crossed the corridor, and used her fob key to get entrance into the secure interview room. A uniformed constable was standing outside. He nodded at Arla.

"Can I help you, Guv?"

"Yes. Knock on the door and ask DI Mehta to come outside."

CHAPTER 50

Both Harry and Lisa emerged. They followed Arla outside and into the viewing room. Arla made sure all the speakers and microphones were turned off.

"I don't think he did it," she said. "I think he's telling the truth."

Harry frowned. "We've only spoken to him once."

"And he's broken down already. Yes, he could be an emotional killer. But did those dead bodies strike you as crimes of passion? No. A lot of premeditation went into organizing the crime scenes. Both the victim's drinks were spiked with Rohypnol. Then the stones, the shrine, all of that points to a cold, calculating mind."

Arla pointed a finger at the interview room. Through the glass, Mike and Wilmshurst were visible, chatting softly.

"Mike looks like a hot mess. He can barely control himself. Sure, he's a sexual deviant. And yes, what he did to me was dangerous. But is he really our man?"

"It could all be an act, Guv," Lisa remarked.

Arla nodded. "Agreed. But it's a bloody good one. Oscar worthy."

Harry said softly, "He could've killed you." His shoulders straightened, and she saw his nostrils flare. She put both hands up.

"I know. But I think that's more a case of him losing it completely. I did smell alcohol on his breath. He stank like a brewery, in fact, when he grabbed me in the telephone box. But," Arla shook her head vigorously, trying to rid herself of that horrid image. "Honestly, I think I had a lucky escape. Because if he was the killer, you might not have seen me for days."

Harry took a couple of steps back, rubbing his jaw and blinking. He obviously didn't like the mental image Arla's words painted. Lisa's eyes moved from Harry to Arla and stayed there.

Arla said, "Ask him about the black rose. And the Rohypnol. Watch his reactions. I hope Jeremy is watching the live feed." Arla sighed. "But it doesn't feel right."

She wanted to give Harry a hug but not in front of Lisa. He gave Arla a cold stare, then both of them trooped out of the room. Arla turned the speakers back on.

Harry asked Mike the questions Arla had posed. As expected, Mike vigorously denied knowing anything about the black roses or the Rohypnol.

Harry asked, "Are you denying you have never used Rohypnol?"

Mike paused for a second or two. It was noticeable. Then he shook his head. "No, I never have."

"Have you ever been up North?"

Mike leaned forward, frowning. "Did you say up North?"

"Yes."

"No," Mike said guardedly, glancing at Wilmshurst. "Why do you ask?"

Harry ignored the question. "Do you know where Kevin Anderson is incarcerated?"

Mike seemed lost by the question. Arla gripped the sill of the viewing box tighter, her breath condensing on the glass. If Mike was acting, he would put a professional to shame. Mike stared at his lawyer, and they both shrugged. Arla's eyebrows lowered, and her heart thudded.

What the....

Mike's shoulders were low, relaxed. His face impassive. "Who's Kevin Anderson?"

"You don't know who Kevin Anderson is?"

"No."

Seconds ticked by, the sound of the clocking ticking on the wall like waterdrops falling loudly into a deep cistern within Arla's mind.

Was Mike acting? He was suddenly calmer, more composed. From her rudimentary knowledge of personality disorders, she knew that serial killers could adopt a split character with ease. Perhaps Mike was doing that now. He was coming into his own as the interview progressed.

She suddenly wished Rochelle had been sent a live link to watch this. Thankfully, Jeremy was watching it, and she would catch up with him later.

"Can you confirm that you don't know of, or about, Kevin Anderson?"

"Should I?" Mike sounded a bit amused. Again, that sudden shift in his character. It had Arla fumbling, and she could see the perplexity in Harry and Lisa's faces as well.

"Is he famous, like Kevin Bacon?" Mike asked. He snorted and shook his head. "You coppers. Where do you get this bollocks from?"

Lisa took over. "You said you've never been up north. How about Nottingham? Or a place called Rampton?"

Mike leaned back in his chair. "No. Never been there."

Harry and Lisa glanced at each other. It was Lisa who carried on with the questioning.

"Both the victims' blood test results showed the presence of Rohypnol, the so-called date rape drug. Have you ever brought or used Rohypnol?"

Mike narrowed his eyes. "No. I haven't."

And we didn't find any in your house either, Arla thought to herself. She knew that Das and Rob were going through Mike's bank statements to see if they could find anything suspicious. So far, they'd drawn a blank.

CHAPTER 51

Arla left the room and walked outside. She came out of the station, using the front doors. There was cloud cover today, and it was humid. There was a fresh breeze as well, and she smelt rain in the air. Arla clasped her jacket tightly around herself as she walked. She needed some distance and space to think. The pastel and brick Lego blocks of council houses reared all around her like trees in a forest. She walked briskly, head down, hands thrust into coat pockets.

After a brisk ten minute walk, she came to the street corner where Angelo's café was placed. A few people sat outside, staring up at the sky as they sipped their coffee. Rain was coming. Arla went inside. Angelo, a big, burly Italian guy, was at the counter, wiping his hands on a white apron.

"Bellissima," he smiled at Arla when she got closer. *"Va bene?"*

Angelo had the sort of Italian accent that made common words sexy. Even when he spoke in English, and in Italian, it sounded heavenly.

"Si," Arla replied with a grin. She took out her purse.

"What can I do for you?" Angelo asked.

"A mocha, please. With chocolate on top."

"And an almond *cantuccini biscotti* on the side?" Angelo winked.

Arla hesitated. It was her favourite biscuit by far, but she was mindful of the calories, too.

Angelo said, "Go on; it's on the house."

She nodded, then got the coffee and sat down on a window table. She took out her notebook and opened up a blank page. Through the window, she could see two men smoking. She followed the smoke rings as they wisped upwards, then disappeared. Connections came, then went nowhere in her mind.

She wrote down black rose, Rohypnol and Kevin Anderson in large capital letters. Then she circled each one.

She dealt with Kevin first. When she met him, he was confident, at ease. It was an act to put her off balance. Kevin knew there was a reason for her coming. Even if he didn't know what the reason was.

Arla had the whole transcript of their meeting in an email, but she remembered with vivid clarity what Kevin had said at the end, in relation to the murders.

You're fishing, Inspector. In very deep waters, I might add.

Men like Kevin played mind games. Part of what he said was intended to increase her self-doubt. To make himself appear more mysterious and cryptic. But was that all?

Did Kevin mean something else?

They were meant to happen.

Arla thought of how Kevin was tracked down. The grease around the bodies had come from a car garage. Kevin's house was close to the victims, and he had known them socially. They had sung karaoke songs in the local pub, done pub quizzes. Kevin was known to the local community. And the only car mechanic who had a garage in his own drive.

They were meant to happen.

Kevin was talking about the current murders. Why were they meant to happen? What did he mean?

He had no contact with the outside world, save the few people on his visitor's list. Arla got her phone out and rang Das. She asked the DC to forward her Kevin's visitor list. The phone pinged a while later.

There were five names on the visitor's list. All of them were OPVs and had been vetted extensively. Arla rang Das back.

"Are we sure that Kevin had no family?"

"Yes, Guv. Not as far as we know."

They were meant to happen.

The words were humming in Arla's brain, the sound getting louder, like a swarm of bees slowly emerging from their nest.

"Conviction," Arla whispered, her eyes suddenly wide. "He said those words with conviction."

Das said, "Sorry Guv?"

Synapses fired in Arla's brain, and the soft boom of hushed explosions reverberated around her skull. Her vision rocked, her mind convulsed in sudden shock.

"He knew. Or at least he expected," she whispered again.

"Sorry, you've lost me completely now. Who's he?"

"Kevin. He knew what was going to happen."

CHAPTER 52

Das was silent. Arla hung up the phone, her breaths fast and shallow, a mad pulse slamming in her ears like waves crashing against a barrier.

She picked up the phone again and called Das back.

"Get Kevin's files up for me. Go back to his place of birth. I want details, the place, and time. I think he was adopted from an orphan house."

"I'm getting them up now, Guv."

Arla hung up, then grabbed her things. She paid Angelo, thanking him for the coffee. She promised him to be back soon, whenever a case needed solving. Leaving a bemused Angelo, Arla literally ran the short distance back to the station.

She barged into Harry as he was coming out of the office.

"Whoa," he said. "Was looking for you. Where did you go?"

"Come with me," Arla said, short of breath. She walked over to Das's desk. Das handed her a folder, and Arla sat down to read it.

Harry and Das observed her in silence. When Arla looked up, her eyes were shining.

"Right," she said, a note of triumph in her voice. "This is what I'm thinking. Kevin hardly has any contact with the outside world, right? But what if he knew someone from many years ago? A person so close to him that they would know what the other was thinking."

Harry frowned at her. "Sorry, you lost me."

"Okay, let me go back to the murders. Kevin told us he met them in the pub. They came to his home. There, he overpowered them, then killed them in his garage. Then he took them to Balham Common, and left them to die."

"Right."

"What I remembered today was a case note from ten years ago. I thought Kevin had a helper. Someone as twisted and devious as him. A partner that he trusted and probably loved as well. If people like Kevin know what love is."

Harry pulled up a chair and sat down. "Carry on."

Das was listening with rapt attention. Lisa strolled up, and Arla waved her over. She approached hurriedly.

"Now, Kevin always maintained his innocence, but we know the truth. However, what if Kevin was telling the truth about the murders?" Arla held her hands up as all of them started protesting.

"Hang on. I didn't say Kevin was innocent. But is it possible he didn't commit the murders? That he brought the women over, charmed them, and someone else killed them? Then Kevin and this other person took the bodies to the common?"

"What struck me at the time was how much Kevin managed on his own. He's a strong guy, but even then, there were hardly any signs of struggle in his house or the garage. Then he had to load the bodies in his car, then take them from his car to the Common. A lot of work for one man. I wasn't the only one who thought Kevin had a partner. Johnson thought so too. Here, it's all written in the report."

Arla held out the page, underlined it with a pen and gave it to Harry. He read, then passed it to Das and Lisa.

Harry narrowed his eyes. "Let me get this straight. Are you saying the real killer from ten years ago is still out there? That he was never captured?"

Arla put her hands on her thighs and rubbed her palms on them. "I'm saying it's possible. Kevin is guilty, no question. For being an accomplice to murder, if nothing else."

Lisa asked, "Did you search for this other suspect at the time? No clues in Kevin's house?"

"We found no samples of any other person, apart from Kevin and the two women. No other DNA or prints. Mind you, the labs weren't as developed as they are now. But regardless, SOCO turned his house and car upside down."

Arla continued. "And think about now. When we went up to see Kevin, he told me – It was meant to happen. What if Kevin and his partner at the time made a pact? For their tenth anniversary, this sicko would do something twisted and evil?"

Das said, "And that's why you think Kevin knew about this? Hence, he said it was meant to happen?"

Arla looked at her and nodded. "Yes, maybe. All of it points in that direction. What other explanation is there?" She broke off, then said, "Are we sure Mike didn't go up north?"

Das said, "That would fit with his employment history and electoral roll data. He's only been registered in Dorking, Surrey, and south London. If he went up north two days ago when Rochelle was attacked, he didn't buy a ticket on his credit card either."

An alarm bell rang deep inside Arla's mind. "Hang on," she said to Das. "Didn't you find a cold case from 5 years ago, in Mansfield, near Nottingham? A woman murdered with a black rose painted on her ankle?"

"Yes," Das said, her eyes lighting up. "She was found in a park as well. Stripped naked, no sexual assault, and her nails were intact. But she had the black rose."

Arla stared at her. "It could be the same killer. And he could have moved from the north to down here."

Harry said, "Hang on a minute. Rochelle was attacked near Rampton. What if it was the same guy?"

All of them looked at each other. Harry said, "Rochelle doesn't drive anymore. She has security with her at all times. Not a long-term solution obviously."

Arla asked, "Has Governor Beasley been told about Mike?"

"Yes.

Arla stood, pushing her chair back. "Call him and Rochelle again. They could be under more danger than we realised. Lisa, call the orphan shelter where Kevin was found. Arrange a visit there and also to Kevin's first foster home, if possible. Let's locate all of Kevin's foster homes, and see if we come up with anything. In addition, keep up the background search on Mike Robert. Work on his school and childhood contacts. You never know what the past can hide."

CHAPTER 53

He wore a black jacket and preferred to sit rather than stand. He was tall and wide-shouldered and when he stood, it attracted attention. Sitting, with his shoulders hunched, kneeling forward, made him look smaller. He finished his fourth cigarette, crushing it in the ashtray.

When he saw Arla Baker approaching the café called Angelo's, his heart did a somersault. Very slowly, he turned his back to her. Had she seen him? Did she know he was here? The thought filled him with panic, till he realized she was alone. He took a hard look at the parked cars opposite, the pedestrians walking past, and the small industrial estate with two warehouses in the corner. All the cars were empty. No suspicious figures loitering, keeping an eye on the café.

Arla went inside the café, and he relaxed. With shaking hands, he lit another cigarette. Two men were smoking next to him, and they shielded his view of the entrance. Through the windows, he caught sight of Arla, chatting to the Italian owner. What were the chances of her coming here, today? Not Providence. He looked up at the sky, thinking of Kevin, encapsulated within the walls of Rampton, or Full Sutton, for life. Kevin was looking down on him.

The plan was working out perfectly. That highly strung, emotional idiot Mike had been the perfect foil. Now it was time to draw the plot to its conclusion.

Arla surprised him by taking a window side table. The light fell on her face as she sat there, almost facing him at an angle. Her jaws, chin, nose were all hard, sharp angles, but the nose was small, the eyes large, and so were the lips. It worked in harmony, with her dark hair, to make her face easy to look at. She was pretty, no doubt. He felt an erection stir in his pants. He had waited for this moment, for so long. He couldn't wait any longer.

He came to Angelo's as the café was frequented by police officers. On occasion, he had got close to them and heard them discussing a case. It gave him a thrill, having this proximity to the very people hell-bent on catching him. If only they knew! They were trying to climb a greasy pole. They would never get to the top.

But he also knew the peak, the summit had arrived. Mike wouldn't hold it together in prison for long. He would break down, wail and cry, and these hardened police officers weren't fools; they would grow suspicious. An emotional wreck couldn't carry out the masterpieces he had created. Yes, he regarded the women as his canvas, his creation. What else? Kevin would be proud of him.

He watched Arla write something in her diary, then sit there with her eyes closed, thinking. He opened his mouth and drew some deep breaths. She was definitely alone. No one else was coming. He got up. He went up the steps of the main door and walked in. She was on his left, sitting with her back to him. Three, maybe five feet away. Two steps, and he could reach out and touch her. Feel her.

Clamp his hand over her mouth. Squeeze that soft throat.

Feel that warm body against his. Struggling till he subdued her.

Without knowing, his feet had moved towards her. Then he stopped. Angelo, the café owner, was wiping the counter.

He went past the counter and to the men's. He splashed cold water on his face, then stared at the deep blue eyes in the mirror, the brown hair falling over his handsome face.

He was so close to Arla. He could smell her, almost. He closed his eyes and exhaled. No, he couldn't wait anymore. When he came out, she was speaking on the phone. Her movements were jerky, fast like she was excited. She hung up, picked up the book she was writing on, and stood.

She waved goodbye to Angelo, and for a fleeting moment, he was sure her eyes fell on him, lurking in the shadows by the bathroom door.

Then she was gone. He gave her five seconds, then followed.

CHAPTER 54

Arla and Harry were in Jeremy Melville's office, where the psychologist was playing back the video of Mike's interview. He paused the part where Mike was denying he knew Kevin Anderson.

"Look at his forehead. Right in the middle, at the frown lines. The lines women have botox for."

Arla squinted. Mike was frowning, and his eyebrows were knotted together.

"What about it?"

"It's called the glabellar muscle. That muscle contracts just before the rest of the forehead muscles do. In fact, the glabellar contracts a lot during our lives, without us being aware of it. It's an involuntary action. Which means its automatic. Therefore, a reliable indicator that he was speaking the truth."

"It contracts so much we need botox injections to get rid of the frown lines," Arla said drily.

"Correct. Mike was obviously surprised by the name. Either he didn't know who it was, or he didn't understand what it had to do with the case."

Jeremy turned to Arla. "Did Mike work here when Kevin was caught?"

"No. But that doesn't mean he can't find out."

"Well, his surprise is genuine. Whether that means he knows nothing about Kevin, that I can't tell you."

"So, he wasn't expecting the question," Arla said slowly. "And if he was involved, I think he would have expected it."

Harry said, "Actually, he also denied being in the Kevin Anderson fan club website. With a fake name, I mean."

Jeremy said, "Overall, his manner is suspect. He shows extremes of emotion, and I don't like the way he became cool and suave at the ending. Like he was trying to make up for his earlier burst of emotion."

Arla said, "You just said he was showing surprise when asked about Kevin Anderson."

"He moved all the involuntary muscles, yes. But that only means he was caught off guard by the questions. It hardly indicates innocence."

Jeremy continued. "And by the way, he showed the same response when he saw the photos of the victims in the park. Genuine surprise."

Arla sighed, getting irritated. "So you can't tell if he's lying or not?"

Jeremy shook his head. "He doesn't exhibit a great deal of calm, restrained behavior, until the ending. He was easier to read then. I think he was speaking the truth at the time. His body posture, feet movement, hand position, all spoke of ease. But in the beginning, it's hard to say if it was an act."

There was a knock on the door, and Das poked her head in. Her cheeks were red, and she breathed rapidly.

"Important news, Guv. The lab got back to us with the DNA results."

Arla rose from her seat. "That was super quick! And?"

Das had come inside the room. "We have a match! Semen sample from the victims matches that of Mike Robert."

There was a palpable air of excitement in the room. Arla felt light, giddy. After a long period of fumbling around in the darkness, a switch had flicked on, and there was sudden, sharp clarity.

Excitement straightened Arla's spine. "You sure?"

"Yes," Das had a broad smile. "I'm sure. The email's been delivered to you as well. And Harry, as he's the SIO now."

This was a major breakthrough. Arla and Harry scrambled downstairs with Das, taking the stairs. A crowd had already gathered around Lisa's desk. The detectives moved around to let Harry and Arla get to Lisa.

Harry bent over to see the email on Lisa's laptop screen. Banerjee had written as well, confirming the DNA results.

"You got him," Harry said to Arla. "If he hadn't been in your house that night, we might never have caught him."

The officers around them murmured in consent. Arla was letting it all sink in. It seemed more than likely now that Mike was the missing link. Had he been Kevin's partner all those years ago? They both came from south London, lived close to each other. They could've been friends, certainly. Kevin killed those women close to his home, and Mike could certainly have helped.

But then, who attached Rochelle? Was that unrelated to the case?

No, Arla thought. It couldn't be. The man who attacked Rochelle came close to killing her. He even asked to see her nails. If that farmer hadn't arrived, she would be dead today.

And then there was the cold case in Mansfield, from five years ago.

Despite the final nail in the coffin of Mike's defense, Arla couldn't shake off a nagging feeling, a persistent gnawing at the back of her mind.

Jason Beauregard said, "Well, well, looks like the nail collector copy cat shot himself in the foot. Shagging the women before he killed them. What an idiot."

No one laughed at his crude comment, and Arla frowned at him. She noted Jason had a smirk on his face; his eyes lit up with a mischievous gleam.

"What's your point, Jason?"

"Slam dunk case now, isn't it? He had the opportunity and also the means. His motive for Jane Crouch was jealousy, and for Debbie Jones, well, he is a serial killer after all. Who knows how many other women he's done. Shame he operated from here though, and no one knew anything about it."

Jason directed his comment at Arla. It was meant as a barb, but she ignored it. She turned to Harry.

"Meeting in my room. Now."

CHAPTER 55

Harry And Arla were crossing the office floor when Johnson's voice boomed from behind them.

"DCI Baker."

Both stopped in their tracks. Johnson walked quickly, for a big man. The smile on his face was even bigger.

"I heard the good news," he said, his teeth dazzling. He looked at Harry. "Well done."

"Thank you, sir," Harry said, glancing at Arla. "We just need to fine tune all the details now, for the prosecution."

"Sure. But come up to my office please; there's someone I want you to meet."

With that mysterious comment, Johnson left. Arla had a sense of foreboding, and it intensified as she and Harry rode up the elevators in silence. When she stepped inside Johnson's fourth-floor office, she knew her intuition had been correct.

Deputy Assistant Commissioner Deakins was sitting at the table. He had silvery hair, a hooked nose, and glasses that rested on the bridge of that protruding nose. He was slim, slightly built, and always reminded Arla of a fox.

Deakins put down the paper in his hand and took off his glasses. Arla and Harry stood stiffly to attention in front of the table.

"Sit, please." Deakins had a rare smile on his face.

"DCI Baker, I'm so glad to see you well and healthy. Awful to hear what happened at your apartment. On behalf of the Met, my apologies."

"No need to apologise, sir, these things happen."

"But looks like you came through. As you always do." Deakins leaned forward. "I know that DI Mehta is the SIO now, but I've had a word with the other Deputy Assistant Commissioners. You are reinstated as the SIO and take full responsibility for the prosecution. How would you like that?"

Now that we have conclusive proof Mike did it, I am back to being the SIO, Arla thought to herself.

"Thank you, sir."

"So, I guess the DNA match settles in then. Open and shut case, now."

Johnson beamed at her, along with Deakins. Arla felt Harry stiffen. She glanced at him, and she read the warning in his eyes.

Tread carefully.

Arla took a deep breath. "I know there's been a lot of media attention over this case. But nothing compared to what will happen when the media find out one of our own staff was responsible."

"I know," Deakins said in a somber tone. "And that's why a swift conclusion is so desirable. Can you have the files ready for tomorrow? To transfer to the CPS, I mean. As soon as a date for the trial is booked, I can do a press meeting." CPS – Crown Prosecution Service.

"But we haven't charged him yet."

Johnson said, "Then do so. Without delay."

"Uh.." Arla swallowed, then decided to just come out with it. "I'm not entirely sure Mike is our man, sir."

The air in the room seemed to deflate, like a balloon punctured. Silence fell like a layer of lead.

"What do you mean, DCI Baker?" Deakins asked in a stiff voice. "We have a motive, reels of CCTV and phone data, and also a DNA match. What more do we need?"

"For one, we don't know who went up north and attacked Rochelle. Mike didn't do it. Unless he has telepathic powers. He couldn't have known we were going up north because we told no one but Governor Beasley. He couldn't have known where Rochelle would be driving to and from, on some country lane in the middle of nowhere."

"Second, there's no evidence of him buying Rohypnol. Dr. Banerjee said this was highly concentrated, medical grade Rohypnol, not easily available. How could Mike have the connections to get that?"

"Given the deviant practices he indulged in, is it so unrealistic that he could have?" Johnson grumbled.

"No," Arla conceded. "But we should be able to find a trail, in that case."

Deakins sighed loudly and leaned back in his chair. "DCI Baker. You always find a sticking point, don't you?"

"I'm sorry, sir." *No, I'm bloody not.*

"I also think that whoever the murderer was, he wasn't acting alone. He had help." She glanced at Johnson. "Like ten years ago, we thought Kevin Anderson had a helper. A person we never caught."

Johnson was scowling. "What are you trying to say?"

"Mike Roberts had sex with the victims. He admitted that. And now we have his DNA from the semen inside them. That only proves he had sex. Not that he murdered them as well."

"Then who did?" Deakins said, a steeliness creeping into his voice. He tapped his glasses on the table. "You admitted that we need to bring this case to a speedy conclusion, DCI Baker. Is that what you call this?"

"I just need some more time, sir. A couple of days. We can charge Mike with murder, and hold him for that time."

The two senior officers looked at each other. Frank irritation shone from their faces when they turned back to Arla and Harry.

Deakins said, "As soon as we charge him, the clock is ticking. The CPS will be waiting for the case files. We cannot delay this."

"Just two more days, sir. Please." Arla implored.

Deakins said, "You have one day, DCI Baker. No more. After that, we go ahead with getting a trial date."

CHAPTER 56

Arla could feel time slipping through her hands like sand. Her mind was in a maelstrom as she strode back to her office, but a few shapes had formed from the murkiness, and she could feel them calling out to her, their voices louder by the minute.

"Get the Incident Room ready," she said to Harry when they got back, raising her eyebrows. "I'm the SIO again now."

"Yes boss," Harry gave a mock salute. Arla suppressed a smile and turned to Lisa.

"Get me Kevin's files again. Specifically, I want his childhood history. Call Governor Beasley and Rochelle up, and make them a telephone appointment with me today."

"Yes, Guv." Lisa left, and Arla sat down at her desk. She called Banerjee, and his erstwhile assistant Lorna answered. She said the pathologist was busy, but Arla insisted it was urgent.

"It's always urgent with you, isn't it?" Banerjee's voice came down the line after a while.

"I'm sorry, Doc. This one really is. I don't think Mike Robert is guilty of murder." Arla explained to him quickly what she was thinking.

"You remember the Rohypnol in the victims' blood tests? You said it was medical grade, highly purified."

"Yes. So pure it could be for intravenous use. Why do you ask?"

"Can we trace the supplier?"

Banerjee was silent for a few seconds. "Rohypnol is available on a prescription. But it's an illegal drug, so no doctor will prescribe it for fear of losing their licence unless the doctor was crooked himself. That can happen, as you know. If the doctor is paid a lot of money. But I think it's unlikely."

"So, what's the other option? Online?"

"Yes, the holy grail to obtain illicit drugs is online. That also narrows the search down. Only a few sellers will have Rohypnol at this strength. I mean, an overdose can kill someone. So, while you may find a few Rohypnol sellers online, only one or two will be selling the batch found in the victims' bodies."

Arla gripped her forehead. "I should have looked for this sooner."

"It's not your fault. You had other problems to deal with," Banerjee's voice was kind. If anything, I should have reminded you."

"Thanks, Doc, I'll get on the case."

"Let me know if I can help."

Arla hung up. The Incident Room wasn't full when she got there, but everyone she wanted was present. She looked at the expectant faces of Warren, Das, Rob, Darren, Toby and the other half a dozen officers assigned to her case.

"Welcome back, Guv," Darren said.

"I was never really away," Arla said. "DI Mehta did a good job, though, don't you think?"

There were a few smiles, then Arla got down to business.

Under Kevin's photo, she wrote down Childhood, in block capital letters. "This is what we need to clarify. His old history, something we never really delved into. We found his DNA in the victims' bodies, and the case was done and dusted. Much like the current case."

Arla swept her eyes over everyone. They were listening to her with rapt attention.

"But, today, I admit we might have made a mistake. There was more to the case then one deranged killer. I suspected this at the time, but then, as now, we needed a speedy resolution. The media was shrieking headlines every day about the Nail Collector Murderer on a daily basis. London was gripped in terror."

"I know we have only one day, but let's make every hour count. Lisa, you have the address of the adoption center where Kevin was first registered?"

"Yes," Lisa replied. "It's called Lightness Home, in Battersea. Not from where he lived as an adult. They should have his records. I contacted them just now, but they want to see ID and so on, so it might be easier to pay them a visit."

"Good. That's my job this morning."

"Did you get in touch with Beasley and Rochelle?"

Rob took over. "I did, Guv. Beasley is waiting for a call back from you, and Rochelle said she was coming to London for a psychiatry convention. So she might well have time to meet you."

"Is she coming down with security?"

"Yes. They're aware of our findings."

"Good, DC Das. You're in charge of finding out the Rohypnol supplier." Arla gave Das the details of her conversation with Banerjee.

"This is an important job because if we can find the source of the Rohypnol, then we can get hold of their customers. Hopefully, our guy is one of them."

Arla turned to Harry. "Anything more from the phone data?"

Lisa answered. "Pamela," she indicated DC Das, "and I have been through Jane Crouch's second phone, the only phone we found so far. Apart from Mike's phone, there is another number she had called regularly in the last four weeks. It's a Pay as you go number. The phone is switched off. But I have called Cyber Crime labs to see if they can get hold of the IMEI number, or trace where the phone was brought from."

"Good," Arla said. "If it was purchased with a card, then that's a big breakthrough. We have a name and address."

"Anything from Mike's records?"

"He has no PCN or former convictions. No fingerprint matches on Ident-1, and his DNA was only a match with the semen from the victims. Nothing in the DNA database."

Arla turned to Harry. "What about his movements on the days of the murder?"

"He was at work till 18:00. There are CCTV logs of him leaving the station. He says he went to a strip club called Brown's in Leicester Square. He's down on the guest list, and he paid with a card. Warren's also seen CCTV footage of him going into and leaving the club. Brown's is on a main street, and there are cameras everywhere."

Arla nodded. "What time did he leave?"

Warren spoke up. "He went in there for 20:00 and left around midnight."

Arla hid the sense of satisfaction she felt. "That settles it then. Good work, Warren and Harry. There's no way Mike could be in two places at the same time."

"Right." Arla glanced at her watch. The day had been an avalanche of action, going to her wrecked home, then coming to work. She felt like she'd run a marathon, but the race was just beginning.

"It's already 16:00 hours. Let's see what we can get done today. Harry and I are off to the Lightness Care Home. All of you know what to do. We have till 16:00 tomorrow to come up with some firm leads that I can show the bosses upstairs."

The meeting dispersed, and Harry headed to Lisa's desk to get the address and phone number of the care home.

Once they were in the car and driving, Arla rang Governor Beasley. She updated him, and he promised to keep a close eye on Kevin if any closer was possible. Arla told him of the cold case in Mansfield from five years ago which Beasley wasn't aware of. He reassured her that his own personal protection would be raised as well.

Rochelle's line was engaged, but she called back almost as soon as Arla hung up.

"How are you, Arla? I've been meaning to speak to you, after what you went through."

"Thanks. I'm better now thanks. I guess both of us have been through the mill recently. But don't worry, I'm getting closer to him, I think."

"Oh, good. So you don't think it's Mike?"

Arla explained to her what she thought. Rochelle listened in silence. When she spoke, her voice was shaky. "That means this guy is definitely around."

Arla caught the insecurity in her voice. "You still have security, correct?"

"Yes, I do. And one of them is coming down with me on the train. Which makes me feel very foolish, but I guess that's just the way it is."

"Better to be safe than sorry," Arla said.

"Will I see you when I'm down for the conference? It's tomorrow, and I'll be free by late afternoon."

"Where is it?"

"The conference is in Park Lane, but I'll be living in Southfields, near Wimbledon."

"That's not far from where I am," Arla said. "And by late afternoon tomorrow, I think we'll have a better idea of what's going on."

"I hope so too. This dreadful business has to come to an end. I can't live like this anymore."

"It is coming to an end, I promise," Arla said. She hung up and rested her head back on the seat.

"How's she coping?" Harry asked.

"Not very well. Can't blame her."

Harry glanced at her swiftly. "And how about you?"

Arla caught his askance eyes, and only sighed in response.

CHAPTER 57

The Lightness Care Home was three streets down from the Battersea Dogs Home. Harry parked and put up his police permit on the dashboard to allow the parking guy an easy view.

The care home was a terraced house, one of the squat, larger ones on the block. A frail, slight woman with wrinkled skin on her hand and face opened the door. Arla guessed she was in her fifties, but the sun had taken its toll on her skin.

She showed the woman her warrant card. "DCI Baker from the London Met. We have an inquiry about a boy who was adopted from here in 1979. My colleague Lisa Moran rang, but she was told we would need to meet face to face?"

"Oh, I see. Come in," the woman opened the door. When Arla and Harry stepped inside the hallway, she shut the door and locked it firmly. "Follow me please."

The woman was dressed in a dark grey dress that fell to her ankles. Her hair was full, brown, and long, falling past her shoulders.

They passed a children's playing area and what looked like two kindergarten classrooms. Children were being taught by teachers, but most of the children were only old enough to be just past the nursery stage.

The woman knocked on a door at the end of the corridor. The name on the door said Violet Asquith, Head Coordinator. A younger woman, in her mid to late forties, opened the door. She was dressed more smartly, in a blue business skirt suit, bare legs, and blue heeled shoes.

She stared at Arla and Harry, then listened to the woman who introduced them. They had to show their warrant cards again.

"Thank you, Martha," Violet Asquith said finally. "Please come in officers."

They walked into a comfortable room with oak paneled walls and gilt leather armchairs. Photos of old men hung on the wall. The carpet was worn, but colourful rugs were put on them. The window behind the main desk was open, flooding the room with sunlight, and there was framed artwork by children placed on the window sills.

"This place used to belong to a well-known tea company in the Victorian days. A lot of the rooms haven't changed much," Violet explained. "Please take a seat."

When they sat down opposite her, Violet said, "I'm sorry we have to do things this way. Of course, you can ask for an FOI release, but due to safeguarding and legal issues, we cannot release all the data. And I thought that you would want all the data we had."

Violet was a straight-talking woman, Arla noted with approval. "Yes. We need information on Kevin Anderson. I'm sure you've heard of him"

"From my predecessor, yes. John Bartlett. John had been here for almost three decades and watched care home regulation go through many changes. When John first started, this place was actually an orphanage."

"When was that?"

Violet pursed her lips and furrowed her forehead. "1972 I believe. Sometime in the early 70s. The regulation to abolish orphanages came around that time as well. Children were widely abused in these orphanages, as you know."

"So what happens now?"

"Social workers bring children to us. We only care up to the age of ten. From the day the children arrive here, we try to match them up with adoptive parents. When they are older, it's foster parents or for adoption."

"I see."

Violet reached for a folder on her desk and pulled it over. It was a thick file, Arla noticed, the type of paper files kept in hospitals as patient notes.

"These are the notes of Kevin Anderson. They were last seen ten years ago, when the police investigation on him was undergoing."

Harry commented, "It's a thick folder for a child, isn't it?"

Violet nodded. "Yes, but you have to remember we get a lot of children who have been treated badly. It's heartbreaking in fact, to see toddlers who have been neglected. No child should have to suffer. It's one of the reasons I do my job."

Both Arla and Harry nodded in silent agreement. Harry said, "So, what was the problem with Kevin?"

Arla remembered vaguely that he had behavior issues. Violet patted the folder. "It's all in here. Before I left last night, owing to your request, the files landed on my desk, and I looked through them."

"In summary, Kevin was brought here when he was three years old. His mother was a drug addict, and she died from an overdose. Social workers found him and brought him here."

"What were his problems?"

Violet took a deep breath. When she looked at Arla, her eyes had a hard glitter on them. "Did you know Kevin had cigarette burns on his body when he arrived? He also had two fractured ribs and was in hospital for several days before he was transferred to our care. He showed signs of starvation, and his liver was failing. He was jaundiced when admitted to hospital."

There was silence for a while. Arla said, "He was abused." It was a statement and a perfunctory one.

"Yes," Violet said. "It's lucky the social workers found him when they did, or he might have died."

She continued. "From day one, the files say he wasn't able to sleep. He was the only child who walked around at night. But not just walking. He threw objects like glass jars and vases down the stairs, just to disturb others, wake them up. In the daytime, he hit other children, like he resented being with them. When he was seven years old, he tortured, then killed a cat."

Arla felt a cold hollow settling inside her stomach. "Was this a pet cat or…"

"Yes, a pet cat of this Home, well looked after. He started by trying to stab the cat with a pencil, then an envelope opener. Then he got access to a hammer from the cupboard and cornered the cat in a room. He hit the cat on the head, smashing its skull."

Arla covered her mouth with her hand. Violet looked down, then away. "And that's not all. We have a large garden at the back. A bird had fallen with broken wings. Kevin was caught torturing the bird. He had a hiding place inside a tree. The bird couldn't fly away, and Kevin got pleasure from breaking its legs, stabbing its eye. Again, a carer caught him in the act one day."

Arla's limbs were cold, fingertips and toes freezing. "Then what happened?"

"He was seen by a child psychiatrist, several times. He used to attend a day centre for disturbed children like him. It's one of the reasons why getting him adopted was difficult. No one wanted a child as troubled as him. He did go into foster care, but he kept running away and back to us."

Harry said, "At least he came back to you. That must mean something."

"We are the only family he had if you know what I mean. Please understand that this is what I've gained from reading through his notes. I never knew Kevin personally, but his case is one of the most tragic and disturbing ones we have."

Violet paused, and her eyes shifted from Harry to Arla. "But that wasn't the only reason why Kevin kept coming back to us."

"Oh? What was the other reason?"

Violet took a deep breath, and Arla was surprised to see a wave of scarlet dance up her throat.

"This was a surprise to me as well. But it seems Kevin had a brother."

CHAPTER 58

Arla's pulse quickened, marching to a sudden, urgent drumbeat. Lightning flashed in the sky, drenching her mind with brilliant incandescence.

"Did you say brother?"

Violet looked uncomfortable. "Uh, yes, I think so."

"Why didn't this come out at the time? We requested his old files, didn't we?"

"Yes," Violet smoothed her hair down with one hand. "And you were given the files. But back then, no one had made the connection why Kevin was best friends with this other boy, two years younger than him."

Harry was leaning forward. "What do you mean, exactly?"

Violet closed her eyes briefly, like she was trying to deal with an uncomfortable thought.

"In Kevin's notes, there are frequent references to another boy who lived with us at the same time. You have to understand this is the early eighties I'm talking about. Record keeping wasn't as good as it was these days. Nothing was computerised. Connections that are made automatically now had to be made manually."

Violet reached forward and took a sip from a glass of water. "Sorry, where are my manners. Can I offer you something? Tea or coffee?"

"No," Arla spoke for both of them. She hadn't eaten since morning, but her appetite had vanished. "Can you please clarify? Who was this other boy?"

"According to the notes, his name was Blake. He was Kevin's partner in all the torture games they played. They were best friends."

"But you said brother."

"Yes, I'm coming to that. Blake's last name was Whiley. It turns out that was the last name of his grandmother, whose care he was under. But the grandmother had re-married, and Whiley was her new husband's name. Her previous name was Anderson. Judith Anderson."

Arla's mouth fell open. Violet held her eyes and nodded slowly. "Judith was the mother of Marianne Anderson, the woman who gave birth to Kevin."

Violet exhaled loudly. "I made the connection last night when I realised Judith Whiley had lived two doors down from the house where Kevin was found. Same road, same address, only number 32, instead of 30."

For a while, no one spoke. Arla was grappling with the enormity of what was being revealed to her. "So, how did Blake turn up here?"

"Judith Whiley died. Her husband, an old man himself, had grown tired of Blake's violent behaviour. Even though he was five years old, he swore like a trooper. Broke plates, hit his grandfather, got up to all sorts of trouble. He even got banned from school for trying to gouge another boy's eyes out." She reached to the left of her large desk and pulled down another large folder. "It's all in here."

Violet continued. "When Blake came here, he and Kevin became best buddies. It was very noticeable because the children we get here find it hard to form bonds. Life has been cruel to them, and they don't trust others."

Arla asked, "When Kevin tortured the animals, did Blake help him?"

Violet set her jaw in a tight line and nodded. "Very much so. It was actually Blake who found the broken wing bird. Kevin admitted that to the psychiatrist. And it was also Blake who helped to corner the cat in the room. Kevin wielded the hammer."

Arla closed her eyes and lowered her head, nightmare visions rising to the fore of her mind. The picture Violet's words were painting was ghastly.

Harry asked, "So after the age of ten, what happened? If Kevin was ten, Blake was eight, right?"

"Yes. No one would adopt them. They were sent to a juvenile residential correction facility. Sorry, Kevin was sent there. Blake remained and did manage to get adopted by a family."

"He did? Do you have the details of that family?"

"Yes, I do." Violet pulled down the folder that said Blake Whiley in large letters on the front and side spine. A puff of dust hit their nostrils as she flicked through to the last page. She extracted a sheet and spread it out in front of them.

"There you go. Mr. and Mrs. Brown, in Purley, Croydon. That's the last record we have of Blake Whiley."

CHAPTER 59

Harry was weaving through traffic as Arla spoke on the phone. "...Yes, Blake Whiley, legal name. I want his passport, driving licence, NI number, last address, everything. I have his birth certificate already. He was born as Blake Anderson, so look under that name as well. But he could well have adopted Whiley as his last name."

Lisa hung up, and Arla focused on the road. It was peak time, almost six pm. There was little chance the Browns would leave home, as they were elderly. They hadn't answered their phones, so going to check on them was the only option. Arla had tried several times already, and she had told switchboard to keep trying every half hour till they got there. A deep sense of worry was eating away inside her. What would she find when she got to the Brown household?

"Put the siren on, Harry," Arla said.

Arla rolled the window up as the blast from the siren hit. It took a while, but the cars indicated to let them pass. It took them half an hour to get to the Brown's house, during which time Arla made calls to Beasley and Rochelle to let them know the latest news. Neither had ever heard of Blake Whiley or Anderson.

The Browns lived in a single story bungalow at the end of a cul de sac. All the buildings were bungalows. It was still bright, and a few of the elderly residents were sitting in their front gardens. They looked up as Arla strode up the path of number 48.

Garden gnomes stood at regular intervals along the short walk, with a well-tended garden on either side. Arla knocked on the door and waited.

Eventually, a woman's voice rasped, "If you're trying to sell something, then get lost!"

"Ma'am this is the police. I can show you my ID."

There was a brief sound like a rug scraping across the floor. "Slide it under the door," the woman said. Arla sighed, then bent over and obliged. Harry did the same.

After an interminable wait, there was the sound of a chain rattling. Finally, the door opened a crack. Arla saw an ancient, weather-beaten face, carved with deep lines, eyes sagging with bags under them. She also smelt cigarette smoke.

"What do yer want?" Mrs. Brown had an Irish accent.

"Can we please talk to you about a foster child you once had? Blake Whiley."

Mrs. Brown's face went bone white. Her eyes bulged, and her mouth dropped open. She started shaking, the type of whole body tremor that makes standing impossible.

Harry moved swiftly. He stepped past Arla and grabbed Mrs. Brown's arm, then her shoulder.

"Whoa, easy. Easy. Shall we sit down?"

Mrs. Brown spit out the words. "Get yer filthy fuckin hands off me!" She tried to move away, but stumbled backwards and would have fallen if Harry hadn't grabbed her.

"Mrs. Brown, please. We just want to talk."

There was a chair by the door. Harry lowered Mrs Brown on to it, then wiped his forehead.

Mrs. Brown gripped her walking stick and shook it in Arla's face. "How dare you come in here sayin that guttersnipe's name?"

"Blake Whiley?"

"Don't!" Mrs. Brown's face creased in pain, making the lines deeper, like cuts on her face. Her head fell on her chest.

Arla knelt by her. "I'm sorry, Mrs. Brown, but this is an urgent police matter. We are looking for Blake Whiley in relation to a serious crime. Anything you can tell us will be important."

Mrs. Brown didn't raise her head. Her voice was muffled. "You're twenty years too late."

"What do you mean?"

The elderly woman raised her head. Tears had reddened her eyes and spilled onto her cheeks. Arla felt her heart twist. She didn't mean to upset Mrs Brown.

"That vermin killed my husband. Everyone said it was an accident, but I know the truth. The police didn't believe me. No one believed me. But that lad was the devil incarnate."

Arla and Harry looked at each other. Arla said, "How did your husband pass away?"

"He was found at the bottom of the stairs. Fell by accident was the verdict. The boy was meant to be at school. But he bunked off school all the time. He went around sniffing glue in the parks and god knows what else."

"Why do you think Blake killed him?"

"Because John stopped the boy from setting fire in the house, that's why! He caught Blake pouring kerosene under the sofa and bed. Had a box of matches and all. Good job John caught him in time. Blake he said that he was going to kill John then," Mrs. Brown screeched, wiping her eyes.

"He also killed our cat. Even told us he did it. Tied a weight around its neck and chucked it in the pond."

Mrs. Brown shook her head. "That boy was evil. Pure evil. But no one believed me. I know he came home from school and pushed my John down the stairs."

Harry was kneeling as well, facing Mrs. Brown. "How can you be so sure?"

"Because he told me, the rotten scoundrel! He wanted to see me suffer. And I believe him. John had a knee replacement, but no way would he fall down the stairs. I was at home. Heard the noise and went to check. Blake used to climb in through the windows without anyone knowing, like. I know he was at home. I know he did it. "

Mrs. Brown dried her eyes. "And that's why I want you out of here. You're a blot on the name of justice! I told the coppers everything back then. But you didn't believe me."

She blew her nose, then her eyes narrowed. "That bastard's done something awful, hasn't he? That's why you're here." She shook her head bitterly. "After twenty bloody years, you come down. Fat lot of good you are."

"Mrs. Brown, can you tell us where he went when he left here?"

"He ran off one day. I was glad to see the back of him. Devil incarnate he was. I told the social services, then the cops he'd gone. Never saw him again." Mrs. Brown crossed herself. "So help me god."

*****

Lisa called on the way back. Her voice was excited.

"Guv, we have good news. You know the PAYG phone that both victims called? Not Mike's phone, the other frequent caller."

"Yes, what about it?" Arla held the phone tightly against her ear.

"Well, the phone's off, but we have the last signal from five days ago. The signal triangulates to a location in Wandsworth, SW18 postcode."

"How wide is the location radius?"

"One hundred meters. We have it down to one street."

Arla felt blood churn inside her veins. This was a real breakthrough. They'd been so busy tracking Mike down, this phone number had been ignored.

"Did this number call Jane's second phone as well? The one she hid?"

"Yes."

"We're going to head down there now. Get two squad cars and meet us there. And Lisa?"

"Yes, Guv?"

"What about the Rohypnol supplier?"

"No luck. We've been trying, but the few suppliers are big customers who buy in bulk."

"Just keep looking. You stay at base, but get Darren to meet us at the address now."

Harry put the alarm on again. Croydon was on the other side of town from Wandsworth. It would take a while to get through peak traffic.

CHAPTER 60

Blake Whiley had followed Arla from Angelo's café back to Clapham police station. Every step of the way, he wanted to make a move. He walked on the opposite side of the road from Arla, far enough not to arouse suspicion, but he could run up to her in a few seconds. His fingers trembled with anticipation. But he had to bide his time. That fool, Mike Robert, had barged in like an idiot. Arla was a tough cookie. She would be a challenge for him. The thought made Blake smile. He loved it when they fought back.

His phone chirped. Without taking his eyes off Arla, he took the phone out. He spoke on it briefly, then hung up. When Arla went inside the station, Blake walked past and took a left after three streets down. He had parked his dark blue Volkswagen here. He liked the Golf VW because it matched the colour of his eyes. He got in, then drove carefully to a point where he had a good view of the station's rear car park.

By now, he knew the black BMW well. The one that lanky gimp, Harry Mehta, drove. The one who followed Arla around like a puppet on a string. Blake felt nothing but scorn for such men. Despite his size, Blake knew he could take Harry down easily. It was getting time to put his theory to the test.

It was a long wait, but Blake didn't mind. For him, the chase was an integral part of the game. It was part of the thrill. The chase sharpened his anticipation. When he had gone after Debbie Jones and Jane Crouch, it had taken weeks of planning. Mike Robert's involvement had been crucial to the selection.

He saw the couple emerge from the rear exit and head for the car. Blake ducked below the dashboard as the BMW came out. He followed shortly, staying three cars behind. The traffic made it easy to stay hidden.

His hands tightened on the steering wheel as he recognized the route they were taking. Past the Battersea Dogs Home. For him, a trip down memory lane. It made him miss Kevin. When the BMW stopped outside Lightness Care Home, Blake's breath was shorter, and a thin film of sweat lined his forehead.

This was where it all begun. His first meeting with his soulmate. His brother. How did Kevin know? Somehow, he remembered. He recognized Blake. Then he protected him, taught him. Soon, Blake had no doubt they were brothers.

Emotion choked Blake's throat as he stared at the tall, wide Victorian terraced building. Battersea had many of these. In the old days, Battersea used to be the home of London's wealthy. The place was full of handsome buildings. And inside this one, Blake had learnt to play his first games. Kevin taught him everything, and Blake brought his own skill. It was Blake's idea to hit the cat's head with a hammer. It was Blake who had seen the broken-winged bird in the garden.

Later, when they were separated, it wasn't for long. Again, Kevin had run away to find him at the Brown's house. He smiled fondly at the memory. Kevin coming to his school, plotting to kill that old idiot. It had to look like an accident. It was Kevin's idea this time, and Blake executed the plan.

They ran away together, back to this care home. Foster home after foster home followed, and in each one, they left a trail of destruction, so cleverly planned they left no evidence behind to incriminate themselves.

Till Kevin wanted to go out in a blaze of glory. Blake didn't want to do it because he knew they could get caught. In the end, Kevin had sacrificed himself. He didn't say a word to the police when he was caught ten years ago. Blake was left heartbroken. He fell into depression, and it claimed years of his life.

The memories were like a moth-eaten film rolling out of an old projector. Blake sat in the sunlight, decades-old sights, sounds and emotions washing over him like a soundless tsunami. Tears dampened his eyes. Kevin had sacrificed so much. He would make sure it wouldn't be in vain.

He didn't like the fact that Arla Baker had come this far. It meant she was on the right trail. Sooner or later, she would discover his true identity. The time for waiting around was gone. The moment of truth had arrived. He had to take the fight to Arla.

Kevin took one last, longing look at the Care Home. Then he backed the car up and started driving home. He needed to get prepared for tonight.

CHAPTER 61

The squad cars had cut their headlights but kept the engines running. They had stopped on both ends of the road, which was a residential street of terraced buildings. The road was effectively sealed off. Harry eased to a stop behind one of the squad cars, and Arla jumped out.

Darren was standing at the corner, speaking on his radio. He waved at Arla. "I kept the helicopter out as you requested. No lights at number 26 now, but the windows are open."

Keeping herself pressed to the edge of the wall, she peeked out. It was past 19:30, and lights were coming on in houses. Number 26 was less than fifty-sixty meters away.

"Good," Arla said. "Did the two extra squads arrive?"

"Warren's at the other end. We have one unit at the back if he decides to leg it. But he can only go through someone's garden. If he comes out the front, then both Warren and I have him. If he gets in the car, then it's us again, but the fourth unit is on the main road. You told us not to hold up traffic."

"Yes, not yet. That'll only make him more suspicious."

Harry appeared behind them. "I suggest we let the uniforms handle this, Guv. Chances are he knows what you and I look like."

"Makes sense," Arla said. "Darren, we need to hit this guy hard. If the windows are open, someone's in. We can't let him know we're here. Use the Enforcer."

The enforcer was the nickname for the battering ram used by the police forces. It could go through any residential wooden door with a few blows.

"Move quickly. We'll be right behind you. He won't have time to get in the car. Alert the units at the back. Do we have an SFO with us?"

Darren indicated the Specialist Firearms Officer who was leaning against the squad car. The man wore a blue striped cap. He waved at them, then opened his coat to show the compact automatic rifle slung over his shoulder.

"You follow the enforcer. I don't trust this guy. What we don't want today is any more casualties than we have already."

The man tipped his cap at Arla and took up position.

Darren was busy on the radio. Arla made sure she was on the same frequency as them, then turned the knob on to soft mode. She could still hear.

"Approach on my count to zero," Darren said on the radio. "Five, four, three…

Arla watched them run down the street, silent but swift. The man with the enforcer was the lead, and he was the biggest of the pack, as tall as Harry.

It aroused attention. Pedestrians were few, thankfully, but all of them stopped to stare. It couldn't be helped. Within seconds, all four officers had congregated at the door. Arla heard the loud crashing sound as the door was breached.

She heard Darren's muffled voice, screaming, "Police, you're surrounded."

Harry sprinted down the road, and she followed hard on his heels. All the officers were inside the house. Loud thuds and shouts came from upstairs.

"Stay behind me," Harry said and went up the stairs. But Arla didn't. She let Harry go and walked into the ground floor hallway.

At the broken front door, she found some utility bill envelopes. They were made out to Mr. B Whiley. She tore into them. The latest gas bill covered the last six months. Blake had been living here for a while.

The sitting room was empty. It was badly decorated with dark paint, and there was a TV with a sofa set. On the table, there was a mug of coffee. She touched it, still warm.

A crash came from upstairs, followed by the sound of cursing. Arla crossed over to the small kitchen. On the counter, she saw a magazine. She picked it up, frowning.

"Guv, we got him," Harry shouted down the stairs.

Arla went upstairs. Darren and Harry were holding a man face down on the floor. The SFO stood with his gun pointed at the prostrate figure.

Arla knelt before him. Floppy brown hair fell over his face. The deep blue eyes sparkled as his lips curved upwards in a snarl.

"Bitch," he whispered.

Arla smirked. "Blake Whiley. We get to meet at last."

CHAPTER 62

Arla had a spring in her step. Blake was in custody at the station. His DNA swabs were on their way to the lab, and Arla was certain a match would be found from the victims' bodies and also their homes.

His photos could now be matched to the CCTV images, and all his movements traced. For the first time in weeks, Arla had slept well. She was still living at Harry's apartment. Last night had been exhausting. She didn't finish all the paperwork pertaining to the case till almost two in the morning. But she passed out as soon as her head hit the pillow. It was ten am now, and she was walking down Southfields, past the tube stop, to where Rochelle Griffiths was staying.

It was an apartment block, and Rochelle was in the ground floor flat. It was close to the train lines, and Arla could hear the tube trains bumping along slowly on their rickety old lines.

Rochelle took her time opening the door. She looked sleek and beautiful as ever, dressed in nice blue trousers and matching vest. Blue gemstone earrings sparkled on her ears. Her green eyes glittered at Arla.

"Can I come in?" Arla smiled.

"Of course," Rochelle stood to one side. Arla walked in, clutching her shoulder bag.

"Straight down the hallway to the kitchen lounge," Rochelle said.

From the sliding glass doors at the back, a small garden was visible. Fences separated the building from the train tracks.

Rochelle came in, and Arla turned to face her. "Nice place."

"It's simple," Rochelle shrugged. "The Royal College of Psychiatry is paying for it, so I don't mind. You've never been to my house in Nottingham, have you?"

"You never invited me," Arla grinned.

Rochelle laughed. "I must apologise. It was so rushed when you came up north, anyway. Not to mention the near death experience I had." Her face became somber. The green eyes dulled.

"I can't believe what happened. For all these years, we didn't know the truth about Kevin, did we?"

"Well, they acted as a partnership. I'm sure both of them did some of the killing years ago. But all will be revealed now."

Arla stared at Rochelle who nodded back. "Exactly. I guess we all owe you a debt of gratitude."

Arla waved it off.

Rochelle said, "Please sit. Tea or coffee?"

"Coffee, please. Milk no sugar."

Rochelle went to the kitchen counter. She opened the fridge and shut it. Arla couldn't see what she was doing as she had her back turned.

Arla played with her phone till Rochelle came back. She put a cup in front of Arla and one for herself.

"Are you drinking coffee as well?" Arla asked.

Rochelle nodded. "Why?"

Arla held her coffee cup to Rochelle. "Why don't you have mine, and I can have yours?"

They stared at each other for a few seconds. Then Rochelle blinked. The faint suggestion of a wrinkle appeared on her forehead.

"Why would you want to do that?"

"Just to see if your coffee tastes different to mine."

Rochelle was still standing, staring at Arla without any expression on her face.

Arla's tone was granite hard when she spoke. "Why don't you sit down, Rochelle. I have something to tell you."

Rochelle stood still as a statue.

Arla grit her teeth. "Sit down, Rochelle."

A light came alive in Rochelle's eyes. They flashed, like lit from inside with a spark. Her jaw set tight. Her lips were pressed tight together. Without taking her eyes off Arla, she sat down.

Arla said, "Blake Whiley's psychiatric history is interesting. After Kevin Anderson was convicted, he was diagnosed with psychotic depression. Blake was admitted to Ashworth Hospital in Merseyside, Liverpool. Ashworth is one of three high secure hospitals in the UK, as you know. Rampton is another."

Rochelle said nothing, but her eyes burned with hate.

Arla continued. "He was in Ashworth for many years, and during this time, his care was conducted by you."

Arla tapped her phone. "Governor Beasley sent us all the reports last night. You got to know Blake quite well over the years, didn't you?"

Rochelle remained silent. Arla said, "I don't know which one of the brothers you really loved, Kevin or Blake. But you signed Blake off as healthy and discharged him from Ashworth. At the same time, you remained Kevin's doctor. You had hundreds of one to one sessions with Kevin at Full Sutton and then at Rampton. Am I right so far?"

Rochelle's spine was erect, and her eyes were fixed on Arla. She looked like a statue, only her chest rose and fell.

"Personally, I think you fell in love with Kevin. You wanted revenge against the police officer who convicted him. That was me. That's why you released Blake, making up some crap about him being healthy. Or did Kevin put the idea in your head? Was Kevin always in charge?"

Rochelle smiled, a stiff parting of the lips that didn't touch the rest of her face. "This is all very interesting, Arla. I treated Blake

Whiley for acute severe, psychotic depression, yes. But how does that make me a serial killer?"

Arla smiled as well. "Remember the Rohypnol that Blake used? It was medical grade. There was no way anyone could get that drug in such pure form apart from a doctor. And not just any doctor. It's usually doctors who work in prisons or high secure hospitals where Flunitrazepam is still used to sedate prisoners. You had access to the medical cabinet in Rampton. Governor Beasley told us that room has CCTV, like everywhere in Rampton. Guess what Beasley's team found when they looked at the footage? You, putting a vial of Flunitrazepam in your pocket."

The smile faltered on Rochelle's face, like a crack appearing down the middle of a painting.

Arla said, "I always knew these murders were planned and done by a team. In Blake's house, we found two things. First, a magazine called Psychology Today. It doesn't have your name on it, but I'm willing to bet it has your fingerprints. Second, from all the knives in Blake's kitchen, we found one that had a tiny speck of blood that hasn't washed off yet. That blood has already been sent for DNA analysis. As for the fingerprints – they aren't Blake's. Again, I'm willing to bet they are yours."

The smile had now vanished from Rochelle's face completely. Her cheeks were blood red, and her eyes were wider, larger. Her nostrils flared as she breathed hard.

Arla leaned forward. "I think you made the cuts that caused Debbie and Jane to bleed to death. You used that knife in Blake's kitchen. You killed them, and then also cut their nails off. You killed them because they worked with me. Maybe I was the final target. You realized that Mike was a good cover, one who could be played easily. You kept in touch with him, seduced him."

Rochelle snarled. "You think you're so clever, don't you?"

"We showed Mike your photo. He doesn't want a conviction. He's cooperating with us. He identified you yesterday, Rochelle."

Arla continued. "I must say, that car accident was a masterstroke. It could've gone very wrong for you. But Blake and you took a risk to throw us off scent. You almost succeeded as well."

Arla stood. Rochelle remained seated, glaring at Arla, her teeth bared.

Rochelle spat the words out. "You had the nerve to put my Kevin behind bars. For life. Do you know how sad he is? How lonely he was till he met me? I nursed him back to health. That's when the idea formed in my head. Why should you get away scot free? Kevin has a lifetime of suffering, and you get nothing?"

"Kevin was a cold-blooded murderer. And so are you and Blake. You started the Kevin Anderson fan page, didn't you?"

Rochelle sat in silence, her eyes darting daggers at Arla. "Yes, we did. And Mike was the best foil we could have. That idiot almost did our job for us. He tried to finish you off."

"You came down here to stay with Blake, while you murdered the women. West Midlands Police sent over CCTV images of you boarding the London train from Nottingham."

Rochelle stood, teeth clenched, hands balled into fists.

Arla said, "Rochelle Griffiths, I'm arresting you for the murder of Debbie Jones and Jane Crouch. You do not have to say anything, but anything you do say can be used against you as a statement in a court of law. Do you understand?"

There was a noise from the back garden. The long legs of Harry, then two uniformed officers appeared as they scaled the back wall, then dropped into the garden. They hurried towards the sliding door, Harry at full tilt. His anxious face relaxed when he caught sight of Arla as she opened the door for them.

The officers put handcuffs on Rochelle, who didn't resist. For one last time, her eyes lingered on Arla's, who stared back unflinchingly. Then she was dragged away.

Harry looked at Arla, his chestnut eyes boring into her.

"That was very risky."

"So is smoking cigarettes." Arla put her hand out. "But I feel like having one. That's an order, Harry."

CHAPTER 63

Rampton High Security Prison
Nottingham

Arla and Harry were sitting with Governor Beasley in his office. Sunlight streamed in through the open windows.

"Thank you for your help," Arla said. "Without the evidence we got from the CCTV at Rampton, we might not have got a prosecution."

Beasley nodded, "Glad to be of assistance."

"Thanks also for forming a relationship, so to speak, with Kevin. Gaining an insight into his mind was crucial."

Beasley smiled at that. "It was your idea, remember?"

Arla had a quiet word with Beasley before she had arrived in Rampton the first time. Beasley had been the Governor when Kevin came to Rampton ten years ago. After one year Kevin was transferred to Full Sutton.

Beasley had used that old relationship to get closer to Kevin, after being encouraged by Arla. It had been immensely helpful. Kevin had told Beasley things about him and Rochelle that would never have come to light.

Beasley said, "So Rochelle was obviously in love with Kevin."

Arla nodded. "It happens. There are intelligent, well educated women who fall in love with serial killers. It's a condition called hybristophilia, as Jeremy has just informed me."

"How strange."

Arla said, "Very strange. Typically, these women have seen all the evidence, but they lust for the killer precisely *because* he is such a bad person. They adore the fact that he can be bad enough to carry out his senseless carnage, only because of the strength of his beliefs.

It's like a dark, twisted alpha male love. Doesn't make sense to me, but there are many things in this world that don't."

Harry said, "But Rochelle didn't stop with loving him. She became a killer, too."

"Yes," Arla said. "That murder in Mansfield five years ago, with the same MO but with the nails on the victim intact, Rochelle did that. She was here at the time, and her DNA is present on the victim."

Beasley shook his head slowly. "I wonder if there are more. West Midlands Police are turning over all their cold cases now, to see if any could be connected to Rochelle." He gave Arla a tired smile. "I don't think you're the favourite person in that police department right now."

Arla shrugged. Beasley asked, "So Rochelle went on this mad spree because she had it in for you?"

"To take revenge on me, yes. I'm sure she always had these tendencies. Kevin just brought it out. During all those one to one meetings, he bared his heart to her, and she fell in love. She told him about Blake, and the stars aligned."

Harry said, "Maybe Kevin moulded Rochelle like he had moulded Blake. The three formed this evil triangle. A genius plan, really."

Arla shook her head. "I think it was Rochelle's idea all along. She found a kindred soul in Kevin. Then she used Blake and Mike Roberts to get what she wanted – her dangerous desire to make me pay."

Beasley grimaced. "Coincidence brought Blake and Rochelle together. Just sheer luck. Who could have thought, she would be Kevin's psychiatrist as well?"

They pondered the question in silence.

Arla said eventually, "I'm glad it's all over now. Let's hope all your other inmates are behaving themselves, Governor."

All three smiled. Beasley said, "I'll be keeping a closer eye on them, and the doctor's treating them, that's for sure."

"Good," Arla said, tapping her forehead. "You never know what's hiding in here. We can look all we want, but a killer's mind is always closed to us."

THE END

HAVE YOU READ THEM ALL?

The Lost Sister – Arla Baker Series 1 (Click here)

Did a serial killer take her lost sister? Secrets of the past reach out to claim Arla Baker's life. Can she save herself from this vicious killer?

The Keeper of Secrets – Arla Baker Series 2 (Click here)

A teenage girl is dead in the park. The killer leaves a note. Ask Detective Arla Baker what happened. This killer knows about Nicole, Arla's lost sister. Now he's coming for Arla.

The Forgotten Mother – Arla Baker Series 3 (Click here)

They took her children. Took her sanity. One mother didn't forget. She didn't forgive. Now she's back for revenge. Can Arla Baker stop her before it's too late?

AUTHOR'S NOTE

Thank you for reading this book. I hope you enjoyed reading it as much I enjoyed writing it!

If you did, would you please mind leaving a review on Amazon? It takes 2 minutes to leave a review, but guides other readers forever.

Here is the link for Amazon:

https://www.amazon.com/gp/product/B07QH5QQXT/ref=series_r w_dp_sw

Thanks Again,

ML Rose

ACKNOWLEDGEMENTS

A book germinates and flowers in isolation, but it only revealed in full glory after the beta readers send their feedback.

I am fortunate to have several people who offer their time and expertise.

Colin Spencer is a retired police officer, and his comments on various police matters is invaluable. Good having a former cop on the team!

The following readers have spotted errors and provided suggestions – Teresa Fronek, Dale Allen, Annalisa Alberti, Linda, June, Gita (also my aunt's name!) Sturtevant, Bernadette Harrison, Ken Ligenfelter, Cathie Jones, Grace Smith, Joan Zee, Carol Butler, Paul McGovern, Rob Ashman and Adele Embrey.

There are others, and if I haven't mentioned every name, then the fault is mine alone.

Thank you for being there, and for pushing Arla to new heights!

Till next time,

ML Rose.

Made in the USA
Middletown, DE
29 May 2021

40630225R00165